LOTTERY

YOU TOO CAN BE A WINNER!

Turn to page 5 for details of our great
lottery competition

DEDICATION

To the committee

LOTTERY

MICHAEL SCOTT

THE O'BRIEN PRESS
DUBLIN

Lottery is fiction. All the characters in *Lottery* are fictional. The characters are not meant in any way to represent lottery winners. Although many of the institutions and retail premises mentioned in *Lottery* are real, they are used in a fictional context, and are not meant to represent the actions of those institutions or any employees.

I would like to express my gratitude to all those lottery winners, in Ireland and abroad, who were willing to discuss how their lottery win changed their lives.

First published 1993 by The O'Brien Press Ltd.,
20 Victoria Road, Rathgar, Dublin 6, Ireland

Copyright © Michael Scott

British Library Cataloguing-in-publication Data
A catalogue reference for this book is available
from the British Library.

ISBN 0-86278-344-5

10 9 8 7 6 5 4 3 2 1

Typesetting and layout: The O'Brien Press
Cover illustration: Katharine White
Cover design: Neasa ní Chianáin & Michael O'Brien
Printing: Cox & Wyman Ltd., Reading

LOTTERY COMPETITION

BE A WINNER WITH YOUR LUCKY NUMBERS

CHRISTINE'S numbers are
turning points in her life.
What do your numbers mean?
Tell us, in not more than fifty words why
your six numbers are special to you.
The best entry will win a fabulous
holiday for two in 1994.

Send your entry on this page to:

THE O'BRIEN PRESS
20 Victoria Road, Dublin 6.

To reach us no later than 31 December 1993

Prologue

The grains of sand were soft and warm beneath her naked skin. Without opening her eyes, Christine Quinn shifted, reaching around to unclip her bikini top, exposing her smooth back, then pressed her face back against the folded towel. A trickle of sweat curled down from her hair-line and ran along her nose. She'd give herself a few more minutes, before making her way back up the beach to the hotel for lunch.

Behind her, she could hear the roar and hiss of the surf as it pounded onto Bondi Beach mingling with the faint squeals of children's laughter and overloud Australian voices.

She gasped as cold oil slid down her back, trickling along the line of her spine. 'You bastard,' she mumbled sleepily, 'you should have warmed it first.'

Strong fingers pressed the oil into her hot, deeply tanned flesh, massaging taut shoulders, sliding along her arms, deliberately, sensuously brushing the sides of her breasts.

She felt a hot breath on her ear and she lifted herself, turning to meet his lips, pressing her breasts against his chest.

'Happy Christmas, sweetheart,' he said, kissing her deeply.

Christine Quinn wrapped her arms around his neck pulling him down on top of her. Christmas Day. She should be at home in cold, wet Dublin, huddled before a fire, watching old movies on the television, as she had last year and the year before and every year before that ...

But this hadn't been like any other year. This was the year she had won the lottery ... and nothing had been the same since.

'Happy Christmas, my love,' she whispered, tears in her eyes.

Saturday, 10 July

Chapter 1

Twelve ...

Sixteen ...

Twenty-three ...

Three ...

Twenty-seven ...

Thirty-four ...

Christine Quinn was only half-listening to the numbers coming from the other room as she poured boiling water into the teapot. The television was turned up loud to drown out the sounds of the usual Saturday night drunken argument in the house next door and the ever-present squalling of the baby in the house on the other side.

Twelve ...

She was twelve when she lost her mother.

Sixteen ...

She was sixteen when she had her first child.

Twenty-three ...

She was twenty-three when she married.

Three ...

Her second baby was three when it died.

Twenty-seven ...

She was twenty-seven before she finally got sense and walked away from the bastard.

Thirty-four ...

She was thirty-four last birthday.

The realisation came suddenly, shockingly, and then she screamed aloud as the steaming water splashed onto her hand.

The numbers. Dearest Jesus, the numbers! They were her numbers!

Those six numbers – twelve, sixteen, twenty-three, three, twenty-seven, thirty-four – were the numbers she'd been using week after week. Magical numbers, special numbers, relevant numbers. Numbers with a story, a history, each number a turning point in her life.

Her numbers.

And tonight the lottery was worth over two million ...

Christine barely made it to the toilet before she threw up.

Sunday, 11 July

Chapter 2

Christine Quinn slowly surfaced from a dream in which she'd been running naked through a forest. Damp mist coiled up around her feet, beading on her skin. It was autumn and the leaves from the trees drifted down around her, soft and green and golden. In her dream, she slipped on a pile of damp leaves and rolled down a gentle incline, tumbling over and over, the leaves flying up all around her, covering her damp body, sticking to her flesh. At the bottom of the hill she rolled to her feet and she was laughing and crying at the same time as she brushed the leaves off her breasts and belly, and picked them off her arms and thighs.

But when she looked down, she discovered that she was covered in money, hundreds – no, thousands – of notes. More and more money was spinning out of the heavens, spiralling past her face, the miniature faces on the notes mocking her. But when she reached for them, they dissolved into crackling dust, crumbling beneath her touch into gritty powder. She tried to gather them up into her arms, bundling them together, hugging them close to her breasts, but they disintegrated, scattering in a fine haze before her. She kept turning round and round, but a wind had blown up, a chill, bitter wind that gathered the money into an enormous swirling ball and then swept it away, leaving her with nothing.

Christine awoke. She was convinced she'd cried out, but the house was silent, the street outside still with the early Sunday-morning quiet. She sat up in the single bed and brushed her hands across her face. Her cheeks were damp; she'd been crying in her sleep. She dropped back onto the pillow and breathed deeply, trying to calm her pounding heart. Maybe she was having a heart attack! Two of her uncles had died of heart attacks.

She shook her head quickly. She wasn't having a heart attack, she was simply frightened – no, she was terrified – to admit that there was a possibility she had won or shared in a lottery that came to more than two million pounds.

Two million! It was an impossible figure, like the distances between stars, or the grains of sand on a beach.

Her social welfare came to just over fifty pounds a week.

She did the sums quickly in her head. Two million pounds was the same as forty thousand weeks' payment ... or ten thousand months or eight hundred and thirty-three years! She laughed, giggling like a schoolgirl. It was like one of those sums: if a single parent with a seventeen-year-old son can live on fifty pounds a week, then how long can the same family live on two million? There were tears in her eyes again but she brushed them away quickly.

Anyway, she still wasn't sure that she'd won. She probably hadn't.

But she couldn't have mis-heard all six numbers, could she? And even if she hadn't got all the six numbers, then she might have got five, and five numbers would be worth a couple of hundred pounds – and even that amount would make all the difference. Of course, she might only have got four numbers and won ten or twelve pounds, but God knows, even that would be great.

This was getting her nowhere! She must find out for certain.

Christine threw back the duvet and rolled out of bed. Pulling on the ragged towelling dressing gown that she'd thrown over the end of the bed, she padded barefoot across the worn carpet to pull back the curtains and look out the window. Lines of identical, featureless houses faced her across the narrow road. Beyond them she could see a dozen rows of equally anonymous houses. The Dublin mountains rose blue and hazy in the distance. She'd grown so used to the view over the years that she no longer looked at the houses, only at the mountains beyond.

She'd learned to tell the weather by the colours of light on the mountain slopes. Purples, greens, golds and bronzes. Today was going to be warm and wet, she decided.

Opening her bedroom door, she stepped out onto the landing and stopped, listening. The house was silent, and she knew, even before she poked her head into Kevin's room, that he hadn't come home last night. This was the second night in a row. She'd have to talk to him again ... and he'd remind her that he was seventeen going on eighteen.

The bathroom was cold, the shadow cast by the house that backed onto hers keeping it in perpetual shade. There was still some hot water left over from the night before, and she stripped naked, and washed quickly, using a facecloth to scrub at her goose-pimpled flesh. When she was finished she turned to the mirror on the wall above the bath and began to drag the hairbrush through her straggly hair. It felt slightly greasy to her touch.

It hadn't always been like that though; once she'd considered it her finest feature, flowing blond, cut shoulder-length. But over the years – like the rest of her – it had just become tired. Tired and worn. She put her hands on her hips and looked at herself critically in the mirror. She was thirty-four ... and looked much older, she decided. And small. That was the immediate impression people got. Small face, blue eyes, long narrow neck, small breasts, narrow waist, a flat stomach – even after two children – and tiny feet. She knew she sometimes projected an air of child-like innocence, but those people who thought her a push-over very quickly realised their mistake. She could be hard and ruthless when she needed to be. Christine touched her hair; if she had won a few bob in the lottery, maybe she'd be frivolous and get her hair done. It was a long time since she had money to treat herself to anything.

Christine hurried back into the bedroom and dressed quickly

in jeans, a baggy tee-shirt she'd bought for a pound in a bargain shop in Henry Street, and a pair of open-toed sandals.

Two million pounds.

It had gone round and round in her head in an endless refrain last night.

Two million pounds.

And what was worse was the uncertainty. Had she won or hadn't she? At least if she hadn't won, she could settle back into her routine and her life would return to normal. She'd tell Kevin about it and they'd laugh and maybe fantasise about what they would have done if they'd won two million.

But what if she had?

Just suppose she had ...

* * *

The church bells were ringing out for a quarter-past nine when Christine left the house, blinking in the early-morning sunshine. The old couple who lived up the street said Hello as they passed by on their way down to the church for half-nine mass. Christine waited until they were well ahead of her, then fell into step behind them. She was reluctant to engage in empty conversation – not now, not while her thoughts were in turmoil.

She didn't go to mass herself. She hadn't since she was sixteen years old. Half a lifetime ago. Still, the memories were as clear as if they'd happened only yesterday. She was sixteen then and in trouble, in desperate, terrible trouble. She was looking for help, someone to talk to, someone to say: It's all right. Now here's what we'll do. So, she went to confession to the old parish priest; he was ten years dead now, and she had neither the pity nor the compassion to say: God rest him. He hadn't listened, hadn't cared, when she told him what had happened. He called her a lying Jezebel. She didn't know what a Jezebel was, but she knew what he meant. As she stumbled from the dark-

15

ened confession box, she swore she'd never set foot in a church again, and she hadn't even married in a church. But it was a vow she broke three times in all those years, when she had Kevin and little Margaret baptised, and then later for the funeral, the tiny white coffin lost in the gloom of the big church, the circular stained-glass window casting blood-like speckles across the white marble steps leading up to the altar.

Funny how the memories came back. She hadn't thought about that terrible time for years. But her thoughts were so chaotic just now ...

Christine hung back on the street corner, watching the mass-goers streaming into the church. There were very few young people among them, she noticed, hardly any of Kevin's age. Maybe they'd come down to the later masses, but somehow she didn't think so. She thought again of Kevin, wondering where he'd spent the night. He said he was going out to a party and although he was seventeen, she still worried about him. She knew he drank and she occasionally smelt smoke from him. But sometimes she got the whiff of a sweet odour that made her suspicious. She hoped and prayed it was from some foreign tobacco, but she was afraid to ask.

She watched him when he pushed up the sleeves of his sweater at the sink; she was looking for the tell-tale marks on the insides of his arms, but they were clean and unbruised.

She didn't think he was using drugs, but who could tell these days? He told her he was too smart to take drugs. He'd seen what it had done to far too many of the kids on the estate. And he even told her about one of the guys he knew who was HIV positive from sharing needles.

There were a few girls who hung around with him, but Christine didn't think there was anyone special. She had a long talk with him about sex and she told him he had been conceived when she was only sixteen; she didn't tell him his father's name, however, even though he questioned her closely. She pointed out that it had changed her life totally. Plans which she'd made – to go to England, to America, to au pair, to become a singer, a dancer – were all shelved. Instead she became a mother.

Maybe it was time to have another talk with him ... maybe when he got home today.

The crowd was gone now, only a few stragglers hurrying up the church steps as the priest's voice, faint in the distance, began the mass. Christine dashed across the road and stopped in front of a young man selling the Sunday newspapers out of the back of a car.

'*Independent*, please,' she muttered, handing him a pound coin. Usually she didn't buy papers; they were too expensive and she'd given up looking through the jobs pages a long time ago.

There was surprisingly little change and for a moment she thought the man had made a mistake until she checked the price on the paper. She turned away with a grim smile: when you were living on welfare, every penny had to count.

The paper seller watched the small blond woman walk slowly down the sunlit street, head bent as she flicked through the newspaper, turning the pages furiously. He was reaching back into the car when he heard a sound, and he raised his head, trying to identify the noise.

It was a long shriek, like someone in mortal agony, or an animal in pain. A cat? he wondered. The woman who'd bought the newspaper was standing rigid in the middle of the street, sheets of newspaper tumbling down around her, until only one sheet remained in her hand. She was holding it so tightly that it began to tear down the middle.

The shriek stopped and the paper seller realised that the sound had come from the woman. He took a couple of steps towards her. 'Missus ... are you all right ... Missus?'

Christine looked over her shoulder, and the man stood still. Her expression was terrifying – her face deathly pale, eyes wide and staring.

'Missus, are you okay?'

Clutching a torn scrap of paper, the woman turned suddenly and ran away.

Chapter 3

It was a mistake. There had to be some mistake. Christine hurried along at a half-run, the scrap of paper clutched in her ink-smudged, sweat-damp hands.

It had to be a mistake ... or if it wasn't, then something else was wrong. It had to be.

The numbers were definitely hers. They were the numbers she used every week – 12, 16, 23, 03, 27, 34 – but maybe she hadn't used them this week, maybe she'd chosen different numbers, or not all the numbers, or marked up new numbers by mistake. She'd been thinking about changing them; often weeks went by and not even one came up.

The sun hit her as she turned down the street. Blinking furiously, black spots dancing before her eyes, she stopped and re-read the small square of paper in her hands, not even realising that the rest of the newspaper had vanished.

LOTTERY WINNER

There was one winner of last night's Lottery, which amounted to £2,225,795. The ticket was purchased on the east coast. Match five winners each receive £1,024, while match four winners win £12.

And they *were* her numbers!

Even if she'd got one of the numbers wrong, she would win just over a thousand pounds, she consoled herself.

The ticket!

The thought hit her as she stood on the doorstep, fumbling with the key: where had she put the lottery ticket? Usually it went on the mantelpiece, or on top of the television. But she couldn't remember putting it there ... in fact, she couldn't remember the last time she had it.

Jesus Christ, where had she put the ticket?

Had she even bought it in the first place?

The door opened so suddenly she stumbled into the hall. Without bothering to close it, Christine raced into the tiny sitting room. The room was in total darkness. Her hands shook so much she could barely draw the curtains and pull open the dusty venetian blinds. Slatted sunlight sliced into the room.

The lottery ticket was in its usual place, on top of the mantelpiece, tucked in behind the clock that had once belonged to her mother. Now that she was this close, she felt almost reluctant to touch it, to check and see if indeed the numbers matched. The last few hours had been terrifying, but they'd been exciting too. She knew – deep in her heart and soul – she knew she hadn't won the lottery, but wouldn't it have been wonderful if she had? Fantasies, which she'd consciously suppressed since she heard the news, came flooding to the surface now, brief, vivid images of wealth, of luxury, of never having to worry again. She smiled suddenly, remembering how excited she'd been last night ... how stupid she'd been.

Christine Quinn picked up the ticket and turned it over.

The shaking began then, a shivering tremble that forced both the scrap of paper and the ticket from her numb fingers. She gently eased herself to the floor and carefully picked up the two pieces of paper. With infinite care, she pressed them flat on the carpet, smoothing them with the palm of her hand, and compared both sets of numbers, speaking them aloud into the silence, each whispered number sounding like a shout.

'Twelve ...'

'12.'

'Sixteen ...'

'16.'

'Twenty-three ...'

'23.'

'Three ...'

'3.'

'Twenty-seven ...'

'27.'

'Thirty-four ...'

'34.'

Christine looked at the paper again, but she couldn't focus on it, and it took her a moment to notice that tears were streaming down her face. There was a sound in the room, a strange gasping sobbing sound that she finally realised was coming from herself. She was neither laughing nor crying but something in-between.

She pinched the flesh of her cheek and flinched, the sudden pain stripping away her hysteria. Taking a deep breath, she rubbed the heels of both hands into her eyes before she looked at the figures again, checking them a second time.

They matched!

She then read out loud the amount of money she'd won: two million, two hundred and twenty-five thousand, seven hundred and ninety-five pounds. Tax free.

Christine carefully folded the scrap of newspaper and the

lottery ticket, and turning the clock around on the mantelpiece, she opened the back and slipped both inside.

Then she suddenly changed her mind, removed them and slid them into the back pocket of her jeans.

She headed back into the kitchen and automatically moved to the sink to fill the kettle, giving her thoughts time to settle.

Two million, two hundred and twenty-five thousand, seven hundred and ninety-five pounds.

She needed time to think; she needed to be calm ... or as calm as she could be in the circumstances. The decisions she made now were going to have repercussions for the rest of her life.

She had often dreamt of winning money. In her deepest, darkest moments, it had been her secret fantasy, to win a few thousand to settle her debts.

But there was a world of difference between a few thousand and two and a quarter million. That sort of money brought danger, made enemies, lots of enemies. Family and friends – even total strangers – would expect a slice of her good fortune. They'd reason that if she had so much she wasn't going to miss a few thousand here or there, was she?

Putting the kettle on to boil, Christine Quinn sat down at the kitchen table. It was at times like this that she wished she still smoked. It would give her something to do with her hands. She had decisions to make.

The first decision was the easiest. She would tell no-one. And that meant no-one. The fewer people who knew, the less chance there was of the news getting out. She knew that the lottery people guaranteed total anonymity. She also knew that they helped with investment advice. She'd need an accountant and a solicitor, but again maybe the lottery people could help there. If the money was invested properly, she'd be able to live in luxury off the interest for the rest of her life. Kevin would have the freedom to do whatever he wanted with his life; his future and his children's futures were assured.

Thinking of her son made her stop. Should she tell Kevin? Could she risk telling him?

If she told him the truth, he'd be sure to tell one of his friends and within hours the news would be all over the estate. But he was no fool; he was bound to know that something was up. Anyway, there was no way she was going to be able to disguise the fact that she'd come into some money.

Could she say that a relative had left it to her?

No. Kevin knew all her relatives, living and dead. She couldn't say she'd won it at bingo, because he knew she hadn't the money to go to bingo anymore.

Robert?

The name flickered at the corner of her consciousness, but she shook her head savagely. Her ex-husband was a bastard through and through. He'd want her money and besides, she didn't want Kevin to even start thinking about him again.

She was left with no alternative; she was going to have to tell Kevin something. She'd tell him that she'd won some money in the lottery, but not how much. Maybe she'd tell him she had matched five numbers. That meant a win of just over a thousand pounds. To a boy of his age that was a fortune.

There was an ache in her face and she realised she was smiling like an idiot. Folding her arms across her chest, she hugged herself tightly. Things were looking up. She could feel it. She certainly deserved a bit of good luck. She was thirty-four and already she'd experienced more misery in her few years than most people did in their entire lives.

First things first.

She was going to move house, get out of this warren and buy herself a house in the country or close to the sea. Maybe not the sea ... she remembered childhood holidays spent in Salthill and Skerries. They should have been the happiest days of her life:

instead they had been terrifying. With no work to go to the following morning, her father drank much too much and he was always in a dark rage when he returned from the pub. Whenever she thought of school holidays, she thought of him ...

Forcing her mind away from those dark memories, she wondered if there was anyone else she'd tell. She had friends of course, but really they were mostly acquaintances, women from the estate, neighbours who had helped her out, whom she had helped out; but there was no-one to whom she could tell this magical news. No-one she could trust ... except Helen.

Helen was a few years older than Christine, a large-boned Cork woman, who was unfailingly cheerful and optimistic. She and Christine had moved into the estate at about the same time, and while other women had come and gone – most of them driven away by Robert's brutish behaviour or Christine's defensive reserve – Helen had always remained, was always there when she needed her. If anyone deserved to share in her good fortune, then surely Helen did.

Christine stopped.

But would Helen be able to keep the news to herself? As much as Christine loved her, she realised that Helen could sometimes be a bit of a gossip, although, unlike many of the other women on the estate, she delighted in gossiping good news rather than scandal.

Christine shook her head. If she told Helen, then she would probably tell her husband Tommy, and Tommy would tell the lads in the pub ... No, not now. She wouldn't tell her now. Maybe when she got used to the idea herself, she'd take Helen out for a meal, tell her then. She smiled at the image. She would wait until Helen had her mouth full of something sticky – chocolate, she loved chocolate – and then she'd tell her. Helen had played the same trick on her in the bingo hall once, waiting until Christine had her mouth full of a cream bun, before telling her the most outrageously dirty story. Christine had almost choked.

She nodded. That's when she'd tell Helen. Who else would she – could she – tell? There was her family. Her father. They hadn't spoken for nearly twenty years. There was Sheila, her sister. Christine shook her head quickly; Sheila was a stuck-up bitch, with a perfect husband who had a perfect job and they had two perfect children. Christine and Sheila had never been close. No, there was no-one else she'd think of telling, no-one she felt she could trust with the news.

She was calm and controlled as she made the tea. Her hands didn't even tremble as she poured. She would tell no-one. That was best. Yet, she knew there was something unnatural about such a decision. She wanted to tell everyone. She wanted to run down the street and scream the news at the top of her voice. She wanted to run into the social welfare office and shout it at their blank, uncaring faces, and to all those so-sympathetic social workers, then to all of those people who had simply dismissed her, writing her off as an unimportant nobody. She wanted to rub their noses in it. With six magical numbers she'd gone from being a nobody to becoming a member of a very *élite* club, a very special group. She'd become a millionaire.

Christine Quinn said the words slowly, savouring each syllable.

I.

Have.

Become.

A.

Millionaire.

And by God, she thought, I'm going to enjoy it.

Chapter 4

It was early afternoon before Kevin Quinn finally came home. He had spent the night with a girl he met at Tony's party.

She lived on the other side of the estate and they knew each other vaguely. Tony had done his usual trick of inviting far too many people, most of them his yuppie college friends, and Kevin felt decidedly out of place, so he was thrown together with this girl. He hadn't consciously tried to get her into bed, but she'd had far too much to drink, and he'd had just a little too much to smoke, and it had sort of ended up that way. He could remember very little about it now, and he wasn't even sure if he'd enjoyed it at the time, but he definitely wasn't enjoying it now. He was hung-over from too many beers, bruised and sore after a night of sex with ... with? ... Sandra. That was her name. Sandra Miller.

He slowed as he turned down the road which led to the terraced house. He wasn't looking forward to this. He knew his mother worried about him but – Jesus! – he was seventeen now. He was old enough to look after himself. When she was his age she'd already given birth to a child. Him.

Slipping his leather jacket over his shoulders to hide the beer-stained tee-shirt, he brought his hands to his face and breathed out. His breath was stale with alcohol and sour with the odour of the hash he'd smoked, and he could smell a mixture of stale sweat and sex off his body. He needed to get into the house and grab a shower before his mother saw him. He patted the pocket of his jacket, feeling the reassuring weight of the keys in the inside pocket.

If he could just open the door, creep in, and get upstairs to the landing, he could shout down a hello, then pop into the bathroom and turn on the shower.

The hall door was open when he reached it.

The young man stopped, surprised. His mother was paranoid about locking the doors behind her, ever since ...

Aware that his heart was beginning to thump, he pressed the flat of his hand against the door and pushed slowly inwards.

The house was silent. There was no radio on, no stereo, no television. That was unusual: sometimes his mother had all three going at the one time because she couldn't stand the silence. Even when she was going out, she generally left the radio on. There was something wrong here.

Leaving the door ajar – just in case he had to make a quick escape – Kevin looked around quickly and saw that the sitting room door was open too. This surprised him because it was rarely used. But the room was empty. Dust motes circled in the air, and the room smelt musty. Moving cautiously now, unaccountably frightened, he looked into the kitchen. It too was empty. He put his hand against the kettle: it was still hot, and there was one cup on the draining board. The dining room – the room they always used – was also empty.

Stepping back into the kitchen he lifted a carving knife off the rack beside the sink and headed for the stairs. He could smell his fear in the air now, remembering the last time he had come home to a silent house. He had only been a child, but the memories remained, and they were vivid and unpleasant: his mother lying on the bedroom floor, her face almost unrecognisable after the beating she'd received. He had sworn then that it would never happen again.

He stopped outside his mother's bedroom, the carving knife pressed flat against his left leg, his hands slick with sweat, sour beer churning in his stomach. There were faint noises coming from within. Suddenly he was eleven years old again.

Listening at the door, Kevin heard cloth being torn with a long ragged rip inside the room, and this sound spurred him to

26

action. Full of fear and holding his breath, he pushed open the door.

And stopped in amazement.

His mother was standing in the middle of the bedroom. On the floor, piled up around her feet, were the torn remnants of most of her dresses, the hand-me-downs and the second-hand clothes she bought at charity sales. Her face was streaked with tears and he couldn't make up his mind whether she was laughing or crying as she wrenched a hideous blue-and-white polka dot dress in two, the cloth parting like tearing paper.

'Mum? Mum? Mum, are you okay? What's wrong?'

Christine looked at him blankly for a moment and then smiled in embarrassment, brushing tears off her cheeks with the heels of her hand. 'Don't worry, Kevin. There's nothing wrong. We've had a bit of good news, that's all. We've come in for a bit of money.' She giggled suddenly, unexpectedly.

'Yea ... well, that's great, Mum. A lot?' he asked, looking at the pile of ruined clothing.

'A few bob,' she said, choking back the laughter. 'We won't have to buy second-hand clothes again for a while.'

'That's great,' Kevin said again, backing out of the room, suddenly unwilling to let her see the knife in his hand. 'Look, I'll just grab a quick shower and then we'll talk about it – okay?'

Christine took a deep breath, visibly calming herself. She allowed the torn dress in her hands to flutter on to the floor. 'You do that. I'll go and make us some lunch.'

Kevin nodded. He closed the door behind him and breathed out a great gushing sigh. For a moment there he thought ...

Pulling off his jacket, he stepped into his own bedroom and nudged the door closed with his foot. He dropped the knife on the window-ledge, realising he was going to have to return it to the kitchen. Now that he'd got over his fright, he wondered where the money had come from, and how much there was.

Most of all, he wondered how much there was.

* * *

She'd have to impress on Kevin that if he told his friends, it would be all over Dublin in a matter of hours. She didn't know what would happen then, but she didn't think she wanted to find out. By the time Kevin came down for lunch – showered and shaved and looking a hundred times better – she had her story worked out. What was it politicians were always talking about: a need to know? Well, she'd tell Kevin what she thought he needed to know.

'This is great news, Mum. We could really do with a few bob,' he said, sliding into the plastic seat. He could feel the suppressed excitement coming from his mother. It was evident in the rigid line of her spine, her taut jaw muscles.

How much, he wondered? Obviously enough to excite her. Christine turned back to the cooker, where she was keeping plates of bacon and eggs warm under the grill. Wrapping a cloth around her hand, she passed a plate across to her son and set the second plate down in front of her own place. As usual, she gave him the larger portion. Sitting across from him, she said very quietly, 'First, we need to talk, Kevin.'

'About what?' he asked, suddenly frightened that she was going to question him about the previous night. The wary look in his blue eyes told her he was trying to hide something from her. But she ignored it.

'The money, Kevin. The money. I don't want you talking to your friends about it.'

'I won't.' He started to eat, the smell of the bacon making him ravenous.

'You have to promise me. Word would get out and soon the whole street would know. We'd have people calling to the door looking for money. Robert might even get to hear of it,' she

28

added very quietly. The ultimate threat.

Kevin stopped chewing. Mention of his stepfather sent shivers down his spine. 'I won't tell a soul,' he promised.

'This is the first bit of good luck we've had in a long time. Maybe we can make it work for us.'

Kevin nodded. Even before he spoke she knew he was going to ask how much.

'How much did we win, Mum? And where did you get it?' he persisted.

Christine tried to ignore the questions. 'First, we're going to buy a few things,' she said with a broad smile. 'Clothes ... maybe that video you wanted. Maybe we'll even think about moving.'

Kevin stopped eating, the realisation sinking in that they hadn't won a couple of hundred pounds, but more, maybe much more. 'How much have we won, Mum?' he asked quietly.

Christine concentrated on eating. She could feel him watching her.

'How much?'

She smiled to take the sting from her words. 'Can I trust you? I'm not sure I should tell you ...' she teased.

He poured tea for them both. 'I'm seventeen, Mum; I'll be eighteen in a couple of weeks' time. I'm not stupid ... well, not completely stupid anyway. I know what would happen if the word got out that we'd won a few bob. Everyone would want some ... and you're such a soft touch, you'd probably end up giving it all away,' he added with a quick smile.

Christine smiled back.

'So how much have we won?'

'A lot,' she said, feeling the grin spread across her face.

'How much?'

She didn't want to tell him, but suddenly, against her better judgement, she was reaching into the back pocket of her jeans, sliding the precious lottery ticket across the table. And then she pushed across the ragged scrap of newspaper. She needed to tell someone.

Kevin stared at her for a single moment, and then looked down, eyes flickering from the lottery ticket to the newspaper and back again. She saw the colour drain from his face as the truth sank in.

'Fuck's sake!' he breathed.

'Language!' she snapped.

'Sorry, Mum,' he said automatically. He swallowed hard.

'Two and a quarter million pounds, Mum,' he whispered.

'Two million, two hundred and twenty-five thousand, seven hundred and ninety-five pounds.' She knew the amount by heart. Reaching over, she squeezed his hand. 'We can do a lot with that money, Kevin. An awful lot. We can start again.'

* * *

Christine prayed that night for the first time in years.

Kneeling by the side of the bed, she gave thanks to a God she had long forgotten, and whom she imagined had long since forgotten her. She had a second chance now. She felt she had wasted her life up to this point, but she was determined not to make the same mistakes again. Sitting up in bed, she pulled open the drawer of her bedside cabinet and took out the ticket and the torn scrap of newspaper, the ink now smudged and faded. Spreading them on the duvet, she looked at them yet again; these two scraps of paper meant the difference between being barely alive and actually living. For the past ten years – more probably, ever since Kevin's birth – she had only been existing, but now, with the freedom the money would give her, she could finally begin living.

Twelve

Sixteen

Twenty-three

Three

Twenty-seven

Thirty-four.

All these numbers were pivotal points in her life. She blinked, sudden tears in her eyes: six numbers, six events ... and apart from her wedding day at twenty-three, she didn't think there was one good memory among them.

They were only experiences.

The winning numbers –

T W E L V E

Chapter 5

It was Sunday, 22 June 1969, a special day, a sad day too. Christine Doolin looked at the *Sunday Independent* and read the minor headline carefully. Judy Garland had died in London. Christine had seen her in the *Wizard of Oz* in the Royal Cinema and, for weeks afterwards, she dreamt every night of the Tin Man and the Wizard and the Yellow Brick Road, wishing she could travel over the rainbow to her own Yellow Brick Road and make her own dream come true. She looked at the grainy picture of the sad-looking woman in the newspaper, remembering the bright-eyed clear-faced girl on the screen, and wondered what had made her so sad.

Christine put down the newspaper and stood on her toes to look at her own face in the mirror over the fire. She was thin, with dark shadows under her huge blue eyes: she knew what made people sad. Today was her twelfth birthday, and her mother had been in hospital for exactly six months.

Christine and her father visited her mother every Sunday. Although the Richmond Hospital was within walking distance from Cabra and she could have visited more often, Christine hated the forbidding-looking hospital, the high-ceilinged, old-fashioned wards and the long echoing corridors. Recently her mother had been moved to one of the small wood-and-metal huts in the hospital grounds. The hut was dark and grim and every week when Christine visited, she kept seeing new faces in the beds. At first she thought that the population of the ward changed because people got better and went home ... but the realisation slowly dawned that most of the people in these wards were going to die. Although no-one told her anything, she knew, deep down, that her mother would not be coming out of hospital. All they were doing was waiting.

The clock over the fireplace chimed one. Christine brushed the tangles from her thick blond hair, pulling it back off her face, holding it in place with a hairband that had once belonged to her mother.

She hated the hospital. Hated the waiting.

Maybe it would end soon.

*　*　*

The ward was quiet when Christine and her father visited. Three of the beds were empty, and there were two new faces in the beds on the left-hand side. Her mother was in the corner at the bottom right-hand side. She was sleeping as Christine and her father approached and the young girl was shocked at the change that had taken place over the past week. Moira Doolin had never been a big woman, but now the flesh had fallen off her, leaving her skeletal. Her face was skull-like, her eyes darkly shadowed, deep-sunk, her cheekbones, jaw and nose prominent. Her wispy grey hair lay lank about her face.

Jimmy Doolin leaned over and kissed his wife's forehead. Her eyes flickered open and for a brief moment there was the look of cold determination in them, a determination to survive at all costs. Then the light died, and it was as if the life had gone out of her face.

And in that moment, Christine realised that they wouldn't have long to wait; her mother had fought too long, now she'd given up and the cancer had won.

Moira stretched out her frail trembling hand and Christine took it. Leaning forward to kiss her mother's cheek, the girl smelt a peculiar bitter medicinal odour that she would associate with death for years afterwards. 'Happy Birthday, love,' her mother whispered.

Christine was determined she was not going to cry. She knew that if she broke down, then her mother would cry too, and if she became too upset the nurses would ask them to leave.

'How are you today, Ma?' she asked.

Moira Doolin made an unsuccessful attempt to hoist herself higher on the pillows. 'Getting better,' she lied. 'I'll be out of here soon. The doctors were saying so only this morning.'

Christine glanced back over her shoulder at her father. He had forced a smile to his lips, but she could tell by the look in his eyes that he didn't believe it either.

'And Sheila, how is Sheila?' asked her mother.

Christine's younger sister had gone to stay with an aunt in the Coombe when her mother first went into hospital. Christine hadn't seen her for nearly two weeks. 'She's great, Ma. She wants to come and see you.'

'I don't want her brought here,' her mother said quickly. 'I don't want her seeing me like this.' She looked up at her husband. 'Don't bring her, Jimmy.'

'I won't,' he promised.

'And where is your father taking you for your birthday?' Moira asked, looking at her husband.

'I'm taking her into town later, and we'll get an ice cream.'

Moira touched her daughter's face with ice-cold fingers. 'Get a knickerbocker glory in … in … ' She stopped, unable to remember the name of the café in O'Connell Street.

'Caffola's,' Jimmy muttered, 'or the Palm Grove.'

'I'm sorry I'm not home to make a cake for you.'

'You can make it for me when you get home,' Christine smiled, holding back the tears.

'I will. I promise.'

Jimmy dropped his hand onto his daughter's shoulder. 'Why don't you go and wait outside while I have a chat with your Ma?' He dug into his pocket and pulled out a sixpenny bit. 'Get yourself a packet of sweets.'

Christine leaned over and kissed her mother again. 'I'll be

back soon, Ma,' she whispered. She opened her hand, showing the silver sixpence. 'Is there anything you'd like in the shops?'

'Lots of things I'd like, love. But I'm allowed none of them. Get yourself something.'

Christine walked down the centre of the ward, not looking at the patients on either side. Most of them had visitors, clusters of people gathered around the beds, talking earnestly, or laughing loudly, falsely, and lying to people, telling them how well they looked. She stopped at the door and looked back. Her mother's face was a smudge of shadows against the pillows and in the dim light of the room, it looked like a fleshless skull. Christine raised her hand and her mother lifted her own in farewell.

That was the last time she saw her mother alive. When she came back from the local shop half an hour later, sucking on a liquorice stick, there was a curtain around her mother's bed and the ward seemed unusually hushed. The sweet-tasting liquorice soured in her mouth and she knew, even as she ran down the ward towards the bed, that something was terribly wrong.

Her mother was going to die. She knew that. But not now. Not today. She couldn't.

The striped hospital curtain parted before she reached the bed and her father stepped out. She had a brief glimpse of a still figure lying on the bed, before her father scooped her up in his arms, holding her so tightly that it hurt. His breath was warm against her ear as he whispered, 'Your Ma's gone to heaven, Chrissy. We have to pray for her.'

*　　*　　*

The days that followed took on a curious nightmarish quality. It was like a dream in which you tried to wake up, but couldn't. The house was full of relatives, friends, neighbours, all of them talking in hushed tones, a droning murmuring that made Christine want to scream.

She had no real memory of the day of the funeral. A few scattered incidents remained with her: her father's tear-streaked face – she had never seen him cry before – the feel of the cold clay in her hands as she dropped it onto the coffin, the sense of standing at the edge of the grave with Sheila's small hand in hers, the icy wind that whipped across Glasnevin Cemetery, the shimmer of light off the coffin, the smell of the leather seats in the funeral car.

And then they came back to the house which now felt truly empty.

Christine awoke screaming the night after the funeral, shaking and terrified from a horrible nightmare. She dreamt she was sleeping alongside her dead mother and when she rolled over, she found herself staring into the skull-like face, its jaws moving, teeth clacking. The skeletal hands grasped her, lifting her up, pulling her out of the bed ... and then she realised it was her father cradling her in his strong arms. He carried her into his bed and tucked her in between the warm sheets. When he lay down beside her, she could smell the tobacco smoke and the odour of stale drink off him.

The nightmare returned to haunt her the following night, and every night after that. Finally, she was too frightened to sleep on her own and she simply crept into her father's bed each night.

Jimmy Doolin had worked as a bus driver, but he'd lost the job just after Moira had gone into hospital. He had never told his wife about this. He had crashed the double decker on the way back to the garage after the last run of the day. Four buses were damaged in the collision, and although no-one was hurt, he was suspended and then dismissed when it was discovered that he was drunk that night. The company had warned him a dozen times about his drinking. The unions wanted to fight the case for him, but he wasn't interested. Now he sat at home watching the television and drinking.

Sheila had remained with Moira's sister Bridie in the Coombe; Bridie had offered to take Christine too, but Christine had refused to go. Someone had to stay and look after her father. In the weeks following the funeral, when the visitors and neighbours stopped calling, he started drinking heavily again. By the time Christine got home from school, he was drunk. He rarely washed, avoided the neighbours, and what food they ate came out of cans and jars.

Three months after the funeral he raped her.

At first she thought it was just another nightmare, but then she realised that she was awake and that the hands on her flesh were real. In the darkness she could smell the overpowering odour of drink. There was pain too, terrible tearing fire that made her cry out in agony until a hand was clamped across her mouth. She bit into his flesh, tasting blood in her mouth, and then her head was rocked back as she was struck across the side of the face. She lay in the darkened room, confused, terrified, wondering what was wrong. Wondering what she had done wrong.

The following night she slept in her own bed. He didn't come for her that night, but he came the next. And through the long months ahead, she grew to dread the nights. What was most terrifying to her was the waiting ... waiting to see if he would come, if he would creep into her bedroom and lift her out of her bed and carry her into his own and hurt her again and again ...

Monday, 12 July

Chapter 6

Christine fed another twenty pence into the phone and listened intently to the voice on the other end of the line.

'And that's all I have to do?' she asked. She made a face at Kevin through the glass phone booth, and then shrugged.

'And when can I collect?' she asked. She looked at Kevin who was mouthing 'Today,' at her. 'Can I collect today?'

Kevin shifted nervously from foot to foot, watching his mother on the phone. Yesterday she'd been all fired up to collect the money immediately, but today, when the lottery office was open, she actually wanted to slow things down! He couldn't believe it. As they sat across the table from each other, she gave him a dozen reasons for delaying. She was thinking about putting it off for a day or two, allowing things to settle down ... maybe the media would be watching the lottery office, and she didn't want to be photographed entering or leaving the building; maybe ...

Kevin suggested that they look at how much the daily interest came to on two and a quarter million pounds, and how much they were losing by delaying. Working out the sum on a sheet of paper, they arrived at a figure of just over four thousand pounds a week. Every week! Divided by seven, that came to five hundred and seventy-one pounds a day. If she delayed by two days they would have lost over a thousand pounds. These figures changed her mind; she'd never realised that they could earn that sort of money in interest alone. The two of them walked out the front door and down the road to use the phones outside the shopping centre.

'Well?' he asked, when she came out.

'Nothing to it,' she grinned. Kevin suddenly noticed that she looked younger this morning: the lines around her eyes and across her forehead had vanished. The haunted, hurt look was missing. Even her shoulders were straighter, as if a huge weight had been taken off them.

'So, what do we have to do?' he asked.

'We bring the ticket and some identification to the lottery place in Abbey Street ... and they give us a cheque.'

'Just like that?'

'Just like that.' She searched through her handbag and checked her purse, wondering if she had enough money for the bus fare into town. 'Let's collect our winnings,' she said, pulling out a five-pound note. 'And remember ...' she began.

'Not a word to anyone,' Kevin finished.

*   *   *

It took an hour. And when she walked out of the offices she wasn't the same woman who had gone in.

Christine had been expecting a lot of red tape, but the whole procedure was surprisingly simple. Once her identification – her social welfare card, a couple of bills – had been verified, and she had handed in the winning lottery ticket, she was simply presented with a cheque made out for two million, two hundred and twenty-five thousand, seven hundred and ninety-five pounds.

She didn't wait for advice or help or assistance, declined the offers of tea and coffee, and promised to get back to the smiling official if she wanted help with investments and accounts. She simply walked out of the lottery office with the cheque in her bag and turned left down Abbey Street, heading for the quays.

The screech of tyres brought her back to the present with a heart-thumping start. She was standing in the middle of the street, outside the Irish Life building ... and she hadn't even realised she'd walked out onto the road. She could have been killed. The irony of it made her smile; it would be just her luck to win the money and then be run over.

'Jesus, lady, you drunk or what?'

Christine ignored the taxi-driver and darted across the street and around by Liberty Hall. She waited for the lights to change before she hurried across the quays and down by the Custom House.

Kevin was sitting on one of the new seats in front of the Custom House. He'd spent the hour staring at the oil-scummed rainbowed water, while his thoughts spun round and round. Somewhere at the back of his mind he couldn't help thinking that there was some mistake. Maybe they hadn't won the money. Or maybe they had won it and the lottery people wouldn't give it to his mother because she hadn't got the proper ID. Or maybe she was going to need her husband's signature before she could claim the money, or ...

He finally gave up and stared at the water, forcing his thoughts away from the possibilities two million pounds would bring and back to more mundane matters. He thought about phoning the girl he'd spent Saturday night with ... what was her name again? Sandra, that was it, Sandra Miller. He supposed he should have phoned her yesterday. But Sunday had been a crazy day. His mother had flipped, completely flipped. One minute she knew she'd won and was making plans accordingly, and then in the next breath, she was equally sure that she hadn't won and was in the depths of despair.

Footsteps clattering on the cobblestones made him turn, and even before she spoke, her voice panting, the pulse in her throat throbbing visibly, he knew from the look on her face that she'd won – that they'd won.

Kevin swept her up in his arms, swinging her round. Tears were streaming down Christine's face as she sobbed into his shoulder, and when they finally sat down on the seat, he had to hear everything that had been said in the lottery office. She had been given a little booklet, which they read through together, heads touching, but most of the advice seemed to be common sense.

'I suppose we need an accountant to invest the money for us,' Kevin said eventually.

'We might just put it in the bank for the moment,' Christine said.

'A good accountant would be able to tell us how to earn the highest rates of interest ... and not have the taxman take most of it,' said Kevin.

'But the money is tax free,' Christine protested.

'The win is tax free, but the interest isn't,' Kevin said.

'Where did you get all that great information?' Christine asked him, teasingly.

'Business studies! School comes in useful sometimes!'

'The lottery people said they'd help us, but I think we'll put the money in the bank for the moment and then see about advice,' Christine decided.

She was nervous, trembling with the thought of the cheque in her bag, which she clutched tightly. The last thing she needed was for the bag to be snatched. 'Where will we lodge the money?' she wondered.

'I suppose we should do it close to home,' Kevin suggested.

'Why?' Christine asked, smiling. 'You don't think we're going to stay there, do you? No,' she said, suddenly decisive, 'we'll open a new account here in town. Nobody will know our business then. We'll get cheque books and credit cards and cash. We'll buy ourselves some new clothes.'

'Boots,' Kevin said suddenly. 'I'd really like a pair of cowboy boots.'

Christine nodded happily. Although she had scrimped and saved to give her son as much as she could, there were times – especially Christmas and birthdays – when she had seen the disappointed look in his eyes, and she knew he'd been compar-

43

ing what other children got with the simple presents she had managed to get him. When every other kid in his class had new schoolbooks, he had to make do with second-hand. He had never had a new bike. Many of his clothes were second-hand, picked up at the markets, or the second-hand clothes shops behind the new bank in Dame Street. He never said anything though, never complained. And now she had a chance to make it all right for him.

Christine gripped his hand tightly. 'Let's go and lodge this cheque and get some money.'

*   *   *

Joseph Chambers put on his most professional smile and rose from behind his desk as the curious couple were ushered into his office. Brother and sister was his first evaluation, but when he looked again, he noted that the woman was much older. Mother and son? He came around the desk and shook hands with them both.

'Joseph Chambers. I'm the manager of this branch. I understand you wanted to see me.'

'Yes. My name is Christine Quinn, and this is my son Kevin.'

Chambers was surprised that they had been so insistent on seeing him. They didn't look the sort who would have important business. He indicated two leather chairs, and then moved back behind his desk, sinking into a high-backed leather chair. He placed his perfectly manicured hands flat on the pristine blotting pad on the desk in front of him, watching the pair from behind dark-rimmed glasses. Their clothes were inexpensive, threadbare, the woman's shoes in need of new heels, the boy's runners frayed around the edges; they looked poor, in fact.

'Now, Mrs Quinn, how can I help you? I don't believe you are customers of this branch.'

'We're not.' Christine glanced at Kevin. After they'd decided to go to a city-centre bank they'd chosen this one in O'Connell Street simply because it was the first they came across. 'But I would like to open an account,' Christine said quietly, opening her bag.

Chambers frowned slightly. 'We could very easily have opened an account for you outside, Mrs Quinn. We have staff who would have been able to assist ...'

Christine pulled out the lottery cheque and pushed it across the table.

Joseph Chambers had been working in the bank for thirty years. He had been a manager for the last ten, and in that time he'd seen and heard it all. There were stories – legion amongst bank staff – about millionaires who came in looking like tramps, about old women heaving brown paper bags of fivers up onto the desk, about teenagers with bank accounts that ran into hundreds of thousands. Since the lottery had started up, another tale had been added to bank folklore: the lottery winners. Usually nondescript, ordinary people, they simply wandered into their local bank one day and lodged huge sums. It was quite a feather in any bank manager's cap to have attracted such a large sum on deposit.

'I would like to open an account,' Christine Quinn repeated, trying hard to stop herself from laughing aloud at the stunned expression on the bank manager's face. He had the pinched features of someone who didn't get much enjoyment from life: cold eyes, thin lips, slightly yellowed uneven teeth. 'I also want you to guarantee me total anonymity. That's why I asked to see you rather than do it at the desk.'

Chambers nodded automatically. He pulled the cheque closer with his thin fingers. 'I take it you won the lottery on Saturday night, Mrs Quinn. Congratulations,' he said, his features wooden.

Christine pushed across a business card, emblazoned with the lottery logo. 'You will want to okay the cheque,' she said coolly. 'You should phone this man here. And of course, you will need some identification.' She pulled out the social welfare card and bills which she had shown the lottery people.

'Yes, yes, I'm sure everything is in order.' Chambers smiled quickly; these people may have come in with nothing, but they had suddenly assumed the status of highly-valued customers. 'Some tea, perhaps, while we work out the details?' He looked from Christine to Kevin. They both nodded. He pressed a buzzer on his desk. 'Could we have tea for three, please, Mary?' He looked up. 'Now, if you will excuse me, I'll just go and get the forms for a new account.'

'Current and deposit,' Kevin said, suddenly remembering his business studies class again. 'And a cheque book each.'

'And we'd like some credit cards as well,' Christine added.

'Of course.' Chambers slipped around the side of the desk and disappeared into another office.

'He's taken the cheque and the card with the lottery guy's name on it.' Christine lowered her voice to a whisper.

'He's checking up on us,' Kevin grinned. 'Wouldn't you if someone came into your bank looking like us, with a cheque for two and a quarter million in their bag?'

'What's wrong with us?' Christine demanded, teasing him again.

'We don't look like millionaires,' Kevin grinned.

'Not yet anyway,' she laughed.

Chapter 7

It took longer to sort out the details with the bank than it had to get the money out of the lottery office. There were dozens of forms to be filled in, some of them in duplicate, and the bank needed several copies of sample signatures. Christine's hands were trembling so much that no two of her signatures matched. Chambers spoke at length about high-interest accounts, special interest accounts, tax efficient accounts, bonds, insurance policies, until finally Christine held up her hands and stopped him in full flight.

'Mrs Quinn ...?'

'Please, I'd just like to keep this simple. You've been very helpful, but at the moment, I'm just a little ...' she paused, 'a little addled with winning this huge amount of money. I'd like a couple of days to think about everything you've said, and see where I'll go next.' She held up the bundle of leaflets Chambers had spread across the desk. 'Kevin and I will read through these and come back to you when we've talked things over.'

Chambers smiled quickly. 'Of course, Mrs Quinn. I fully understand. And in the meantime, if there is anything I can do for you, please do not hesitate to contact me.' He pulled out a business card, turned it over and scribbled a number on the back. 'This is my personal extension.'

Christine added the card to the bundle of paper on the desk before her.

Kevin leaned forward. 'And in the meantime, what will happen to our money?' he asked.

Chambers looked from the woman to the young man.

'Well ... we will immediately lodge the greater part of the money to a high-yield deposit account, and though we usually require three months' notice before a withdrawal, I will personally guarantee that you can have access to your money at an hour's notice ...'

'Should we have that in writing?' Kevin asked immediately.

Christine reached out and put her hand on her son's arm. 'I don't think that will be necessary. I'm sure we can trust Mr Chambers. Please go on, Mr Chambers.'

'When you have decided what you want to do with the bulk of your money, we can make those arrangements for you. There are several tax efficient options, which would net you ...' He stopped, smiling. 'But I'm sure you don't want to hear about that just now.'

Christine shook her head.

'In the meantime, I'll get two temporary cheque books ready for you before you leave here, one for each of you. Further cheque books and your credit cards should be with you by the end of the week. Now, I need to know how much you would like me to transfer to your current account?'

Christine looked at Kevin, who grinned and shrugged his shoulders. She turned back to the bank manager. 'Say ... twenty thousand for the moment.'

Joseph Chambers kept his expression completely neutral as he filled out the form, and then pushed it across the table towards her. 'If you could sign, please ...' Christine looked at it blankly, feeling dizzy, and he indicated the line for her signature. 'I will monitor this account personally,' he said. 'If I see the balance falling dangerously low, I'll transfer funds immediately. Or, if you are going to make a large purchase, perhaps you would let me know beforehand, in which case I'll transfer the appropriate amount and ensure that the cheque clears.'

There was a tap on the door and a young woman entered holding two long blue cheque books. She laid them on the desk before Chambers and left the room.

'These are your cheque books. I'll just need you to sign for them here and here ...' He indicated the dotted line on the white slips of paper. 'Now if there is anything else ...'

'Cash, Mum,' Kevin said quickly. 'Shouldn't you get some cash too?'

'Of course,' she nodded. 'How much, I wonder?'

'Five hundred?' Chambers suggested.

'Make it a thousand,' Christine said.

'Of course. If you would just sign here ...' He passed across a withdrawal slip and waited until Christine had filled in her name, pressing heavily with his fountain pen. 'I'll just get this for you now,' he said, rising to his feet.

Christine and Kevin sat in silence for some moments until the bank manager returned with a thick brown envelope in his hand. He opened the envelope and slowly counted out one thousand pounds in fifties, twenties and tens. When he had finished, he shuffled it back into the envelope, passed it across to Christine and sat back into his chair with a smile. He watched as she took a single twenty-pound note out of the envelope and pushed it into her pocket. The envelope went into her shabby purse.

'Have you any idea what you're going to do now, Mrs Quinn?' he asked. 'I'm sure there are big changes ahead of you.'

'We haven't made any long-term plans yet,' Christine smiled, 'but right now, we're going shopping!'

'Enjoy it,' Chambers said, as sincerely as he could.

'We will,' Christine and Kevin said together.

* * *

Christine stood on the steps of the bank and looked up and down O'Connell Street, suddenly seeing it through new eyes. The street seemed brighter, the colours sharper, cleaner. Even the air smelt good.

'What's wrong, Mum?'

Christine reached down and caught her son's hand. 'Nothing's wrong,' she said softly, tears stinging her eyes, 'nothing's wrong at all.' She squeezed his fingers. 'Let's go shopping.'

Kevin shook his head quickly. 'But you look like you're about to fall down.' He glanced at his watch. 'It's after one, and I'm starving. How about some lunch?' He nodded towards a hamburger restaurant.

At the thought of food, Christine felt the sudden pangs of hunger, and she realised that she'd only had a cup of tea for breakfast. She'd been so nervous in the bank manager's office she hadn't been able to drink the tea they'd offered. 'Good idea. I could do with a cuppa.'

As they stepped into the restaurant, Christine gave Kevin the twenty-pound note from her pocket to buy lunch. The smell of food was making her dizzy and slightly nauseous, and she knew that if she didn't sit down soon, she was going to fall down. A young couple were leaving a window seat as she approached and she slid onto the hard plastic chair and stared out into the busy street, only vaguely aware of the crowded restaurant and the young woman clearing off the table. Her head was buzzing, the facts and figures the bank manager had given her still tumbling crazily through her mind, and she couldn't quite shake off the idea that any moment now she was going to wake up and discover that it had all been a dream. Her fingers were trembling violently and she clenched both hands together into a tight knot in an effort to control herself.

Kevin slid the tray across the table and sat down facing his mother. He looked at her face, surprised to discover the lines of stress and anxiety around her eyes and mouth again, shocked at the tears brimming in her eyes. 'Mum? What's wrong?' he whispered.

She shook her head quickly, pulling open her bag to find a tissue. Her fingers touched the thick brown envelope Chambers had given her. With her bag still on her lap, she opened the envelope and peered inside, looking at the wad of ten, twenty and fifty pound notes. 'It's not a dream,' she said very softly.

Kevin grinned widely. 'Oh yes it is, Mum. It's everyone's wildest dream.'

Christine took a deep breath and dabbed quickly at her eyes. When she reached for the styrofoam cup of tea, she was pleased that her hands were no longer trembling. She drank the tea quickly, feeling the hot liquid burn its way down her throat and into her stomach. 'I think I'm in shock,' she explained.

Kevin nodded, his mouth full of burger.

'We need to do some serious thinking,' Christine continued, picking out a long narrow chip and nibbling at it, knowing that if she ate too quickly now, she would have hiccups for the rest of the day. 'We'll need to keep this very quiet. We'll have to be careful how we spend our money. We don't want the neighbours to cop on to anything unusual. You know how they talk around the estate.'

'Were you serious when you said we'd move?'

Christine smiled quickly. 'If we do nothing else with this money, Kevin, we're moving.'

'Where?'

'Somewhere nice and quiet ... beside the sea. I've always wanted to live beside the sea.'

'Howth ... Dun Laoghaire?'

She nodded. 'Someplace like that. We're going to use this money to make a new start. A new home in a new area, new clothes, a car ...'

'You'll be talking about changing our names next,' Kevin grinned.

Christine looked at him seriously. 'That mightn't be such a bad idea. I wonder if we could do it?'

Kevin leaned across the table. 'With money, you can do anything.'

Chapter 8

Habit made them turn down Henry Street. Christine was awed by the fact that she could afford anything – everything – in the shops they passed: clothes, shoes, make up, perfume, jewellery. She could have them all. And yet, she found herself slowing to look at clothes which had been reduced in a closing-down sale. There was a nice cotton dress in red-and-white candy stripe ...

Kevin caught her arm and pulled her away. 'What are you doing, Mum?' he laughed. 'You don't need to look at this junk anymore. You can afford the best.'

'I know that, but I still can't quite believe it,' she said slowly.

'We should go up to Grafton Street,' Kevin said decisively. 'Shop in some of the expensive shops. Buy the best.'

Christine shook her head firmly. 'Not yet. Not today. Let me buy some reasonably good clothes first. I wouldn't feel comfortable going into one of those shops dressed like this.'

'There's nothing wrong with the way you're dressed, Mum.'

Christine silently lifted her left arm to show the tear in the cheap material beneath her armpit.

Kevin looked back at the candy-striped dress in the window. 'That would look well on you,' he said.

'Well, we know it's here; let's have a look in Roches and Dunnes first.' She turned to her son. 'Look, I'm sure you don't want to come traipsing around town with me. Why don't you go and get yourself some clothes too? We'll meet in a couple of hours.'

'That's a great idea, Mum. I need some new jeans.'

'And what about those cowboy boots you've been talking about for weeks?'

'They're about a hundred and fifty quid,' he smiled.

'Oh, I think we can afford it, don't you? Now, stand in front of me so no-one can see what I'm doing.' Christine opened her bag and carefully counted out fifteen twenty-pound notes. Folding them into a small ball, she passed them across to Kevin. 'There's three hundred. Do you think that's enough?'

Kevin tucked the money into an inside pocket. 'More than enough, Mum.' He kissed her quickly on the cheek, surprising her. 'Where'll I meet you?'

'We'll meet at Roches Stores main entrance in two hours.' She glanced at her watch. 'At half-three.'

'I'll see you then, Mum. Don't spend too much,' he laughed before vanishing into the crowd.

Christine turned back to the shop window, smiling at her son's reaction. The last time he had kissed her had been at Christmas, a quick peck on the cheek, out of duty.

She looked critically at the dress again. Reduced from twenty-two pounds to fourteen. She could easily afford it – and another hundred like it. But she wasn't entirely happy with the way the collar was finished and the striped pattern didn't quite match where the sleeves joined the shoulders. She suddenly laughed out loud, startling a woman standing beside her, who quickly moved away. Christine took a deep breath, taking control of herself. Three days ago she would have been delighted to have had the fourteen quid to buy the dress, and would have bought it without a second look. Now that she had a few bob, she could afford to be critical. She could afford the best. She was humming softly to herself as she moved off down the street.

* * *

Kevin turned to the left at the bottom of Henry Street, into Liffey Street. He could actually feel the weight of the three hundred pounds in his inside pocket, a hot and solid pressure just above his heart. And there was a lot more where that came from! He'd be able to get himself some new clothes, pay off a few debts and maybe if he sweet-talked his mother, he'd get her to buy him a motor-bike. He'd suggest a holiday, somewhere hot like the south of Spain or Greece, or maybe even the States. He'd always wanted to visit the States. He was seventeen years old, and he'd never been outside the country, never even been to England. When the school had organised trips abroad, he never had the money.

Kevin darted across the quays onto the Ha'penny Bridge, eyes flicking over the beggars crouched on the stone steps. A couple of years ago, he'd stood on this bridge and begged for money himself. He came into town on a Saturday morning with two pounds in his pocket. He spent – or lost – it, and found himself a long way from home with no money for his bus fare. In desperation, he found a cardboard box and stood on the bridge, head bent, the box outstretched. It took him two excruciating, humiliating hours to make enough for the bus fare home, and he swore then that he would never beg again.

Kevin cut through Merchant's Arch into Temple Bar and stopped outside a shop which specialised in leather boots. He'd had his eye on a pair of tooled leather boots for a long time, but the hundred-and-fifty pound price tag put them way out of his reach. He'd been in to try them on so often that he was sure the staff had come to recognise him. It was going to give him a great deal of pleasure to take the wad of cash out of his pocket and count out the twenties. And he'd have one hundred and fifty left. He'd get a pair of jeans – good Levis, not cheap imitations – and still end up with a hundred quid or so left over. Maybe he'd give Sandra a ring later, ask her out for a date. New jeans, new boots and a hundred pounds in his pocket – he'd make quite an impression.

* * *

The first purchase was the hardest of all. The choice was bewildering. Christine wandered along the racks of dresses in Roches Stores, Arnotts and finally Marks and Spencers, just looking at the colours, feeling the fabrics, trying to imagine what they would look like on her. She was amused and a little bewildered at her own indecisiveness. She'd never had a problem spending money before – well, she'd never had money to spend.

She took a deep breath and tried to come to a decision. She found herself torn between two dresses, one a plain ivory-coloured cotton, the other a warm mustard colour. They were three times the price of the striped dress she had seen earlier, but she could see – and feel – the difference in quality. Taking the two of them off the rails, she stood in front of a long mirror and held them up to herself. In the glass, she could see two young shop assistants looking at her, and she knew that the rather dowdy-looking woman staring at her from the other end of the aisle was probably a store detective. They all thought she hadn't got the money for the dresses. That decided her. It gave her a great deal of satisfaction to carry both dresses up to the counter, and see the looks of surprise on the assistants' faces.

Once she started spending, it became almost a compulsion. Four blouses, one in pure silk, two good skirts, three complete sets of underwear, two pairs of shoes, a stylish tracksuit, a pair of joggers, six pairs of sheer stockings ...

Christine stopped only when she realised that she was having difficulty carrying the numerous bags and packages. When she looked at her watch, she realised that the two hours she'd given Kevin were almost up. A uniformed security guard held the door open for her as she left, weighed down with her purchases. 'Looks like you had a good day,' he grinned.

'The best,' she said sincerely.

As she made her way down Henry Street, she stopped in the Body Shop and bought bath oils, soaps and shampoos. She made a final stop at the beauty counter in Roches Stores and bought herself a complete range of make-up.

Kevin was waiting for her as she came through the shop's main entrance. There was a single black plastic bag on the ground at his feet. He started laughing when he saw the bundle of bags and packages his mother was carrying. 'You don't have to spend it all today, Mum.' He lifted the larger bags off his mother's arm.

'I couldn't make up my mind,' she said, smiling, 'so I bought the lot.' She looked at the bag at his feet. 'Is that all you got?'

'It's a pair of jeans ... real jeans,' he added with a grin. Then he lifted his left foot and hiked up his trousers to show the ornately tooled leather boots. 'And I got these.' Reaching into his pocket, he pulled out the remainder of the money.

'I've got some change.'

'Keep it,' Christine said quickly.

'I felt almost guilty spending so much on a pair of boots,' he admitted, as they walked down the street.

'Me too. And then I realised that what we've spent hasn't even dented the interest we've earned today alone. Let's just enjoy being able to spend. We do have one problem though,' she added seriously.

'What's that?'

'How are we going to get all these bags into the house without the neighbours seeing them?'

Kevin grinned. 'We'll tell them we won the lottery. They'll never believe us!'

Chapter 9

Christine sat on the worn carpet in the middle of the sitting room, surrounded by dozens of packages, the plastic bags and wrapping paper scattered all over the room. The new blouses and dresses were draped over the backs of chairs, shoes lined up neatly beside the fireplace, underwear arranged on the shabby settee, bottles of make-up, shampoo and bath-oils on the floor in front of her. In a neat little pile beside her were the receipts. She began totalling them ... and stopped when she became frightened by the amount of money she'd spent.

The door opened and Kevin looked in. He grinned at the state of the room. 'It looks like a clothes shop in here.'

'I keep expecting them to disappear,' Christine said, laughing shakily.

'This is only the beginning, Mum.' He lifted his right foot, turning it to show off the new boots beneath the crisp new blue-jeans. 'What do you think?'

'Can you walk in them? Those pointed toes must have your feet crippled.'

'Mum! I've seen pictures of the winkle-packers you wore when you were my age.'

'Winkle-*pickers*. And only men wore winkle-pickers,' she smiled. '*And* they were a little before my time. Just how old do you think I am? Are you going out?'

'Yea, I thought I'd take Sandra out for a few drinks. Show off my boots,' he laughed.

Christine looked up, watching her son's face carefully.

'Sandra? Have I met her?'

'I don't think so,' Kevin said quickly. 'I just met her a while ago. She's all right. I might bring her home soon.'

'Is she from around here?'

'Other side of the estate,' he said. 'I'm sure you'll know her to see. Look, I'd better be off,' he added hurriedly, before she could ask him any more questions.

'Don't be too late.'

'I won't.'

'Have you got your key?'

'Key and cash.' He paused by the door. 'Thanks again, Mum.'

'For what?' she asked, genuinely surprised.

'For the money and ...'

'Kevin! Who else am I going to share it with? It's not my money. It's ours, yours and mine. Go on, off you go, but remember ...'

'... not a word to anyone. Trust me,' he smiled as he closed the door.

Christine listened to the hall door rattle shut and remembered that his father – his real father – had used exactly the same phrase when he made love to her, eighteen years ago. 'I'll take care of everything. Trust me.' She did ... only to discover what a fool she'd been. It was one of Robert's favourite phrases too. 'Trust me.' He usually said it when he was cheating on her, or up to some shady business. After a while, she came to the conclusion that when a man said 'Trust me' it meant he was lying.

Thoughts of Robert sent a shiver down her spine. Even though he was gone for nearly seven years now, he still had the ability to terrify her. When she walked away from him, she swore she'd never even think of him again. Paradoxically, she found herself thinking about him nearly all the time, wondering where he was, what he was doing. During the first few years he kept turning up unexpectedly, finger stabbing the bell as he shouted abuse through the letter box. Sometimes, she saw him standing on the corner staring fixedly at the house, and, once, he followed her through Dublin's crowded streets. Every time she turned, she caught glimpses of him, but when she looked again, he was gone. Then two years ago she saw his name in the paper; he was sentenced to eighteen months for a vicious assault on a barman. She breathed a sigh of relief, knowing that she was free of him for a little while at least. But she lived with the fear that he was going to turn up on the doorstep one day. She'd taken out a barring order against him, but she knew it wasn't worth the paper it was written on if Robert appeared in one of his rages. By the time the neighbours got round to calling the police, he could have beaten her to death.

Now she knew that she wasn't going to live with that fear any longer. The money she'd won was going to wipe it away. Christine and Kevin Quinn were going to disappear.

Gathering up the clothes, she carried them upstairs and spread them out on the bed, mixing blouses and skirts, trying out different colour combinations. She ran the back of her hand down the front of the silk blouse, and found her eyes brimming with tears again. The last time she'd worn silk had been on her wedding day, almost eleven years ago. She was twenty-three then and really looking forward to getting married. She loved Robert very much. He was taking her away from the terrors and mistakes of her youth. She saw it as a chance to make a new beginning, a new start.

On impulse now, she tore off her clothes to try on her purchases. When she was completely naked, she reached for the blouse, then stopped, suddenly unwilling to dress in the new clothes until she was completely clean.

Tugging on her dressing gown, slipping her feet into the faded blue slippers Kevin had given her last Christmas, she shuffled into the bathroom and spun the hot tap, wondering if he had left any hot water. It came out steaming, scalding her fingers – which meant he had left the immersion heater on again. Usually the waste infuriated her, but this time she was actually grateful. She used the shower attachment to clean the bath, then stuck in the plug, and turned the hot tap on full, allowing the water to thunder out. While the bath filled, she wandered back into the bedroom and sorted through the bath oils and soaps she had picked up in the Body Shop. The scents were gorgeous, exotic, with wonderful-sounding names. Gathering the whole lot up in her arms, she carried them back into the bathroom.

When she opened the door, steam billowed around her, and the memory of that special time when she stood in a steam-filled bathroom struck her with such vividness that she stopped still in the open doorway, trembling with the recollection. Moisture condensed at her hair-line and ran down along the side of her face, following the line of her jaw. Brushing it away, she broke the moment and the memories faded, leaving her shaken with their intensity. Eighteen years ago, and it might have happened yesterday.

Sitting on the edge of the bath, Christine sorted through the bottles and jars, finally deciding on apple-green bath salts and matching shampoo. She poured half a bottle into the bath, smiling at the sheer extravagance of it, and churned the water to a foam with her arm. Green-tinged bubbles frothed over the side. Throwing off the dressing-gown – she was definitely going to buy a new one, thick and white and fluffy – she slid into the hot water, biting her lips as it stung her flesh, but forcing herself down into it. Then she folded a towel behind her head, lay back in the bath and closed her eyes, breathing in the warm apple-scented air.

When she bought a house, a new house, large and grand, with loads of rooms and wooden floors and glass, the first thing she was going to get was a bath – one of those sunken baths. And a jacuzzi. She'd read about them in magazines and seen them on television, and often wondered what it would be like to lie in the water and feel those jets of bubbling water popping off her skin.

She was going to find out. The lottery win meant that she would be able to do all those things she'd only dreamt of before.

A house first. She wanted to get as far away from this place as possible, for several reasons, but mainly because Robert knew the address. When her ex-husband came calling – as he would, sooner or later, even if she'd never won any money – she wanted him to find either an empty house, with no forwarding address, or else a new family living here.

First thing tomorrow morning, she would dress up in her new clothes and go into the city to look at what some of the estate agents had to offer. She had often looked in the windows of such offices and been amazed at the sizes and the prices of the houses. She used to wonder who could afford to buy them. Now *she* would buy one. A house in .. Howth? Killiney? Dun Laoghaire? Or maybe somewhere out the country, Kildare perhaps. Or she could move further away, down to Cork or over to Galway.

Christine stopped, suddenly realising that she was doing what she always did: she was running. She had started off by running from her father and ended up with Robert, who had become just like her father. And then she ran from him.

No more running. She was making her own decisions now. The time for running was over.

Sweat trickled into her eyes, stinging them. Reaching blindly for a towel, she dried them quickly, and found herself looking at the cracked ceiling. She'd grown up in a house with a cracked bathroom ceiling, and Jimmy Doyle, her first lover and, though she had never admitted it to anyone, Kevin's father, had lived in a house with a cracked bathroom ceiling.

Again, the memories flooded back, of a steam-filled bathroom with a cracked ceiling, eighteen years ago ...

The winning numbers –

SIXTEEN

Chapter 10

As they stepped off the 22 bus, the leaden skies opened.

The sudden downpour caught them unawares, soaking through Christine's thin cheesecloth blouse, moulding it to her skin, outlining her bra, staining her jeans a deeper blue, the flared ends flapping against her ankles. The dye started to run in Jimmy's tee-shirt, purple streaks curling down his arms, the waistband of his white jeans turning a deep purple.

Jimmy Doyle's house was closer than Christine's to the bus-stop and they reached it first, breathless with running and laughter. They were both soaked through, Jimmy's long blond hair – longer than Christine's – plastered to his skull. Christine's boyish pageboy cut clung to her head like a cap. As Jimmy fumbled with the key, his stained fingers left oily purple patches across the new white paintwork.

'I'm home,' he shouted as the door swung open and they stepped into the dim hallway.

The house was silent.

'Anyone home?' he called again. 'There's no-one in,' he said turning back to Christine, a wide smile on his face. Leaning forward, he made to kiss her, but she moved her head back and pointed to the floor. Purple-tinted water was forming into a pool around his feet.

'Aw shit!'

Christine pushed her damp hair out of her eyes. 'I told you not to dye it yourself.'

'Mum'll kill me,' Jimmy muttered, pulling up the tee-shirt to examine his stomach and chest. He shook the tee-shirt, spattering purple spots across the newly decorated hallway.

Christine started laughing. His shoulders and chest were tinted purple, and the dye had now coloured his jeans to his knees.

'It's probably toxic. I'll probably get blood poisoning.'

'It's only vegetable dye,' she reminded him.

'Aw fuck!' He had just noticed the spots on the white wallpaper. He rubbed one, smearing it into a long purple streak. 'Shit!'

'Don't touch it. Let it dry; maybe we can cover it with white paint or something.'

Jimmy nodded, spattering Christine with water. 'What am I going to do? I'll never get this bloody dye off ...'

Christine was laughing so hard she had a stitch in her side. The expression on Jimmy's face reminded her of that cartoon character of the doleful dog with the slow sad voice. 'Stay here, I'll go and get your mother's washing basket.'

'It's all right for you,' Jimmy muttered, pulling the tee shirt over his head, staining his face and hair with purple streaks.

Christine returned from the kitchen with a plastic basket, a newspaper and a tea-towel. 'Put your clothes in here – not the tee-shirt,' she added quickly. Holding out the newspaper, she said, 'Put that in here ... and dry yourself with this.'

Jimmy stepped out of his runners, tugged off sodden socks and then pulled down his trousers. His thighs were a pale lilac colour. The top half of his Y-fronts were a shade of deep plum where the dye from the tee-shirt had run into them.

'You'll have to have a bath,' Christine said decisively. 'Dry yourself off with the towel, while I wash these out in the bath first.' She bundled the clothes into the basket and dropped the newspaper-wrapped tee-shirt in on top of them, before racing upstairs, hoping that Jimmy's mother wouldn't come home for a while. The old bitch would blame her for the mess Jimmy was in. 'My Jim never wore those sort of clothes before he got involved with you ...'

Christine Doolin lived ten doors down from Jimmy Doyle, just off the Old Cabra Road. They were complete opposites in almost every respect – which was probably what had drawn them together. Jimmy's father had a well-paid and pensionable job in Guinness's brewery, and Jimmy was an only child. The family were well-off and Margaret Doyle considered herself a cut above most of the neighbours. Mrs Doyle particularly detested Christine's drunken father, and had forbidden her son to have anything to do with the daughter ... which only conspired to bring them closer together. Tall, blond and handsome, Jimmy could have had his pick of any of the local girls, but he wanted the one who wasn't particularly interested in him, Christine Doolin. Their friendship had grown slowly and hesitantly over a number of months, much to the astonishment of Jimmy's friends who didn't know what he saw in the painfully shy girl with the lonely blue eyes.

Christine was bent over the bath, white steam curling around her as she scrubbed at the tee-shirt, when the door opened behind her. Without turning round, she said, 'How much dye did you use in this?'

'A whole packet,' Jimmy said. 'No, two. I wanted it a really deep purple colour. There's a new band in England called Deep Purple,' he added.

'Maybe you should join,' she muttered. 'This just keeps coming.' She turned and held up purple-stained hands for inspection. And stopped. Jimmy was standing in the doorway, wearing only a small towel wrapped around his waist, holding it closed over his right hip. As she stared, the centre of the towel began jerking upwards. Her heart lurched, and she felt a sour, sick feeling in the pit of her stomach.

'Go and get dressed, Jimmy,' she said as firmly as she could and turned back to the bath. She spun the hot tap, and water thundered onto the enamel, steam billowing around her. 'It's a good job the water is hot ...' she began ... and stopped as Jimmy's hands closed on her hips.

'You should get out of those wet clothes before you catch a

chill,' he said, his voice sounding hoarse and ragged. He pressed himself against her body.

'Jimmy!'

He ignored her and tugged her damp blouse out of her jeans.

'Not now, Jimmy,' she said quickly. 'Your mother could come back,' she added.

'Today's polling day. I remember they said they were going down to the polling station to vote. They won't be back for ages.' His hands were warm on the bare flesh of her belly.

Christine leaned against the edge of the bath and squeezed her eyes shut. She hated him when he was like this. When she first met him she thought he was such a nice quiet boy, not like so many of the others who were only after one thing. By the time she realised her mistake it was too late, they were considered a pair, and peer pressure made breaking up difficult. Jimmy was a toucher, his hands always roving over her body, resting on her shoulders, sliding across her arms, his elbows 'accidentally' brushing her breasts, fingers sliding past her buttocks. They'd kissed of course, even experimented with what the other girls called French kissing, but they'd both been laughing so much they hadn't got anywhere. And then she'd let him touch her breasts through her cardigan, although when he tried to place her hand on his groin, she pulled back. She knew what lay between a man's legs.

Catching her by the shoulders, Jimmy spun her around, and held her tightly to him. She kept her eyes fixed on his face. Turning his head sideways, he attempted to kiss her, but she twisted her head aside and he ended up with a mouthful of hair.

'Look, do you want this tee-shirt washed or not?' she demanded angrily.

'A kiss,' Jimmy urged. 'How about giving me a kiss?'

Christine sighed. 'If I give you a kiss will you go away?'

Jimmy nodded. 'Absolutely.'

As she brought her face close to his, she closed her eyes ... and his hands tightened over her breasts. Christine yelped with pain and surprise and opened her eyes ... to discover that Jimmy had stepped back and allowed the towel to fall to the floor. Her eyes dropped ... and then the memories came flooding back.

It had been a while since ...

Her heart was thundering now, the noise drowning out the pounding of the water in the bath.

Christine had a name for it now, a name for what her father had done to her when she was younger. It hadn't happened for a few years now, and they never spoke about it. But she still locked her bedroom door at night.

It had been a while since he had come to her bed ...

She knew now that what he did was wrong, and although she knew she couldn't have done anything to stop it, still she felt guilty, dirty; she felt that she was partly to blame.

Christine shook her head wordlessly.

Jimmy wrapped his arms around her, mistaking her silence, wide eyes and open mouth for desire. He moved his hands over her breasts, pressing himself against her.

Had squeezed her tiny breasts, pressing himself against her ...

Moving his mouth across hers, tongue moist on her lips and chin.

His tongue foul and harsh on her lips and chin ... Hurting her. Always hurting her. And if she didn't move it was easier.

And if she didn't resist it was easier. And if she let him have his way it was over sooner. 'Don't hurt me ...' the little girl whispered. 'Don't hurt me.'

'Don't hurt me,' Christine whispered.

'I won't hurt you,' Jimmy promised, tugging at her blouse, fumbling with the back of her bra, trying to unhook the catch. 'I won't hurt you,' he repeated, unzipping her jeans, pushing them down. She was tense, rigid with excitement, he thought. He was rigid with excitement too, he thought, grinning.

'Not inside me,' Christine said through gritted teeth.

'I won't,' Jimmy swore. 'Trust me.'

Christine squeezed her eyes shut – then snapped them open as Jimmy pressed hard against her, hurting her, tearing her as he forced his way into her body, his hands tight on her breasts. Condensation beaded on her face, disguising the tears. Christine watched the ceiling, reading the cracks, the pattern of shapes ...

She squeezed her eyes shut as Jimmy pushed, driving deep into her body, hard fingers bruising her breasts, then suddenly shuddering in his passion, throwing his head back, his posture matching hers for a single moment.

'I love you,' he breathed. 'I'll always love you.' His voice was hoarse and low. 'Always.'

* * *

Ten weeks later, when Christine Doolin told Jimmy Doyle that she had missed two periods and thought she was pregnant, he looked at her for a long time – and in those terrifying moments while she waited for his reply, she knew he was going to deny it.

'You can't be ...'

'I am, Jimmy. I know it. It was that day in your bathroom ... the day it rained ... your tee-shirt. The purple tee-shirt.'

'You can't be,' he repeated. 'I mean, I'm sorry if you are ... but you can't be ... and if you are, it can't be mine ...'

'Jimmy, I've never done it with anyone else. There's only you; you've got to accept responsibility ...'

He shook his head savagely. 'I've no responsibility. It can't be mine. It's not mine, and I won't have you trying to put the blame on me,' he added, his newly-broken voice growing higher and higher. 'It's not mine. It's not!'

The sixteen-year-old girl walked home looking at the pattern of cracks on the pavement. They reminded her of the ceiling of Jimmy's bathroom.

Monday night, 12 July

Chapter 11

After the deafening wall of sound in the dark, sour-smelling disco, the silence of the night was an almost physical thing. The couple were temporarily deaf, speech was impossible, and pulsing spots of colour still danced on their retinas.

Kevin Quinn put his arm around Sandra Miller's shoulder. She snuggled in against him, her head against his chest, an arm around his waist. As they came up out of the Leeson Street club, Kevin kicked an empty beer can, sending it clattering off into the shadows. When he could hear it rattle in the distance, he knew that his hearing was coming back.

'Did you enjoy it?' he asked.

Feeling the boy's voice rumbling in his chest, Sandra looked up. 'What?'

'Did you have a good time?'

This time the young woman guessed, rather than heard, the question, and nodded enthusiastically. 'I had a great time, Kev.' She pressed herself against him for emphasis.

'Do you want to go and get something to eat?'

'What?'

He mimed eating with his free hand and she nodded quickly. She tapped the side of her head. 'I'm still a little deaf.'

'It'll wear off.'

'What?'

Kevin grinned and shook his head. He hadn't really enjoyed the nightclub; the room was too small and far too hot and crowded, even for a Monday night. And the drink was incredibly expensive. But he'd never been to a Leeson Street club before, and he was determined to try it at least once, just so that he could say he had. He wouldn't be going back.

However, it had the desired effect. Sandra had been suitably impressed when he told her where they were going, and she was even more impressed when he hailed a taxi as they stood waiting for a bus. He flashed his new boots, and was vaguely disappointed when she didn't notice them, but he knew that she had to be aware that this night was costing him a lot of money. He grinned suddenly; this was the first night in his life he was able to go out and not have to worry about having the bus fare back home. And he'd never have to do that ever again.

'What are you grinning about?'

'Nothing.'

'You look like that cat that's got the cream,' Sandra smiled. She pinched the flesh of his stomach. 'Tell me?' she demanded. Sandra Miller was small and slender to the point of thinness, and this emphasised her large breasts. Her face was tiny and almost triangular, sweeping from a broad low forehead to a pointed chin. She accented her bright blue eyes with eyeliner and eyeshadow. 'Tell me,' she repeated.

'Why shouldn't I smile? I've had a great night out with you.'

'I've really enjoyed myself too.'

They walked out onto Stephen's Green and turned right, heading down towards the Shelbourne Hotel.

'Where do you want to eat?' Kevin asked. He was trying to work out exactly how much he had left from the three hundred pounds his mother had given him earlier that day. He had tucked a twenty pound note into his boot, so that he'd be able to resist the temptation to spend it. He probably had enough left for a meal and a taxi home.

'You've spent a lot of money,' Sandra said quietly, almost as if she could read his thoughts.

'I wanted to show you a good time. Nothing's too good for you.'

'You must have spent at least sixty quid in the club.'

'Did I?' He was genuinely surprised. The club didn't sell

beer, and the cheapest wine had cost twenty pounds a bottle. Sandra had had a cocktail – some concoction with paper umbrellas – which cost him twelve pounds. He nodded, he could easily have dropped sixty notes. He shrugged. 'Well, as I said, nothing's too good for you.'

They turned to the left, passing the brightly-lit facade of the Shelbourne.

'What do you fancy eating?'

'I was just wondering where you got that sort of money,' Sandra continued forcefully.

'I was thinking Chinese. I know there are a couple of good Chinese restaurants in George's Street and Dame Street. Or how about Indian? But maybe you don't like spicy food?'

'Where did the money come from, Kevin?'

Kevin stopped, surprised by the note of seriousness in Sandra's voice. 'It's my money; I've been saving it for a rainy day or a special occasion.' He grinned, his blue eyes wide and innocent. 'Well, this was the special occasion.'

Sandra nudged his foot with the toe of her shoe. 'Are these the boots you were telling me about, Kev? One hundred and fifty quid you said they cost.' Reaching out, she ran the back of her hand down his thigh. 'And these are new jeans; proper five-o-ones too. You're wearing at least two hundred quid's worth of new gear, you spent another sixty on me ... and you're trying to tell me that it's all from savings. Where are you getting the money to save, Kev? You've no job. And your mother's on assistance; she certainly hasn't got it to give to you.'

Kevin looked at her blankly. He couldn't understand what she was arguing about. The night hadn't cost her anything.

'So – where did the money come from?' she demanded.

He reached out and put his hands on her shoulders, but the girl shrugged them off.

'It's legal. The money is legit. I haven't stolen it or anything.'

'I don't believe you,' Sandra said icily, tossing her blond hair over her shoulder. 'Where else would you get that sort of money?' As she walked away, she said, 'And I liked you, I really did. But I won't have anything to do with a thief.'

Kevin stared after her. He didn't know whether to be angry or to laugh. Two nights ago, this girl had been perfectly willing to sleep with him – and at that stage he had maybe one pound in his pocket. Now that he had some money and spent it on her, she didn't want anything more to do with him. He strode after her, caught her arm and spun her around to face him. He released her when a cruising Garda car slowed as it neared the couple, only to speed away again, its radio crackling loudly.

'Listen to me, I didn't steal the money. I swear to you.'

'Well, where did you get it?' she demanded.

'I ... I can't tell you.'

Sandra's face tightened in disgust, her lips disappearing into a thin line. 'I hate liars, probably more than I hate thieves,' she added. 'My father lost a good job because he was a liar and a thief. And when my mother found out, the shame of it nearly killed her. My father stayed indoors for the last six years of his life, watching television, so it was left to my mother to go out and face the neighbours. She lived with the shame of it, but he never had to face it. When I saw what it did to her, I swore that I would never have anything to do with a liar or a thief.'

'We won some money,' he said suddenly.

'What?'

Kevin took a deep breath. 'My mother won some money; she gave me the money for the boots and jeans. I'd a few bob left over so I thought I'd take you out.'

'You're a fucking liar, Kevin Quinn! I don't believe you,' Sandra said, turned, and walked away.

Kevin raced after her. 'Jesus, what will it take to convince you? I've told you the truth.'

'Your mother won some money,' Sandra repeated sarcastically. 'Come on, surely you can do better than that?'

'But it's true!' he insisted.

'It must have been an awful lot of money, if she was able to give you nearly three hundred pounds to spend on yourself.'

'It was.' Even as he was saying the words, Kevin knew he was making a mistake, but they were out before he could stop himself. 'We won Saturday night's lottery. We won over two and a quarter million pounds. We collected it today.'

'You're full of shit ...' Sandra began, and then stopped, open-mouthed. 'You're not lying.'

'I'm not.' He was grinning now, unable to help himself. 'I'm not lying. It's the truth. Gospel.' It would be all right. Sandra wouldn't say anything.

'Two and a quarter million,' the young woman repeated, numbly. 'It said on the radio that the winning ticket was bought in Dublin.' She looked sharply at Kevin. 'You're not lying now, Kev? Swear to me you're not lying.'

'I'm not, Sandra,' he swore. 'I'm not. We're rich, Sandra, we can have anything we want, do anything we like, go anywhere that takes our fancy. And you and me can go out every night of the week. I'll be able to buy you anything you want.'

'You're not lying,' Sandra repeated, mouth dry with the sudden realisation that she was talking to a millionaire. Stepping closer, pressing her large breasts against his chest, she draped her arms around his neck. 'This is fabulous news. You must be thrilled.'

'Yea, absolutely.'

Sandra laughed and kissed him quickly, catching him off guard. 'Come on, I thought we were going to eat. You can tell me everything over dinner.'

Chapter 12

Underwear first. The silk moulded itself to her skin, sending a shudder deep into her groin, setting her heart racing.

Watching herself in the mirror of the wardrobe, Christine pulled on the matching bra. It was flesh-coloured, a delicate filigree of lace around the cups, its touch deeply sensuous. The underwire pushed up her breasts, giving her a cleavage for the first time in her life. Then stockings, sheer and black and feather-soft, costing more than half a dozen packets of the tights she usually wore. The garter belt matched the colour of her bra.

Deliberately not looking at herself now, she put on the gold-coloured silk blouse. It was oily smooth as it settled onto her shoulders and the curves of her breasts. Then she pulled on a pair of tan culottes, cinching them around her waist with a broad leather belt. Finally, she stepped into a pair of butter-soft tan Bally shoes.

When Christine Quinn looked into the mirror again she didn't recognise herself.

The last time she had looked in this mirror – properly looked, that was, not a quick cursory glance – she had seen an old woman. Not old in years, though God knows she looked far older than her thirty-four years, but tired and dispirited, her eyes dead, hopeless. Christine nodded fiercely. That was it: she had been hopeless. The future had been bleak.

But when she looked into the mirror now, she saw that her eyes were bright and wide. The lines that too many hard years and too many bitter experiences had etched around her mouth and forehead and along the side of her nose were no more; even her posture was more positive. And of course the clothes helped; they gave her confidence and poise.

She had a future now.

Looking at the stranger in the mirror, Christine repeated the thought aloud, the words sounding strange to her ears. 'I have a future now.'

* * *

Christine lay in bed, her arms locked behind her head, staring at the clothes hanging in the open wardrobe. She had left the curtains open, and the street lights washed across the silk, painting it black, making it shimmer like oiled metal.

Although it was after two in the morning and it had been such an emotional day that she should have been exhausted, she found she was bright and alert, buzzing with energy, her thoughts tumbling and chaotic. She kept glancing at the clock, watching the digital display tick away the seconds towards the dawn. She couldn't wait for Tuesday. There was so much she wanted to do. So much she could do.

She needed someone to talk to. It was madness trying to keep this huge excitement bottled up inside her. She should have told Helen. Maybe she would have been able to swear her to secrecy. She could have done with the older woman's solid advice now. Helen would know what to do; she always knew what to do. When Kevin had caught the mumps, the chickenpox and measles, Christine had turned to Helen. When Robert had turned dangerously brutal, Helen had been there to advise her, and when Margaret, poor, dear baby Margaret had died, Helen had been there for her, keeping her sane, keeping her together when everything had fallen apart. She wouldn't have survived that period if it hadn't been for Helen. She was like the big sister she never had.

She'd tell Helen. And Helen would be able to advise about clothes and fashions – she'd worked in one of Cork's largest department stores for four years before she moved to Dublin to work in one of the big fabric shops. She had a great sense of colour. Maybe she'd tell Helen in the morning, and then the two of them could go into town and buy some clothes and make-up. She was going to have a completely new image, something bright, cheerful and strong. And Helen would be able to help. She'd know about houses too; maybe they could go house-hunting together. A house. She wanted to do something about a house.

That was a must. Maybe she'd look into that tomorrow. And she could get some more clothes, and she'd get her hair done. Maybe she'd get her hair done before she went looking for houses. She'd spend the day in the city; she'd wander around and enjoy it. Simply enjoy it, knowing that she could walk into any shop and say, 'I'll have that.' She'd get lunch in a fancy restaurant, then tomorrow night, she could go out with Kevin. The cinema. A restaurant. The cinema and a restaurant.

Where was Kevin? It was getting late.

Christine took a deep breath, trying to calm herself. Her heart was thumping again. She realised this was the first time in many years that she actually looked forward to the next day.

In her previous life – she was beginning to think of it as such – there was never any real reason to plan for tomorrow. When you're poor, tomorrow is like today, and today is very much like yesterday. What was it people said about money not being able to buy happiness? Well, they were wrong. Although she had it less than twenty-four hours, the money she won had already made her very happy indeed. It had opened up a whole new lease of life for her and her son.

Kevin was late.

She was happy. The times of real happiness in her life had been so few that she could remember them really clearly. Her wedding day. The day baby Margaret, her second child, had been born. Margaret would be seven now if she had lived. The day she held that little life in her arms had been the happiest in her life. Kevin's birth hadn't been such a pleasant experience. She was sixteen years old, not married and under great pressure to give the child up for adoption. She faced them down; refused to tell them the name of the father, and insisted that she was going to raise the child herself. She did too. She'd discovered her strength then, her stubborn streak. It had served her well ever since.

Where *was* Kevin?

Christine lifted her head off the pillow and looked at the clock. A quarter to three.

He was out with that girl, the new girlfriend. Celebrating, no doubt, enjoying himself. Christine envied him; she'd never really known a childhood or the fun of being a teenager. Well, now she had the chance to give him everything she never had.

This money was going to change both their lives.

Christine looked at the clock again. She hoped he'd be in soon. And she hoped he wouldn't tell anyone about their win. But he wouldn't. He wasn't stupid.

* * *

'Wait,' Sandra hissed, 'the gate squeaks.' She stepped in front of Kevin, deliberately pressing against him, her nipples hard and pointed beneath her blouse, and carefully lifted the gate before pushing it open. 'We can't go in,' she added. She closed the gate between them, then leaned across and kissed him, tongue flickering across his lips. Her breath was warm with spices and soya sauce. 'Everyone's out tomorrow night, though,' she added. 'You could come over early ...'

Kevin nodded. 'About nine?'

'Make it a bit earlier. That'll give us more time together.' She raised her thin eyebrows archly.

'I think that sounds like an indecent proposal,' he smiled.

'It is,' she whispered. 'I'd better go. I hope Ma isn't awake.'

'Sandra ...' Kevin began. 'What I told you earlier ... about winning the lottery. Don't say anything to anyone. Mum doesn't want anyone to know. Promise me.'

'I won't tell anyone,' she promised, and pecked him on the cheek.

Kevin waited until he saw Sandra step into the hallway and close the door behind her before he set off for home. It would take him ten minutes if he cut directly across the estate, through the lanes and narrow passageways between the houses. But at this time of night some of the lanes weren't too safe, and he decided to stick to the main roads. It was ten minutes longer, but safer. As he walked past the rows of identical houses, he wondered where his mother was going to buy their new house.

*　*　*

'And just where have you been until this hour, miss?'

Sandra turned, colour rising to her cheeks. 'Ma ...'

Betty Miller snapped on the hall light. She was standing at the bottom of the stairs, arms folded across her large bosom. 'Do you know what time it is?'

Sandra blinked in the sudden harsh light. 'I know what time it is ...' she said defensively, glancing at the ornamental carriage clock on the hall table.

'You've been out with that Quinn boy. I saw him. I've told you before: stay away from him. But will you listen to me? Oh, no! You stay away from him. He's no good. He has no future. His father ended up in prison – not that he was his real father,' she added. 'And that mother of his thinks she's better than the rest of us ...'

'Ma ...'

'I don't want you seeing him again. Is that understood? You could easily do better for yourself.' Betty Miller's voice was shrill.

'But, Ma ...'

'No buts. You are not to see him again. And that is that.'

'They won the lottery, Ma,' Sandra said quickly. 'The Quinns won the lottery on Saturday. Over two million pounds, Ma. Kevin's a millionaire!'

Tuesday, 13 July

Chapter 13

Christine opened the bedroom door slightly and peered into Kevin's room. She wrinkled her nose at the bitter odours of sour sweat, spicy food and stale alcohol. She'd been awake until three and he hadn't come in. Normally, she'd have been worried sick – with no money and nowhere to go, what was he doing? But now, knowing that he had money in his pocket, money for the cinema, restaurants, discos and a taxi home, she discovered she wasn't so worried. Concerned certainly, but not worried.

Slatted blinds threw horizontal bars of light across the bed which was piled high with clothes and blankets. She had taken a step into the room before she saw that Kevin was lying face down under the clothes. Although he'd pulled off his jacket and shirt, leaving them lying on the floor, he was still wearing the jeans and boots he'd bought yesterday.

Picking her way through the clothes, books and cassettes strewn across the floor, Christine knelt by the bed and shook his shoulder. 'Kevin?'

The boy mumbled in his sleep and instinctively burrowed deeper under the duvet.

'Kevin?' She shook harder.

He opened one eye, stared at her without recognition for a few seconds then made an effort and tried to sit up.

'Mum ...' he said stickily.

'Stay where you are.' She drew the duvet up over his shoulders. 'What time did you get in last night?'

'Two ... half-two,' he muttered, rubbing his eyes.

'I was awake until three, Kevin,' Christine said gently.

'I suppose it might have been closer to half-three,' he admitted. 'I was celebrating,' he added.

'I hope you told no-one,' Christine said quickly.

Kevin yawned widely, then looked into his mother's eyes and shook his head. 'No-one, Mum. I'm not stupid.' Suddenly noticing that his mother was wearing some of the new clothes she'd bought yesterday, he swiftly changed the subject. 'Where are you going?'

'I'm going into town to spend a few bob. I was thinking I might get my hair done in one of those fancy salons.'

'That's a good idea ... but how are you going to get out of the estate without people seeing you dressed like that?' he asked with a grin.

Christine suddenly realised that her son was right. If she strolled through the estate wearing a couple of hundred pounds' worth of new clothes, the news would spread like wildfire. 'I'll wear a coat.'

'Mum, it's the middle of July. You'll be baked. Wear your old clothes.'

'No, I'm not going into a hair salon wearing my usual rags.'

'The grunge look is in. They'll only be interested in your money.'

Christine shook her head firmly. 'No, I'm not getting changed.'

'Can't bear to be parted from the new threads, eh?'

Christine caught a fold of denim and lifted Kevin's leg. 'I'm not the only one who can't bear to be parted from my new clothes.' They were both laughing now.

The young man sat up in bed and ran his hand through his long hair, pulling it back off his face. 'You look real good, Mum.'

Christine nodded, pleased. She had been astonished at the transformation as she glanced in the mirror when she'd finished dressing after breakfast. She chose the simple mustard-coloured dress, held around her narrow waist with a broad leather belt, and a pair of low-heeled shoes. She applied a little of the make-up she'd purchased, a light foundation cream and a touch of eye-shadow to emphasise her eyes. She rarely wore make-up – it was a luxury she could not afford – but she certainly had to admit that not only did she look better, she actually felt better too.

'What time will you be back?'

'Late in the afternoon, I suppose,' Christine said. 'Will you still be here?'

'Yea. I won't be going out until around eight.'

'I thought we could go out together ...' she began, then stopped when she saw the disappointed look in his eyes. 'We can do it tomorrow, if you've made plans for tonight.'

'We'll do it tomorrow night then. It's a date. Don't spend too much,' he called after her, before snuggling down under the duvet again.

Christine stood in the sitting room and pulled on a light mac over her dress. Then she parted the venetian blinds and peered out onto the road. It was just after ten and still fairly quiet; there was a group of young children playing on the green, others racing their bikes up and down the path. Two women stood gossiping on the corner near the bus stop. She tried to make them out, but she was too shortsighted and the shimmering heat waves rising off the street made it impossible to see who they were. She'd have to pass them to get to the bus stop, unless she went the long way round ... but that would take ten minutes.

She glanced at her watch. There was a bus in five minutes' time. She'd miss it if she went around the long way, and if she missed it, she'd have to wait another hour for the next one. No, she'd have to brazen it out and walk past the two women. Maybe she wouldn't know them.

Christine's eyes watered as she stepped out into the brilliant morning sunshine. Sunglasses. As soon as she got into the city, she was going to buy herself a pair of sunglasses, an expensive pair, proper polaroids.

The two women turned as she neared them. She recognised them then: Mrs McKenna and Mrs Harbison. The local news-service. She could feel their eyes travelling up and down her body, lingering at the new shoes, the hem of her dress hanging beneath her coat, the make-up on her face.

'Lovely day, Chrissy.' Mrs McKenna was smiling, but her eyes were cold and calculating.

'Gorgeous,' Christine agreed. She hated being called Chrissy.

'You off out, love?' Mrs Harbison's expression matched her neighbour's.

'Yes, I'm going into town.'

'That's a lovely dress ...'

'You'll be baked with that coat on,' her companion added, letting her know that they were aware that she was trying to disguise the fact that she was wearing a new dress.

Christine smiled through gritted teeth. 'I know. But I didn't want my dress to get dirty on the bus. You know what those seats can be like.'

'You off somewhere special?' Mrs McKenna continued, moving slightly to block the rest of the path.

'Yes ... yes, I'm off for a job interview,' she said quickly, saying the first thing that came to mind.

'Where, love?'

'A secretary's job.' She looked at her watch. 'I have to go. I'll miss the bus.' Stepping out onto the road, she darted past them, then started to run as the bus came round the corner.

The bus pulled away from the stop and Christine settled into a window seat. She turned and looked at the two women. They were both staring at her. She raised her hand and waved at them. She knew they were talking about her. This would be nothing new. They and their like were always watching, always gossip-ing. Anyway, just now she didn't give a damn.

*   *   *

She'd have to get sunglasses.

The last time she'd worn a pair of sunglasses was when Robert had taken them on holiday to Salthill in the west of Ireland. It would have been shortly after they married in 1980. So it would have been that glorious summer of 1981. She had been happy then, truly happy, married to a man she really loved, and who swore he loved her. Kevin was seven, and although he was having some problems adjusting to his stepfather, Robert loved him as his own. She became pregnant on that holiday.

Robert had bought her a pair of sunglasses, cheap plastic things from one of the stalls on the strand. He also bought himself a pair which were like silver mirrors, reflecting back everything he looked at. She hated them, because when he wore them she couldn't see his eyes, and without being able to see his eyes, she couldn't tell when he was lying to her. Although she lost her sunglasses that summer, he kept his mirrored shades long after they'd gone out of fashion.

Christine stopped at Weirs, the jewellers at the bottom of Grafton Street, and looked at their selection of sunglasses, tilting her head to read the names off the arms of the glasses: Ray-Ban, Ferarri, Porsche. Any of those would do, she thought. But she stayed less then a minute inside the shop when she discovered that they cost over a hundred pounds. She might be a millionaire, but she wasn't paying a hundred pounds for a pair of sunglasses! Walking across the street to Hayes, Conyngham and Robinson, the chemists, she bought a pair for twelve pounds that she figured kept out just as much sun as the hundred-pound pair.

Christine Quinn strolled up Grafton Street. She pulled off her mac and squashed it into her shoulder bag. She was amazed at the confidence the clothes and the little bit of make-up gave her and she felt protected behind the dark glasses. She noticed the way men's eyes followed her. It had been a long time since any man had looked at her, but they certainly were looking now.

On impulse, she turned into Brown Thomas department store. The last time she was in here, she was so intimidated by the staff and the surroundings that she promptly walked out again. Now she strolled along the counters at her ease, breathing in the fragrance of countless perfumes.

'Would you care to try ...?'

The woman was in her late forties, immaculately dressed, perhaps just too much make-up and jewellery. She was holding a fat-bodied perfume bottle in her crimson-nailed hands. Christine was suddenly aware that her own nails were ragged and unpainted. She mentally added nail-varnish to her list of things to get.

'Would you care to try this?' the woman smiled. 'A new perfume, Coco, by Chanel ...'

Christine was extending her wrist when a woman darted in front of her. Small and stout, her extended wrist was enclosed in a thick golden chain dangling intricate charms. She turned and glanced witheringly at Christine. 'I'm quite sure this young woman is not interested in such an expensive perfume.'

The saleswoman sprayed a burst of perfume onto the woman's wrist and launched into her sales patter. 'This is the ultimate perfume, it suggests that the wearer is a woman of ...'

'How much?' the woman asked bluntly.

'Thirty-one pounds fifty for fifteen milligrams.'

'That's outrageous! Scandalous.'

Christine leaned forward and caught the woman's chubby arm. Bending her head, she breathed in the perfume's sharp clean fragrance. Then, without a flicker of a smile, she said, 'I'll take it.'

Chapter 14

'It's true, I tell you.' Betty Miller took a deep breath and waited for the crowd of women gathered in the small post office to fall silent. 'My Sandra is doing a line with her son Kevin. He took her out on the town last night to celebrate ... and my Sandra said he spent about two hundred pounds without even blinking.'

'I don't believe it,' the post mistress said, folding her arms on the counter and peering out through the grill. 'I'm sure I would have heard something.'

'I heard on the news that the winning ticket had been sold in Dublin,' someone offered.

'And yesterday's newspaper said the ticket had been bought on the east coast,' someone else said.

'Now that you mention it, I saw her this morning, and she was all dressed up.'

The focus of attention turned to Mrs Harbison who was standing in front of the display of greeting cards.

'I was talking to Joan McKenna when Chrissy Quinn came running up. She was wearing an old mac, but you could see that she had a new dress and shoes on. And she was wearing make-up,' the woman added significantly. 'She said she was going into town to do an interview for a job.'

Determined to bring the spotlight back to herself, Mrs Miller said loudly: 'Two and a half million pounds. That's what she won. Two and a half million pounds. Sure, what would you do with it? Mind you, I'm sure there's many a one on this estate who could do with it more. She has only the lad and herself to look after.'

'But if your Sandra is engaged to the lad, then you'll be all right too,' one of the women said.

Betty Miller smiled happily. She had already thought of that.

Chapter 15

She had bought the perfume on impulse. Over thirty pounds for a bottle of perfume! She often lived for a week on less. She was horrified when she discovered the size of the bottle. It was tiny. Christine rarely wore perfume, though she had a collection of cheap scents Kevin had given her for birthdays and Mother's Day. She never had any reason to wear them, because she never went anywhere ... and the floral-rich liquids always gave her a pounding headache.

Sitting at the window in Bewley's café, looking down over Grafton Street, she placed her new sunglasses down on the table, dipped into the black-and-white Brown Thomas bag, pulled out the small bottle of perfume and prised off the cap. The heady fragrance mingled with the rich dark aroma of coffee. It smelt of money, she decided. She dabbed the scent onto her wrists, behind her ears, and into the hollow of her throat. Then as she placed the bottle back into the bag, she stopped, the sudden image of the three objects – sunglasses, coffee and perfume – abruptly bringing home to her just how much her life had changed in the past three days.

Looking down onto the busy lunch-time street, Christine spotted a lone woman pushing her way through the crowd, laden down with plastic bags. The woman didn't even window-shop as she hurried past. There was something familiar about the dejected slump of her shoulders, the fixed expression in her eyes, the slightly shabby air about her ... and then Christine realised that the woman reminded her of herself, her old self.

There, but for the grace of God ... A few pounds would make all the difference to that woman's life. Christine had a sudden impulse to follow her and give her some money ... but then the young waitress was beside her, coffee pot in hand.

'More coffee, ma'am?'

Christine nodded absently, and when she looked down into the street again, the woman had vanished into the crowd.

As Christine sipped the coffee – real coffee – she decided that she would give some of her winnings to charity. She could easily afford to. She wasn't sure which one yet, nor how much, and it would have to be done anonymously. No-one must ever know she had given the money; she realised that if even a whisper got out her life would be a misery.

Which charities? The Vincent de Paul probably: they helped people in trouble, and Childline, which lent children a listening ear. The Samaritans too; they had helped her once. Her thoughts slid away to the past, to sudden images of a rain-swept phone booth and a lonely frightened girl telling the calm and soothing voice on the other end of the line that there was nothing left to live for.

How much would she give? A thousand, two, maybe ten thousand. Christine smiled into her coffee cup. She wouldn't even miss a hundred thousand. She could ask Kevin – but no, she immediately shook her head: he wouldn't want her to give any of it away.

But first things first and to the *real* reason for her visit to the city. The house. The hair-do could wait. The house was the most important thing of all. Someplace far away from the untidy sprawling estate, someplace where she would be safe, where Robert would never even think of looking for her.

Putting on her sunglasses, Christine picked up the bill without even checking the amount and left a tip of two pounds on the table. As she walked towards the cash register, she realised it was the first time in her life she had left a tip.

*   *   *

There was no point in asking an estate agent to send brochures to her home, Christine figured. They'd look at her address, then look at the price of the type of house she was enquiring about and decide that she was wasting their time. No, far better simply to call to the offices and see what they had on offer.

The windows of the estate agents off Stephen's Green were filled with separate sheets of paper, each advertising a house for sale. Christine ignored most of the details – they meant nothing to her – and concentrated on the picture of the property, and the price. If she liked the picture, then she checked the number of bedrooms – how many bedrooms did she need, anyway? – and the size of the garden. She loved flowers and shrubs, but she lived in a house with a front garden the size of a handkerchief. Over the years she got the odd slip or shrub and made it look good. Robert had cemented over the back garden shortly after their marriage, despite her protests. He'd always hated gardening.

The choice of houses was bewildering.

Some had big gardens, or many rooms, others were beautifully decorated, some were situated beside the sea, or deep in the country, some were new, others old, single-storey bungalows, detached, semi-detached ...

And she liked them all. They appealed to her for different reasons: the space, the size, the privacy ...

In the next window, she discovered another dozen properties she liked.

This was getting her nowhere. Taking a deep breath, Christine Quinn pushed open the door and walked into her future.

*   *   *

Henry Simms had been an estate agent for more than twenty-two years. He had joined the company as a junior and worked his way up to the position of the chief auctioneer and valuer. He confidently expected to become a director within the next five years. He once boasted that he could sell any property – no matter how decrepit or dilapidated, and when he was taken up on the wager by a group of auctioneers from rival firms, he won the thousand-pound bet by selling a derelict plot of land next to the city dump for a phenomenal sum. His colleagues put his success down to his charm, elegant manners and ability to put even the most nervous buyers at their ease. Simms was inclined to agree with them, though he knew that he also possessed an uncanny ability to determine within moments of meeting a buyer, exactly how much they were prepared to spend.

Usually Henry Simms didn't deal with the casual enquirer, people who stepped in off the street out of curiosity to ask the price of a property, with no intention of buying. But when the door opened and warm air, acrid and metallic with traffic fumes, blasted into the office, he looked up from his desk, assessing the woman automatically. She was a curious mixture: new shoes, new dress, new sunglasses, hair recently washed but not styled. Nice make-up. No jewellery. He was about to say mutton dressed as lamb, when he realised that she couldn't be more than mid-thirties. Curiosity – the same curiosity that had driven him into the estate agency business: the desire to see into people's houses – made him stand and approach the desk, waving back one of the junior staff.

Simms smiled easily, showing his perfect teeth. 'How can I help you?'

Christine pulled off the glasses, blinking at the elegant man before her. 'I would like to talk to someone about a house.'

The accent was Dublin, simple, unsophisticated. There was no chance of a sale here, he decided. 'Of course, madam. Was there anything on display which particularly interested you?'

'Well, yes,' Christine admitted.

'Perhaps if you were to give me some details of your requirements and price range ...' Simms suggested.

'Price is not a problem,' Christine said, enjoying the sentence, savouring it like old wine, 'but I'll go up to half a million for the right property.'

Simms swallowed hard, trying to find saliva in a suddenly dry mouth, Adam's apple bobbing beneath taut skin. Under his perfect tan, his skin paled. However, when he spoke again, his voice was smooth and even. 'Certainly, madam. If you would care to step this way, I will show you some of our most desirable properties.' Simms stood back to allow Christine to step past him. The perfume was Coco, he realised with a start. One of the most expensive on the market. He'd bought his mistress a bottle last Christmas, then, when he discovered just how powerful a fragrance it was, he bought a bottle for his wife, just in case she realised he was coming home smelling of a strange perfume.

'Henry Simms,' he said introducing himself, extending a hand when they entered a small office. The pastel walls were covered with framed prints of old Dublin.

'Christine Quinn.' His hand was softer than hers, she realised.

'Please ...' Simms said, indicating a soft leather chair. 'Now, I will just get some details first,' he said, smiling widely as he walked around the broad leather-topped desk and lifted a yellow pad. Reaching into the jacket of his pin-striped suit, he pulled out a thick-bodied Mont Blanc fountain pen. 'Would you care for some coffee ... tea?'

'No, thank you. I've had lunch.'

'Fine.' Simms unscrewed the top of the pen, briefly wondering if he was the victim of a practical joke. Some of his colleagues had a very peculiar sense of humour. 'Now, what sort of property were you interested in?'

'Something by the sea,' Christine said, coming to a decision. 'Detached and private. Five or maybe six bedrooms, and a large garden.'

Simms made a series of cryptic notes, mentally sorting through the properties the company had on their books.

'Furnished or unfurnished?'

'Unfurnished,' Christine said after a moment's hesitation. This was going to be *her* home – in every way.

'A delicate question,' Henry Simms said, 'but it makes things so much easier if I ask it now. You have mentioned a figure in the region of five hundred thousand. I presume you have loan approval?'

'I will be paying cash.'

'Cash,' Simms said. And now he knew it was a practical joke. He allowed his voice to harden. 'Perhaps if madam were to give me an address, I could send on some details of suitable properties.' He smiled insolently, showing his teeth.

Christine stared at the man for a moment, then with a cold expression on her face she leaned forward, took the expensive fountain pen from his chubby fingers and swivelled the pad around. She scribbled a name and a phone number on the pad, then turned it back to Simms. 'This is the name and number of my bank manager. Phone him first, then perhaps you can deal civilly with me.'

Flustered, Simms looked from the pad to the woman's face. 'I assure you, madam ...'

Christine's face was a stone mask. 'Oh, I understand. Someone walks in off the street and wants to spend half a million on a house. Of course you'll want to check them out. It'll speed things up if you contact this man.'

'I'm quite sure it will not be necessary ...'

'Yes it will!' Christine replied coldly. 'I can always take my business elsewhere.'

Simms stood up so suddenly the chair toppled over. When he finally disappeared into another room, Christine allowed her mask to crack and she smiled widely. She was enjoying this.

Chapter 16

Harry Webb heard the snatch of conversation above the lunch-time babble in the pub, and swivelled around on the bar stool to listen to it.

'... it's true, I tell you, she's won it. Aaah, of course you know her ...'

'... husband ran off and left her ...'

'... son was in my Tommy's class ...'

'... over two million ...'

Picking up his drink, Harry Webb slid off the bar stool and moved closer to the small group of women. Mention of the two million had confirmed his suspicions that they were talking about Saturday night's lottery winner and, from what he'd overheard, they seemed to know just who had won it.

And if they knew the identity of the winner, then he was going to find out.

Harry Webb was a failed author turned freelance journalist. He edited the local free newspaper and scraped together a precarious living stringing stories to the national newspapers and magazines. It'd be quite a scoop if he could discover who had won Saturday night's record lottery. The only information anyone had was that the winning ticket had been sold in the Dublin area.

'... I heard her husband's in jail ... murder I think it was ...'

Looking over the group, Harry recognised one of the women, Betty Miller. A fine-looking woman, a widow. He'd known her late husband Joe, vaguely. Lost his job in Guinness's for stealing. Harry had toyed with the idea of doing an article on the story, but abandoned the notion when he remembered that he still had to live in the area. And Betty Miller would make a formidable enemy.

'Well, all I can say is that she sure keeps herself to herself; never has a word for anyone. Stuck-up ...'

Someone turned on the jukebox at the other end of the room and a throbbing drum-beat filled the long smoky bar, drowning out the conversation. Finishing his drink in one long swallow, Webb took up a position by the door. He glanced at his watch. The pub would be closing soon. He'd get his chance to talk to Betty Miller then.

Chapter 17

It had taken less then an hour for Christine to narrow the choices down to three properties. She spread out the three sheets of paper on the desk before her, lining them up side by side. Then, with her elbows propped on the table, chin resting on her clasped hands, she looked at each in turn.

Across the table, Henry Simms silently bundled up the twenty-two properties she had rejected and placed them on the floor. He had done his talking, extolling the virtues of each individual property, pointing out a minor defect or two when he felt it was necessary, encouraging the woman to trust him. Now it was up to her; Simms had been long enough in the business to know when to talk and when to stay silent.

Christine turned her head slightly to look at the property to the left. Seasonstown House was a six-bedroomed mansion on fifteen acres in County Kildare. The colour photograph showed a building that looked as if it came straight off the cover of a romantic novel, ivy-covered walls and a gnarled rambling rose curling over a columned porch. There was an option to purchase the stables separately.

Would Kevin like this house, Christine suddenly wondered?

She looked up and found that Simms was staring hard at her. Only the taut muscles at the side of his jaws revealed his tension. He smiled tightly and looked down, busying himself doodling on the yellow pad.

She was surprised to discover that she hadn't even considered Kevin until now. Maybe she should have him with her now? She should take these sheets and show them to Kevin, get his opinion. After all, he'd have to live there too.

But for how long?

The sudden thought stopped her cold. Kevin would be eighteen next birthday. He was already independent; he was the sort who'd move into a flat as soon as he could afford it ... and they could afford it now.

No, the house wasn't for Kevin – not in the long term anyway – the house was for her. This was her choice.

The middle sheet showed a long, low, sprawling split-level bungalow, just outside the seaside town of Skerries in North County Dublin. The views from the sitting room and master bedroom windows showed a long stretch of golden sandy beach, while the caption explained that the mountains of Mourne could be seen on a clear day. But Skerries brought back painful memories of her childhood, the countless holidays spent on the sandy south beach or the rocky north beach. They'd been on holiday there the year her mother had fallen ill ...

Christine turned to the third sheet: Island View, on Killiney Hill. Physically, the house was the least striking of the three: a six-bedroomed solid Victorian redbrick, with deep bay windows and a box porch. But it had half an acre of mature gardens, which included an ornamental pool, enclosed behind a seven-foot high wall. There was private access through a side gate down onto Killiney beach.

'They're all very attractive,' Christine said finally.

Simms said nothing.

Reaching out, she pushed aside the page describing the bungalow and brought the two remaining pages together, lining them up at the edges. Maybe she shouldn't be making this decision now. Maybe she should take a few days to think it over; let the reality of the money sink in.

The house was the big decision, probably the most important decision she would make. And it represented the reality of winning the lottery. The new clothes, the sudden freedom, all of that was fine ... but at the end of every day she still went back to that house in the estate, and that bedroom, with its sour and bitter memories. Winning the lottery would become more real somehow when she finally closed the door inside her new home.

'It's down to these two. I like them both.'

'Perhaps you would like to view the properties?' Simms suggested. He was more careful with her now though he still couldn't figure her out.

'How soon could I move in?' Christine asked suddenly. 'I mean, how long would it take to ... to ...' she paused, 'to sort things out.'

Simms consulted his notes. 'Seasonstown House is still occupied; it would take three to four months to arrange the conveyancing.'

Christine pointed to the picture of the house on Killiney Hill. 'And this one?'

'It is vacant at the moment. Immediate occupancy. Well, as quickly as the solicitors can process the paperwork.'

'What does that mean in terms of days or weeks?' Christine asked.

Simms shrugged elegantly. 'Six to eight weeks?' he suggested. He saw the disappointed expression flit across Christine's eyes and immediately added, 'However, I am sure we could find someone to speed up matters. It might cost,' he murmured.

'I would like to look at this house.' She picked up the sheet to look at the picture. 'Island View.'

Henry Simms dipped his head so that she wouldn't see the smile. Island View was the most expensive of the properties she had looked at. The asking price was two hundred and seventy-five thousand pounds. Reaching into an inside pocket, he pulled out a wafer-thin leather diary. 'I can arrange a viewing at your convenience ...'

'Today.'

'I beg your pardon?'

'Today.' Christine looked into his wide, startled eyes. 'I want to see it now.'

'Well ... I really ...' Simms began.

Christine Quinn fixed him with a cold smile. 'I am prepared to make a decision today.'

'My car is across the road.'

*　*　*

A car, Christine suddenly decided. She hadn't even thought about a car. Standing back, she watched Henry Simms carefully manoeuvre the fire-engine red BMW out of its parking spot on Stephen's Green. She would have to buy a car.

Simms hopped out of the car and went around to open the passenger door. She saw his eyes linger on her legs as she swung them into the car, and she could hardly keep a straight face. Randy old goat.

He reached forward and touched the radio. 'Do you mind?' he asked.

'No, not at all,' Christine murmured. Lowering the window, she leaned an elbow on the door and put on her new sunglasses. Wind ruffled her hair, reminding her that she still had to do something about getting it cut and styled. She could always do it tomorrow. She smiled quickly; that was another thing the lottery had given her – tomorrows. Two days ago, tomorrow had meant little. Tomorrow was just another day, no different than today. Only the weather and the bills changed. But now she could look forward to tomorrow, she could make plans.

The word 'lottery' brought her back to the present with a start. The lottery advertising jingle was playing on the radio, announcing the estimated total – a quarter of a million – for the draw which would be held on Wednesday night.

'I see someone in Dublin won it on Saturday night,' Simms said, idly gunning the engine as they sat waiting for traffic lights to change. 'Two and a quarter million,' he added, glancing sidelong at her. 'Just think what you could do with that.'

'I'm sure it's made a hell of a difference to someone's life,' Christine said quietly, looking away, unable to hide a smile.

Simms brushed a lock of hair off his forehead as he shook his head. 'Aaah, but you wouldn't be happy with all that money. Unless you were born to it, there's no way you'd ever be able to adjust to having that amount.' The lights changed and the heavy car moved smoothly away. 'And think of all the begging letters you'd get – it'd ruin your life,' he said decisively.

'Oh, I don't know,' Christine said with a smile. 'Think of the freedom money like that brings. The freedom to do anything, go anywhere, buy anything you want without having to wonder if you can afford it.'

Simms pursed his lips. 'I'm sure that would be fine for a while, but you'd get bored very quickly.'

'Do you buy lottery tickets, Mr Simms?' Christine asked.

'Well yes, of course. Doesn't everyone?'

'But if you'd be unhappy winning it – why do you buy the tickets?'

Simms glanced at her, but she had turned away and was watching the passers-by, fingers idly tapping to the tune on the radio.

Chapter 18

He knew it was late afternoon because the bedroom was in complete shadow.

Kevin stretched, joints popping, then rolled out of bed and picked his way through the scattered clothes to the bedroom door. Opening it a crack, he stood still, listening. The house was silent.

'Mum? Mum?'

She was still out. Scratching hard at the side of his head, he pulled open the hot-press and reached inside to flick on the immersion heater switch ... and discovered it was still on. He put his hand against the tank, and felt the heat through the thin lagging jacket. He grinned. Another sure sign that they really had won the lottery! His mother was fanatical about turning off the immersion. Well, at least there would be hot water. Padding back into his bedroom, he picked up a cassette at random and dropped it into the player, then cranked the sound up loud. Iron Maiden pulsed through the speakers.

A compact disk player, Kevin decided, that's what he wanted. Or one of the new digital taping systems. Maybe both. And a TV – one of the big ones, twenty-eight inch flat screen or a wide-screen TV with stereo sound and a stereo video to go with it. And a computer, a proper computer, not a games machine ... well, maybe he'd get a games machine too.

He could have them all and more – much more – everything he ever wanted. All the things his friends had, all those things he'd never had, that he'd only dreamed about. Well, he could have them now. A motor-bike, a car. Both.

Kevin racked Iron Maiden up to the limit, until the speakers were vibrating, the sound wobbling with distortion. He almost didn't hear the bell ring.

'Kevin Quinn?'

Kevin blinked at the short, stout, bald man standing on the step. He didn't know the man, though the face was vaguely familiar; maybe he lived on the estate. He was probably collecting for something.

'Kevin Quinn?' the man asked again. He grinned, showing bad teeth clinging to receding gums. Skin was peeling from his sunburnt skull.

'Who wants to know?' Kevin asked belligerently.

'Is your mother in, Kevin?'

'Why?' Kevin demanded. Social welfare? he wondered. Debt collector?

'I'd like to speak to her.' The man's smile grew wider.

'She's not here,' Kevin said, stepping back, pushing the door closed.

'I've just been speaking with Betty Miller,' the man said quickly.

Kevin stopped.

'You do know Mrs Miller, I believe?' The man pulled out a battered leather-bound notebook, and flipped it open. 'I believe you are engaged to her daughter, Sandra. Is that correct?'

Kevin started to shake his head. What the fuck was going on?

'And I believe you and Sandra celebrated your mother's lottery win with an engagement party last night. Would you care to comment? What's it like to win two and a quarter million pounds, Kevin?'

Kevin Quinn slammed the door shut, then sank down behind it and drew his knees up to his chin. Sandra, the bitch! She'd promised ... she must have gone straight in home and told her mother, and now ... and now ...

Christ, what had he done?

And what was his mother going to say?

Chapter 19

'Electronic security gates,' Simms announced, slowing the car. He pointed up to the left. 'There is a camera on the wall there. You can view all callers on the monitor inside. Even speak to them, if you wish.' He pointed a small black remote control at the tall wrought-iron gates. As Christine watched, they swung silently open on oiled hinges.

The estate agent eased the car forward, gravel crunching beneath the thick wheels.

'Although the house and gardens are surrounded by a seven-foot wall for added security,' Simms continued, 'the mature gardens have been arranged and cultivated so as to conceal it from the house.' Christine noted how his voice had become pompous and professional. As the car moved up the short tree-lined avenue, she ducked her head to look at the house through the greenery.

Henry Simms took a deep breath. 'This is one of our finest properties and, as I'm sure you are aware, it is in an exclusive and much sought-after address.' Rounding a small stand of trees, he stopped the car before it got too close to the house, allowing her to see it fully. 'Now, you will note the ...'

'Okay, okay!' Christine cut across him. 'Let me have a look at it. If I like it, I'll buy it.'

She was excited. She liked the sense of this place. She opened the car door and stepped out onto the gravelled driveway. Pushing her sunglasses up onto her head, she walked towards the house – and in that instant she knew she was going to buy it.

It felt right.

There was a solid comfortable feeling about the house; the dull red brick had weathered and matured, giving the building a russet colour that was now glowing warmly in the late afternoon sunshine. Although the house was quite close to the road that led up to Killiney Hill, the place was still and silent, the sounds absorbed by the trees and bushes, and the air itself smelt salt and fresh with the sea.

Simms stepped out of the car and jingled keys importantly.

'Just a moment,' Christine called over her shoulder. 'I'll let you know when I want to see inside.' Leaving the estate agent looking surprised, she wandered down along the flower beds, around the side of the house.

The gardens – she vaguely remembered that the brochure had said half an acre – were magnificent. And although the house was empty, they were obviously still well looked after. Trees and bushes sloped away from the house towards the wall, layer upon layer of greenery, splashed with colour where a tree or a bush was in flower. Enormous chunks of natural stone had been used for effect, and the path was inset with shells and polished pebbles which she guessed had come from the beach.

The blue-white glint of water through the greenery caught her attention, and she followed the twisting path through a passage of bushes to a tall narrow spiked gate set in the wall. Through the gate she could see down onto Killiney Beach, the water of the bay looking impossibly blue, disturbed only by the white sail of a boat in the distance.

Christine gripped the bars of the gate and looked down onto the golden sands. Just think; when she owned this house, she'd be able to go down onto the beach whenever she wanted, at any hour of the day or night. She could stand on the beach and watch the sun come up in the morning, or walk along the shore at dead of night and listen to the sea moving in and out. When she was a child, she always thought the waves sounded like an ancient sea monster breathing, snoring gently. And then when she'd finished on the beach, she'd be able to come back up here and wander through the gardens ...

Christine caught her breath; there were tears in her eyes. Brushing them away, she folded her arms across her breasts and hugged herself tightly. This was a dream ... a dream. Still hugging herself, she continued down the path, stooping from time to time to read the tags on the plants. Some were in English, but most were in Latin. When she owned this house, she was going to make it her business to know the name of every tree, bush and shrub in the garden. She wondered if the house had a greenhouse; if it didn't, she was going to add one on, so that she could grow beautiful exotic plants and fruits ...

A sudden splash of water stopped her. It sounded so close. Christine looked up and around. She couldn't see any other house nearby and Simms had said that the property was not overlooked. Water splashed again. Christine ducked through the trees, heading towards the sounds which were coming from the back of the house.

She pushed her way through trees and bushes ... and stepped out onto an enormous stretch of green lawn that sloped from a paved patio area at the back of the house down to tall dark trees at the bottom of the garden. In the centre of the lawn was a large ornamental pool. A tall, deeply-tanned young man, wearing nothing but cut-off jeans and tattered running shoes was fishing long strands of clinging green weed from the pool with a stick. Christine moved back and from the concealment of the trees, she watched the ripple and play of the muscles in his shoulders and back as he worked.

'Mrs Quinn ... Mrs Quinn ...?'

The voice made the young man spin round, and Christine abruptly realised that he wasn't as young as she'd first thought. The body was that of a young man, but his face showed his maturity. It was long and square and etched with lines around the eyes and along the sides of his mouth. His eyes seemed to be sunk deep in his head. His thick black hair was streaked with grey. Late thirties, early forties, she guessed. He caught sight of Christine standing under the trees and bent his head to look at her. She saw him smile, the flash of teeth startlingly white against his deep tan. 'Hello there,' he called.

Feeling self-conscious, Christine stepped out from the trees and walked towards the man. 'Hello.'

'You must have come to view the house,' he said, smiling easily. He leaned on his long stick as she approached and she could sense his eyes roving over her body.

'How can you tell that?' she asked.

He raised his chin slightly. 'Simms's voice. Once heard, never forgotten!'

Christine laughed easily. 'I know what you mean. And yes, I've come to look at the house.'

'What do you think?'

'Well ... ' Christine looked around and shrugged. 'I haven't seen inside yet, but I love the gardens. If the house is only half as nice I'll take it.'

'Great!'

'And your job is safe,' she added.

'My job?'

'You've done a great job on the gardens.'

She watched as a delighted smile spread across his face, and then Simms was running up beside her, red-faced and panting, sweat sheening his forehead. 'Aaah, Mrs Quinn. There you are. I was becoming concerned. I see you've met Mr Cunningham. If you buy this property, you will be neighbours.'

'Neighbours?' Christine asked blankly.

The man rubbed his hand on the side of his shorts, then stretched it out as he stepped closer to Christine. 'Mark Cunningham.' His eyes were blue, she noticed.

'Christine Quinn,' she said automatically as she took his hand. She felt colour flood her cheeks. 'I thought ... I'm very sorry, I thought you were the gardener.'

'Not to worry.' He grinned. 'Seeing me like this, it's an easy mistake to make. And I like to garden,' he added. 'This garden has a pond and mine doesn't, so I thought I'd hop over and give it a bit of attention.'

'Mr Cunningham is a surgeon in the Blackrock Clinic,' Simms said quickly. 'I'm sure you've see his picture on the social pages of the newspapers. Best dressed man. One of Ireland's most eligible bachelors,' he added.

'Of course,' Christine said numbly. She had never heard the name before.

'I was probably wearing more clothes the last time you saw me,' Cunningham said easily, realising that the name meant nothing to her, and saving her the embarrassment of having to say something.

'Probably,' she smiled gratefully.

'Perhaps we should have a look inside ...' Simms touched Christine's elbow and she automatically moved away from him. She saw Cunningham watch the exchange and smile.

'I hope you like what you see, Mrs Quinn,' Mark Cunningham said softly. 'If you do, maybe we'll meet again.' He lifted his stick. 'I'll go back to clearing this pond.'

As Christine walked with Simms towards the house, she could feel Cunningham's eyes on her back. She turned once, glancing quickly over her shoulder and discovered her suspicions were correct. The surgeon was staring after her; even when he saw her watching, he made no attempt to look away, and raised a hand in farewell.

'What are the other neighbours like?' Christine asked, turning back to Simms.

'Excellent,' he said immediately. 'Mr Cunningham is your nearest neighbour. On the other side, are the O'Briens, a retired couple. He was in printing, I believe. You will rarely see them;

they spend six months of the year in Portugal.' They walked back around to the front of the house, Simms rattling a set of keys.

'Why are the present owners selling?' Christine wondered.

'Financial problems.' Simms attempted a sympathetic face. 'The owner made a series of unfortunate investments. He was a Lloyds Name,' he added significantly.

'Oh,' Christine murmured. She hadn't a clue what a Lloyds Name was, but it sounded important.

'How negotiable is the price?' she asked.

Simms paused with the key in the lock, and Christine saw the mixed emotions flicker behind his eyes. He wanted a quick sale, and yet he wanted to sell it for as much as possible. She presumed he was on commission.

'The asking price is ...'

'I know what the asking price is,' she reminded him. 'Two hundred and seventy-five thousand. Now tell me what the owners will accept.'

The estate agent turned the key in the lock. Somewhere deep in the house a buzzer went off.

'Cash. Immediate payment,' she added.

Simms opened his mouth to reply, then suddenly realised that the alarm was counting down. Darting in to the hall, he tapped in the four-digit code onto the control pad behind the door.

'Sorry,' he said, reappearing. 'You have forty-five seconds from the moment the door is opened to the time the alarm goes off. The local police station is alerted, and they can have a car here in minutes.'

Christine stepped into the marble hallway. The house smelt dry and musty.

'The floor is Italian marble ...'

'You didn't answer my question.' She smiled dryly at him.

Simms stopped, and she knew he had deliberately chosen to

try and ignore the question. 'I would imagine the owners would be keen to look at an offer of around, say, two seven.'

Christine grinned. 'I would imagine the owners will be looking at an offer of around, say, two five.'

Simms shook his head firmly. 'They may take five or possibly ten off the price, but I cannot see them taking twenty-five thousand pounds off the asking price. In fact, I could not even bring such a low offer to them.'

Christine folded her arms and looked around, not meeting Simms's eyes. Every Saturday evening, she went into Moore Street to buy fruit and vegetables. She always made sure she was amongst the last customers and, because she knew the dealers were unwilling to shut up their stalls with fruit left unsold, she was able to bargain them down. And by never having exactly the right amount, she always managed to shave an extra few pence off the price.

'If the price is not open to negotiation, then I'm no longer interested in looking.'

Simms stared at her blankly. 'But you haven't even viewed the house.'

'There really isn't much point, is there?'

Simms took a deep breath, then stopped himself, realising that he had been about to sigh in exasperation, and nodded. 'What sort of figure are you offering?'

'I've told you: two hundred and fifty thousand. Cash.'

'I'll speak to my client,' he mumbled. 'I will put your offer to them.'

'Good. Now, why don't you show me the house,' she smiled.

Chapter 20

Henry Simms wanted to drive her home, but Christine refused, saying she had to meet someone in the city centre. He insisted on driving her back into town, finally depositing her in O'Connell Street, under Eason's clock just as it was chiming six. Christine waited until his flashy red car had vanished, then turned and headed down the quays for the bus.

There was a long queue, a sure sign that there hadn't been a bus for a while, and she knew that when it came, it would be crowded. Usually Christine hated queuing, the shoving, jostling and pushing, but tonight, she didn't give a damn. She was still thinking about the house.

The house was amazing. It looked like it had been lifted straight out of a television series or off the pages of a magazine. And because it had no furniture, it seemed enormous and it was very easy for her to imagine it filled with the best of everything. Because that's what she was going to have: the best of everything. Her imagination was working furiously already.

Four rooms opened directly off the marble hallway, while the entrance to the kitchen was further back, beside the stairs. To the left was a huge sitting room with a high ceiling. This room had a large black marble fireplace. There was a pale area above the fireplace, the irregular outline edged in black soot. There had been a mirror there, Christine decided, an antique gilt-framed mirror. She'd make sure there was one there in the future. A room like this needed a mirror.

The dining room was to the right, the windows looking out onto the back of the house, while French doors led out onto a paved patio and down into the rear garden. Standing at the windows, she'd been able to see Cunningham still fishing weeds out of the pond.

There was a small room close to the stairs. Simms had grandly called it the library, because it was lined with bare shelves, but Christine could immediately see it as a TV room for Kevin, or a cosy sitting room. Directly across from it was a small ivory-tiled bathroom, complete with wc and handbasin.

The kitchen lay down a narrow corridor to the right of the stairs. It had been laid out in warm golden oak, and the look of polished wood almost took her breath away. She could imagine dried flowers and bunches of herbs dangling from the exposed rafters, lines of gleaming brass pots and pans, the big, heavy ones with the French name. The cooker was huge – only it wasn't just a cooker, it was a hob as well. She'd been looking around for gas rings, until she realised that the flat expanse of what looked like glass concealed the electric cooking plates. She'd never cooked with electricity before. There were two sinks side-by-side, space for a dishwasher, and the space for the fridge was hidden behind what looked like tall cupboard doors. She was just about to ask where the washing machine went, when Simms led her out into what he called the utility room. The utility room was bigger than her present kitchen. It contained the washing machine, tumble drier and chest freezer. Simms told her, almost apologetically, that he thought the present owners would take the various machines with them. But Christine didn't want them; she had lived too long with other people's cast-offs.

The staircase was wide and deep, the banisters' golden glow lost under a coating of dust. The stairs turned twice, almost doubled back on themselves. There was a tall narrow window at the turn of the stairs. It was too high for Christine to look out, and all she could see were the tops of the trees that surrounded the house.

'There are six bedrooms ...' Simms was saying, but Christine wasn't listening to him.

The bathroom was at the top of the stairs. It too was enormous, a vast expanse of gold and white tiles. The triangular-shaped bath took up one corner of the room. Christine ran her hand across its surface; it was ceramic, not plastic like the one they had at home. The bath and handbasin had gold-coloured taps. Alongside the wc was what looked like another, strangely shaped wc. Christine knew it was a bidet, though she'd never used one. She caught a glimpse of herself in the full length mirror that took up one wall, and the image startled her. The blonde in the mirror wasn't the Christine Quinn she knew.

'Jesus,' she muttered. She only had the money for two days and already she was beginning to look and act completely differently.

All the bedrooms had been decorated in a different colour. Simms announced their names as he opened each door, smiling as if at a little joke. Christine didn't see what was funny.

'The Blue Room ...'

This was the smallest bedroom – but still bigger than her room and Kevin's combined. Christine decided that it had once been used as a child's nursery. A pale blue carpet mirrored the blue ceiling, which had been painted with fluffy white clouds. Blue striped wallpaper covered the walls, and she could see the square and rectangular marks where pictures had been removed. The window overlooked the back of the house.

The next room – the Pink Room – had obviously been a girl's. The Yellow Room, the Green Room, the White Room, all looked and felt as if they had belonged to boys. Christine wondered which one Kevin would take ... and what colour he'd paint it. Black probably.

Simms had kept the largest bedroom at the end of the landing until last. 'The master bedroom,' he said grandly, throwing open the door, stepping back to allow her to precede him into the room.

The room was huge, made even more so by the wall of built-in wardrobes, their mirrored doors reflecting the room, giving it added depth. There were windows to left and right. Three large windows on the left overlooked the front of the house, while two full-length windows to the right looked out over the back lawn. The predominant colours, gold and white, reflected back the late afternoon sunlight, lending the room a gentle warmth.

This was going to be her room. As a child, cowering and terrified in the dark, she had dreamt of a room like this: white and gold, bright and warm, a princess's room.

'Sun in the morning and in the evening,' Simms said softly.

The white carpet showed the indentations of furniture; two single beds, Christine noted. She was going to buy herself the biggest bed she could find – king sized, emperor sized, if there was such a thing.

'And here we have another of the unique features of the house,' Simms said, throwing open the full-length windows and stepping back, allowing Christine to walk out onto a small balcony. Honeysuckle twisted and curled over one side of the wrought-iron rail, yellow-and-white flowers in full bloom. Leaning against the rail, Christine breathed in the warm, scented air as she looked down over the garden. She searched for Cunningham, but he was gone, the waters of the ornamental pool shimmering golden and undisturbed. She was vaguely disappointed that he wasn't there.

There was a bathroom en-suite, a miniature version of the bathroom just down the hall. She couldn't see the need for it, but the sheer extravagance amused her. Three bathrooms in the house!

She had seen enough. 'If I wanted to buy this house, Mr Simms, how soon would I be able to move in?'

Simms ran a hand across his head, patting stray hairs into

place. 'Well, you would have to make an offer, which my clients would have to approve ... or not, as the case may be. If they did accept your offer, it would have to go to the solicitors, then they would look into the title and it would finally go to contract stage. Realistically, three months.'

'Too long,' Christine said firmly. 'You told me back in your office that it might be done in six to eight weeks. And that it might be possible to do it sooner.'

'Well yes, of course, it might be possible...' he said cautiously.

'I am paying in cash, Mr Simms.'

'I appreciate that, Mrs Quinn ...'

Christine folded her arms and looked at the estate agent. 'I'm sure you would be able to help me, Mr Simms. You would be able to find me a solicitor who would hurry things along. I will be paying cash,' she said again. 'And that includes your commission.' She saw the flicker of greed behind the man's eyes and she knew he'd bite. 'My offer on the house – two hundred and fifty thousand pounds – is subject to a quick sale.'

'I suppose we might be able to bring the time down to a month, maybe six weeks,' Simms said doubtfully.

'Make it two,' Christine said firmly. 'Make it shorter, and you'll earn yourself a bonus. Cash,' she added.

* * *

Two hundred and fifty thousand pounds, Christine repeated silently, sitting on the bus, staring out through a filthy window. She had just made an offer of a quarter of a million pounds and here she was still travelling by bus. She needed to get herself a car.

It was now Tuesday, 13 July. If Simms could put the deal together in the two weeks, that would mean she and Kevin could be moving into the new house by the first week in August.

Two weeks.

Lost in her day-dream, Christine almost missed her stop and had to scramble down the bus before it pulled away.

Pulling on her mac, she tucked the new sunglasses into the pocket as she turned into the housing estate. Of course, she'd have to make sure that neither she nor Kevin did anything out of the ordinary for the next two weeks. She didn't want to alert the neighbours that something was up. Maybe she wouldn't buy that new car just yet. Everything had to remain exactly as it was.

She was still smiling at the thought as she rounded the corner into her road and saw the crowd of people. She slowed, then quickened her pace when she realised they were gathered outside her gate. Someone spotted her and the crowd turned and surged forward, a man with a camera and a man with a microphone breaking out of the centre of the group. Another man with cameras strung around his neck, hurried along beside them.

'Mrs Quinn ... can you tell us ...'

'Mrs Quinn ... congratulations ... '

'This way, Mrs Quinn ...'

A camera flash.

'Christine ...'

Another flash.

She knew then. The damage was done.

Chapter 21

The dream had turned into a nightmare.

Christine dozed off and on during the night, awakening from terrifying dreams in which leering faces and grasping hands had been thrust towards her, mouths opening and closing, lips twisting in smiles, eyes cold and envious. Long-nailed claws grasped for her, tearing at her clothes, the hands coming away filled not with cloth and material, but with crumpled currency notes. When she was naked the claws tore at her flesh.

She finally realised sometime after three that she wasn't going to get any sleep. Rolling out of bed, she pulled on her dressing gown, pushed her feet into slippers and padded downstairs to make herself some tea. She was plugging in the kettle when Kevin appeared in the kitchen, rubbing sleep out of his eyes.

'I didn't mean to wake you,' Christine said shortly.

'You didn't wake me,' he mumbled, slumping at the kitchen table. 'I couldn't sleep. We've got to talk, Mum,' he added.

'You've done enough talking already.' She turned away before she could say any more, say anything she would regret later. She had a sharp tongue; Robert had said that she never knew when to stop, never knew when she'd said enough.

'Okay. Okay. Let's start again,' she said, taking a deep breath. The kettle whistled and she poured boiling water into the small teapot and added a single teabag. Pouring two cups of weak tea, she turned back to the table and pushed Kevin's cup in front of him.

'When I came home last night, I thought ...' she began, and stopped. She wasn't sure what she'd thought. She had seen the crowd gathered in front of her gate, and immediately thought that there had been an accident, but there was no ambulance, and then the thoughts came tumbling quickly ... a fire ... Robert had returned ... police ... Kevin. But when the crowd turned to her, and she saw the cameras, the flashing lightbulbs, she knew, even before the shouted questions had begun, she knew what had happened. The news had got out ... which meant that Kevin had told someone. The little bastard! Despite everything she'd said, despite all his promises, he hadn't been able to keep his big mouth shut.

Tucking her elbows in, she shouldered her way through the crowd, ignoring the questions, barely feeling the hands that patted her back and touched her sleeve, twisting her head to avoid the smiling faces, the puckered lips, the cold envious eyes as people tried to congratulate her.

Most of the crowd fell back as she pushed open the gate. One reporter persisted, a small, stout, balding man, with bad teeth and foul breath. She thought his face was vaguely familiar. He scurried up the footpath alongside her, insistent, demanding, shouting questions: 'What does it feel like ... how do you feel ... what will you do ... what will ... what ... what ... what!' As she fumbled with the key, he pushed a tape recorder into her face and smiled widely. 'Harry Webb, Mrs Quinn. You must have a comment for the local press please, Mrs Quinn.'

Christine bit back her response, snatched the small recorder from the man's nicotine-stained fingers, and dropped it in the bush by the side of the door, the place which next door's dog used as a toilet. As she was pushing the hall door closed, she heard Webb mutter, 'Aw shit!' She wasn't sure if he was swearing or simply making a discovery.

Kevin was waiting for her in the hall. His eyes were red against his pale skin, and she knew he'd been crying, though he'd never have admitted it to her. She had been about to shout and scream, but suddenly all the anger drained away from her, and she simply said, 'Go to bed. We'll talk about this in the morning.'

Kevin climbed the stairs without a word, not even looking back when the doorbell rang and the letter box flicked open. Christine knocked it closed with the flat of her hand. When she heard Kevin's bedroom door click closed, she made sure the hall door was locked and the chain was on, before she took a tea towel from the kitchen and stuffed it into the letter box to prevent people peering in.

When the ringing doorbell became too much for her, she simply unscrewed the bell from the wall, leaving the clapper buzzing against thin air. She was suddenly thankful that she didn't have a phone.

When it became obvious that she wasn't going to come out and make a statement, the press disappeared and the crowd thinned out, leaving a few gossiping neighbours standing at a gate further down the road, while the bald reporter – Webb, the persistent one – moved amongst them. Peeping through her bedroom window, Christine noted with a smile that he wasn't using his tape recorder to take notes.

She'd gone through the rest of the evening feeling numb and detached, making herself endless cups of tea, unable to settle to anything, finally heating the water for a bath. She was in bed by ten – no wonder she couldn't sleep.

The news was out. The secret discovered. The entire estate would know before the night was over, and the press photographers had been here, which meant her picture in one of the morning papers ... which meant ...

Just what did it mean?

While the win had been secret, they had little or nothing to fear. But now that the press had got hold of it, now that the neighbours knew ... then everything changed. The story of my life, she thought bitterly, the first piece of good luck in a long time, and it had to go sour.

At least she still had the money.

But for how much longer?

Christine looked across the table at her son in the early-morning gloom. 'Do you want to tell me how the word got out?' she asked, very quietly.

He started to shake his head, his eyes suddenly shifty. 'I don't know ...'

'I didn't tell anyone, Kevin. Outside of the lottery people and the bank manager, no-one knows.'

Kevin opened his mouth and Christine knew he was going to try to blame someone else. Just like his father, Jimmy Doyle. He had never been able to accept responsibility for his own actions either.

'The truth!' she snapped.

'I told no-one except Sandra,' he muttered, wrapping his hands around the chipped cup, not looking into her eyes.

'Sandra?'

'Sandra Miller. You know her, she lives ...'

'I know her,' Christine said bitterly. She also knew her mother, Betty Miller, one of the local gossips. 'After all we talked about, Kevin, and you couldn't keep it a secret for five minutes. Why, Kevin? Why?'

'We went out together last night. I suppose I was spending too much ... she thought I'd stolen the money. She didn't want to have anything to do with me if the money was stolen ... so I told her, but she swore she'd say nothing.'

'And you believed her?'

He nodded.

'She didn't keep her promise.'

'I know that,' he sighed. 'And then earlier this afternoon, a man called to the door, a bald guy. He was asking for you. Then he said he was a reporter, and he said he'd been speaking to Betty Miller, and she told him that Sandra was engaged to me and that we had an engagement party last night.' He looked at his mother now, and there were unshed tears sparkling in his eyes. 'But we're not engaged, Mum. We're not. But she told the reporter we were.'

'Did she now?' Christine said grimly. She could see immediately where this was going.

'And then all those people turned up, and there were people taking photographs of the house, and ...'

Christine held up her hand. She had heard enough.

'We'll have to move out,' she said decisively. 'We'll stay in a hotel or guest house or something until we find someplace new to live. Oh, Kevin,' she sighed miserably, 'why couldn't you keep your big mouth shut?'

'I'm sorry, Mum, I ...'

'It's done,' she said quickly, 'and there's nothing we can do about it now.'

'Where were you today?' Kevin asked, breaking the long silence that followed.

'I was looking at houses,' she said quietly.

'Where?'

'Do you honestly expect me to tell you? You'll find out when we move in!'

Wednesday, 14 July

Chapter 22

DUBLIN WOMAN WINS £2.25 MILLION

Mrs Christine Quinn (36) is the latest lottery multi-millionaire. Mrs Quinn and her son, Kevin (17) who were said to be still in a state of shock by close friends and neighbours, were unavailable for comment.

THE LOTTERY MILLIONAIRE

Dublin has a new lottery millionaire. Christine Quinn (37) won Saturday night's jackpot lottery of £2,225,795. Mrs Quinn, who lives with her son, Kevin (17), is estranged from her husband, Robert. She is currently unemployed and close friends say that she has no immediate plans for her record win.

TWO-AND-A-HALF MILLION
REASONS TO CELEBRATE

Christine Quinn (38) has extra reasons to celebrate her lottery win. She will now be able to give her son Kevin (18) the wedding celebration of a lifetime. Kevin's fiancée, Sandra Miller (18), said that they had been putting off naming the day until Kevin found a job. 'But the lottery win changes all that,' she said today. She was hoping they would be able to arrange a date in September or early October.

Chapter 23

Robert Quinn stood in the shower and gradually turned the hot water down to cold, allowing the needle spray to beat at his body, and bring a red flush to his skin.

'Why do you do that?' The naked woman standing in the doorway folded her arms across her breasts and drew on the cigarette, her first of the day.

Quinn ignored her. Stepping closer to the shower nozzle, he turned the water up full, ice-cold needles of pain pricking at his flesh. He clamped his jaws together to keep his teeth from chattering. Finally, when his entire body was tingling, and he felt awake and alive, he turned the water off and stood in the bath, dripping.

'Why do you do that?'

Robert Quinn turned, brushing water from his cropped grey hair. He smiled at the woman. 'In prison, if you've got a problem with someone, you usually settle it in the showers. Most people close their eyes in warm water; it relaxes them ... and that's when you get them.'

'You're not in prison now, Bob,' Rachel Farmer gently reminded him.

'You can get used to showering in cold water. It wakes you up, gets the blood circulating,' he continued, ignoring the interruption. Realising that he was beginning to shiver, he stepped out of the bath, pulled a towel off the radiator and started drying himself vigorously.

Rachel Farmer leaned against the doorway and watched the big man. He'd spent eighteen months in prison and obviously a lot of that time in the gym. She could see newly-defined muscles in his chest, shoulders and forearms, and his stomach was flat and hard. He had adopted the bodybuilder's trick of removing all his body hair to highlight his muscles, and she found the overall effect startling. Like a little boy with a man's body. Reaching forward, she traced a semi-circular scar on Robert's left shoulder. 'That's new.'

'Bottle,' he grunted.

'What happened?'

Quinn smiled mirthlessly. 'An argument which went too far. The little shit got a bottle from the kitchens, broke it and attacked me from behind.' The smile broadened. 'He needed a new face when I was finished with him.'

'Didn't you get into trouble?' Rachel wondered.

'Officially he fell. That's what he told the screws and the doctors.' Robert Quinn laughed, a dry wheezing cough. 'He fell several times.' He turned quickly, catching her and pulling her to him, her breasts flattening against his hairless chest. He plucked the cigarette from her fingers and flicked it into the bath. He kissed her savagely, teeth bruising her lips, while his hands roved down her back, tracing her spine, squeezing her buttocks.

Finally, gasping, Rachel pushed him away. 'Let me catch my breath. I thought you got enough last night!'

'I've got a lot of catching up to do,' he grinned. He slapped her bottom as he stepped into the bedroom, leaving a distinct red impression of his palm and fingers on her flesh.

'I hope you kept my clothes,' he called.

'In the suitcase on top of the wardrobe,' Rachel said. She was standing before the bathroom mirror examining the bruises and scratches on her body, the tokens of their lovemaking. He had been like an animal last night, biting, clawing, pounding into her, releasing the frustrations of an eighteen-month spell in prison. There were fingermarks on her stomach and thighs, bruises on her hips and arms where he had clutched at her in his passion, and her large nipples were hard and tender where he had sucked and bitten.

'Tell me how you've been,' Robert called from the bedroom. 'You never visited me,' he added ominously.

'You told me not to,' Rachel said immediately. 'You said you didn't want the police making a connection between us.'

'Did I? I suppose I did,' he said, answering his own question.

Plucking the cigarette butt from the bath, she dropped it into the wastepaper basket and turned on the shower, washing the bath clean. Then she put the plug in and allowed the bath to fill. A hot bath would ease her aching muscles.

Leaving the bath filling, she went back into the bedroom and watched Robert dressing in the clothes he had left with her a year and a half ago. 'You look good,' she said. 'Fit. Healthy.'

'I am.' He pulled on a pair of boxer shorts and stepped into black jeans. 'I hate to say it, but the stay inside actually did me good. You look good yourself,' he added. 'You've lost that skinny look. I can't see your ribs anymore.'

Unsure whether to take it as a compliment or not, she reached for the packet of cigarettes on the dressing table. Rachel Farmer had been twenty-six when she first met Robert Quinn at a night-club, four years before. He danced close with her on that first night – very close. She was skinny then, but she used her thinness to emphasise her long legs. They were her best asset. She knew her features were unremarkable. Her eyes were a muddy brown, her face was too broad, chin too square. Her hair had once been red, but she had bleached and dyed it so often that it now assumed a yellowish colour and had the consistency of straw.

She knew him for six months before she realised what he was: a brutal, often violent, man. But by then she was in love with him, and she excused his brutality as passion, his violence as just another demonstration of love.

She knew him a year before she discovered that he was married, and that his wife was still living in a housing estate just outside the city.

She knew him for eighteen months before she discovered that he was a petty criminal with a violent record. She was determined to split up with him then, but he swore that he'd changed, reformed, that all that was in the past, the mistakes of his youth. She believed him, because she wanted to believe him. She wanted to believe that he wasn't a violent petty criminal ... though deep in her heart she still suspected that he was. It was about this time that she realised she was actually frightened of him.

She knew him for two years when she realised that she wasn't the only woman in his life. She almost broke with him then, but when she tackled him, he flew into a terrible rage, and pointed out that she didn't own him, they weren't married, she had no hold over him ... and besides, these other women were only one-night stands, they meant nothing to him ... and he always came back to her ... and didn't that mean that he loved her?

It had been a terrible shock when he was arrested for assault. He pleaded self-defence, but the barman's injuries were of such a serious nature and inconsistent with the plea, and when the judge took several other cases into consideration, he sent Robert Quinn to prison.

Robert made Rachel swear that she'd wait for him and, although she agreed, as the months went by she began hoping that he would forget about her. When she realised that he'd been out of prison for nearly a month and hadn't contacted her, she finally breathed a sigh of relief – he had forgotten about her. She was relieved. Although she could honestly say that she loved him, she was also aware that she was frightened of him. And she knew that no relationship built on fear could survive and flourish.

Then, last night, just after ten, there was a knock on the door of the flat. Thinking it was one of the other residents of the house, she opened the door ... and discovered Robert Quinn standing on the landing. Before she could say a word, he stepped into the room, closing the door with his heel, swept her up in his arms and carried her into the bedroom. In the sweat-soaked hours that followed, she had rediscovered the passion that had first brought them together. And when he whispered, 'I love you,' she believed him, and believed that he meant it.

'Are you still working in that office?'

Rachel nodded. She worked as a secretary in an accountant's office, just off the quays. The pay wasn't great, there was no chance of advancement, but the work was undemanding, and she knew that these days just having a job was an achievement.

'I thought you got out a month ago,' she said, drawing hard on a cigarette, watching the way his eyes lingered on the swell of her breasts.

'I did. I had a few things to do,' he said, and she knew from the tone of his voice that she wouldn't get any more out of him on that subject. 'I wasn't sure you'd still be here,' he added. 'You were thinking of moving the last time I was here.'

'Good flats are hard to find,' she said, going back into the bathroom to turn off the hot tap.

She felt the water, wincing as it stung her fingers, then spun the cold tap. She'd had this flat in Glasnevin, close to the cemetery, for the past eight years. She occasionally thought about moving, but realised that it would be difficult to find a place so close to town at a reasonable rent. 'Anyway,' she said, coming back to stand in the doorway, 'it suits me. I can walk into the office in twenty minutes.'

Robert stood up and pulled on a black polo-neck. It stretched across his chest, outlining his muscles.

'You must have done nothing but exercise in prison,' she said.

'There's not a lot else to do.'

'Have you any plans?' she asked. 'Any jobs lined up?'

He laughed hoarsely. 'Jobs? What do you think about the chances of an ex-con getting a job?'

'What will you do?'

'I'll find something.'

'Will you be staying long?' She was careful to keep her voice neutral.

'As long as ...' He stopped, eyes narrowing. 'Is there a problem? Maybe you've a boyfriend?' he laughed, but there was no humour in the sound.

'There's no boyfriend.'

'If you don't want me here, I can move on.'

'No, no, it's nothing like that.'

'Well then, I'll stay for a while.' He gave her a crooked smile. 'The bath's overflowing.'

Rachel squealed with alarm and darted back into the bathroom. If she didn't mop it up immediately, water would drip down onto Mrs Corcoran's flat below, staining her ceiling, blowing the light bulb. The last time it happened the old woman almost died of a heart attack. It cost Rachel a week of presents before she calmed down.

Robert's grin widened as he watched Rachel on her hands and knees frantically mopping up the bathwater with a towel. 'I'll go and make us some breakfast. What time do you have to be in to work?'

'Nine.'

'It's just eight now,' he said, snapping on the radio as he stepped into the tiny kitchen.

He rooted through the fridge looking for something to cook, idly listening to the news.

'... rise in the mortgage rates ...

'... renewed fighting in Bosnia ...

'... South Africa ...

'... bomb in ...

'... lottery multi-millionaire ...

'... Christine Quinn ...'

Robert straightened, the name shocking him motionless, and turned on the radio, but the newscaster moved on and began the first story.

'The Central Bank today announced a drop in the commercial lending rate ...'

Robert turned back to the cooker and cracked two eggs into the greasy pan. Christine Quinn. Coincidence. A name from his past. He hadn't thought about Christine for a while. He wondered if she was still living in the house on the estate. The same house she had him barred from.

Fat spat, stinging the back of his hand.

'Christine Quinn.'

He spun round to look at the radio, fragments of the newsreader's sentences falling into place like tumbling cards. 'Lottery winner ... Christine Quinn ... record lottery win of two million, two hundred and twenty-five thousand seven hundred and ninety-five pounds.'

He shook his head. Lucky bitch, whoever she was. But it couldn't be the same Christine ...

'... seventeen-year-old son, Kevin, just finished his leaving certificate.'

Robert's mouth opened and closed silently.

The discussion moved on, panellists speaking about the need to cap the lottery wins, a spokesman from the lottery arguing that bigger wins meant more people playing. But Robert heard none of it.

Christine had won.

His Christine.

The pinched-mouthed, flat-chested, razor-tongued bitch had won two and a quarter million.

A slow smile spread across the big man's face.

It was time he saw Christine again. She owed him.

Now she could afford to pay.

And she would.

Chapter 24

'Oh Jesus,' Christine sighed and turned off the radio. She had never thought that her name would be broadcast on the radio. She wondered how they'd found out ... that reporter, Webb, no doubt. Little bastard.

Christine leaned back against the sink and stared at the faded lino. Robert. Her immediate thoughts were of Robert. He bought that lino when they first moved into the house, back in ... 1982, two years after they married. It had never been changed, and she couldn't even remember what the pattern had been. Robert. It he heard her name on the radio, he would come looking for her; he would want some money. Never mind that he had no right to it; he would want some. He'd probably want it all.

Kevin pushed open the door. 'Did you hear the radio?' he mumbled. Christine nodded fiercely, determined not to say anything rash.

'What are we going to do?'

She shook her head, brushing stray strands of hair from her dry lips. She didn't know.

'I don't think we should stay here,' he said quietly.

Christine looked at him blankly.

'I mean, now that people know we've won the money and where we live, there might be callers, newspaper people, beggars, neighbours. Maybe we should go into town for the day,' he suggested finally.

Christine stared at her son, trying hard to prevent herself from saying something she would regret. At this moment, she hated him: hated him for what he had done. Everything had been perfect, just perfect, until he betrayed her trust …

'You're right,' she said. She looked at her watch. Twenty past eight. There was a bus at half past. 'We'll go into town, maybe spend a few bob'…

'I'm sorry, Mum,' Kevin began.

'Forget it. What's done is done. It can't be undone,' she snapped, turning away so that he wouldn't see the tears in her eyes.

What's done is done. And cannot be undone.

The story of her life.

The winning numbers –

TWENTY-THREE

Chapter 25

Christine Doolin stood and stared at the oversized Bank of Ireland calendar pinned to the back of the bedroom door. The first half of the month of June was scored through with heavy lines. Saturday, 21 June 1980 was circled in red lipstick.

Two more days.

Well, one really, because you couldn't count Saturday.

On Saturday, 21 June 1980, the day before her twenty-third birthday, Christine Doolin was marrying Robert Quinn.

The young woman smiled, saying the name aloud, giving herself the title, 'Mrs Christine Quinn. Mrs Christine Doolin-Quinn.' She shook her head. No, not Doolin-Quinn, just Quinn. Christine Quinn.

Opening her handbag, she took out her lipstick and twisted it up, then stopped and turned to look at the clock on the wall above the sink. When the second hand swept past midnight, she slowly and deliberately ran a line through Thursday, 19 June.

Thirty-nine hours.

Christine moved slowly around the small flat. She was exhausted but unable to settle, and she knew she was too excited to sleep. Opening the bedroom door, she looked in on Kevin. He had crept into her bed again, and was sleeping curled up in a tight little ball at the foot of the bed, wrapped around Mr Ted. Smoothing strands of blond hair off his forehead, she wondered how he was going to get on with Robert. There was no male role model in the boy's life and Christine had to be both mother and father to him. In the three years she'd known Robert, the two had got along really well, even when Robert sometimes stayed over for a night. Still, it would be only natural if he was jealous because of this new figure in his mother's life. Yet, there were no signs of the jealousy she'd been expecting. But she wondered how the boy would react when he discovered that Uncle Bob wasn't just a casual visitor anymore. She expected that he would be confused and probably resentful of Robert's presence, but she was determined she was going to pay extra attention to the boy, just to show him that he still had a special place in her heart.

Bending over, she pressed her lips to his damp forehead. 'Good night,' she breathed.

The boy's bright blue eyes snapped open, looking at her blankly before they focused. 'Is it time?' he asked immediately. She sometimes thought that Kevin was even more excited about the wedding than she was. 'Not yet,' she smiled. 'Soon. One more day. Go back to sleep.'

Kevin obediently turned over and drifted back to sleep.

Christine stood over the bed, looking down at the sleeping figure. In the past seven years – and they had been hard and difficult years – she had never once regretted having the baby. There had been enormous pressure on her when she announced she was pregnant. When she refused to name the father, that pressure increased, and without Jimmy Doyle's support, she was forced to carry the burden herself. Her father threatened to throw her out when she told him. She dared him to do it, staring him straight in the eye, her own responding threat unspoken; but they both realised it was there. Though they never talked about what had happened in the years following her mother's death, it was always there, lurking, festering.

Eight weeks before the birth of her baby, she had moved into a flat with a friend in Fownes Street, in the heart of Dublin, just off the quays.

Christine never went back to the house in Cabra and, although she kept up a tentative relationship with her sister, and had spoken briefly to her father, there was no love between them, and they were little more than casual acquaintances.

They wouldn't be coming to the wedding on Saturday.

She had invited them, but only because Robert insisted. He had no family of his own, and found it difficult to understand how someone with living family could actively cut themselves off. Christine tried to explain, speaking frankly about her experiences as a pregnant sixteen-year-old girl, though unable to bring herself to tell him of her father's abuse.

Robert seemed genuinely sorry when the simple note of regret came from Sheila. On the bottom of the card, in her tight crabbed writing, she wrote that her father was unwell and wouldn't be coming either. But she was unable to leave it at that, and added that it was a pity Christine wasn't getting married in a church. The ceremony was to be held in the Registry Office in Molesworth Street.

Robert offered to go and see Sheila, and try to convince her to come, but Christine would have none of it. She hadn't been invited to her sister's wedding and was secretly pleased that Sheila wouldn't be coming to hers. If she had any regrets, it was not being able to show off Robert to her family. He was everything she wanted in a man, tall, darkly handsome with a quick smile that lit up his whole face and his teeth were the whitest she had ever seen.

Sheila's husband Nick, at twenty-seven, was exactly the same age as Robert. But he was short, stout and balding. He was humourless now, and Christine knew that in ten years' time he would be dour. Sheila gave him the grand title of area sales manager, but Christine knew he was nothing more than a commercial traveller for a package food company.

Robert worked as a free-lance publishers' rep. He represented a dozen of the smaller British and Irish publishers, selling their books to bookshops and wholesalers around the country.

They first met in the bookshop on the quays where Christine worked part-time, covering the lunch breaks and the days off, the meagre pay helping to supplement her paltry social welfare payments from the state.

It took her a while to realise that he made a point of coming in on the days she was on duty. He usually arrived mid-morning when it wasn't busy. He would spend some time chatting with her and always gave her free samples of his stock. It took him the best part of three months before he plucked up the courage to ask her out for a date.

Christine had a rule with boyfriends. She made a point of telling them, straight off, on the first date, that she had a child. Some ran a mile and never came back; others said they didn't mind, but she could see in their eyes that they did, and they eventually drifted away. A few assumed that because she had a child she was either promiscuous or available and came on fast to her.

Robert seemed different though ... she could see that from the start. He didn't back away when she told him she had a young son, nor did he take it as an indication that she was available. He seemed kind and considerate, genuinely sympathetic and gentle too. And he listened. He listened so intently. Most of the young men she knew just wanted to talk – usually about themselves. But Robert listened, giving her his full attention. They spent most of the first date talking about Kevin and the following day he came into the shop with a bundle of children's books for him. They had been out on three dates before he plucked up the courage to kiss her, and even then she had to initiate it, standing so close, with her face turned to his, that he could not mistake her intentions. She knew she was taking a terrible risk – if he refused her, the embarrassment could easily shatter their growing relationship. But he didn't refuse her. He wrapped his arms around her and lowered his lips onto hers, and in that instant she knew that here was the gentle man she could allow herself to fall in love with.

She had never allowed it to happen before. She didn't hate men, as some women she knew did. But she was wary of them. Defensive. Distrusting. There had been a couple of occasions in the past when she found herself drawn to one or other of the young men who came into the shop but, even when everything seemed to be going well, she always held back part of herself, watching, waiting.

It didn't take her long to realise that she *was* falling in love with the big man, but Christine Doolin was practical. She knew that though he might be fond of her and Kevin, there was no way it would go any further. She had nothing going for her, no great looks, she was stuck in a dead-end job and, after all, what man would take on the responsibility of another man's child? She was resigned to the fact that Robert Quinn would never be more than a short-term relationship.

They had been seeing each other for six months when Robert asked her to marry him, on Christmas Eve, 1979. They were in her flat, standing under mistletoe. He said it casually, softly, the words almost whispered, and yet she heard them as distinctly as if he'd shouted them.

'Would you think of marrying me?'

Six months ago ...

Those months simply flew, until the end of May and then, paradoxically, time seemed to stop and the last three weeks crept by, until she was now counting every hour.

Christine stood up and moved around the two-roomed flat. It would be cramped when Robert moved in, and Kevin would have to sleep in the sitting room. But Robert promised they would buy a house as soon as he saved enough money for a deposit.

In one corner of the bedroom were the presents they had received: a toaster from the staff in the bookshop, a kettle, some cutlery, a block of steak knives, blankets and pillow-cases from her few friends. In another pile was another kettle, a food mixer, a juice extractor and a weighing scales from Robert's friends and colleagues. She was tempted to use them, especially one of the new kettles, but held off. They were hers and Robert's; they would use them together.

What she grandly called her wedding dress was hanging on a hook on the back of the door. She hadn't even considered getting married in white, and they only discussed a church wedding briefly. Neither was particularly religious and without the pressure of parents or family to bow to, they preferred to put the money they'd save on the function towards a deposit for a house. Christine's outfit was an ivory-coloured linen suit, worn over a beautiful silk blouse, and a tiny pillbox hat with a scrap of a black veil. Overall, it cost nearly one hundred and fifty pounds; she didn't want to spend the money, but Robert insisted. It was only one day, he said. The first day of the rest of her life.

Pressing her face to the cool linen, she breathed in the cloth's crisp fragrance.

Thirty-nine hours.

For the first time in her life Christine Doolin – soon it would be Christine Quinn – felt safe and loved. She would never forget her twenty-third birthday.

Chapter 26

Harry Webb yawned and checked his watch again. Eight twenty-two. He had taken up position outside the Quinn house shortly after seven, parking his battered red Toyota Corolla at an angle which would allow him to move away quickly as soon as the Quinns left the house.

Eight twenty-three.

Because they would be leaving, he knew that. There was no way they were going to stay in the house for the day. If he'd read them right – and he would lay money on it that he had – they would probably spend as little time as possible in the house until the fuss died down, or they moved out of the area. He wondered if they had any relatives they could lie low with.

Well, he grinned, they could run, but they couldn't hide. Not from Harry Webb, investigative reporter.

Eight twenty-four.

He sighed. It could be a long wait. Neither of them was working; they probably wouldn't get up until noon. Well, he would wait, and when they appeared he was ready for them.

The camera on the passenger seat was a twenty-year-old Nikon F, fitted with an eight-year-old motor-drive, which allowed him to shoot off multiple films with a single press of a button. His spare tape-recorder sat alongside it. Last night when the woman dropped his small recorder into the bush, it had landed in a pile of dog shit. Webb scowled, suddenly wondering if she knew what was in the bush. He wouldn't be at all surprised if she did. He lifted his left hand to his face and sniffed at his fingers. He'd scrubbed at them with every available washing-up liquid at home, but he still thought he could smell the foul odour off his flesh. He'd read somewhere that dog shit could make you blind. Or was it cat shit? Still, maybe he could sue her. Webb brightened at the thought. He could sue her for a new tape recorder, one of the latest voice-activated ones that the professional journalists used. And maybe he'd add on the damage to his suit. And he was sure he'd catch a disease from the filth. A skin disease, or maybe blood poisoning. He wondered if you could catch AIDS from animal shit. He lifted his fingers again: they did look a bit red ... but that could have been from the scrubbing. There was a cut there at the side of his nail; something could have got into that wound ...

He added mental anguish to his list. The worry about whether he'd caught a disease. He flexed his fingers. Were they beginning to stiffen up? His career – such as it was – would be ruined if he couldn't type. The amount of damages went up. It might be worth the cost of a solicitor's letter; she'd probably pay up just to avoid the publicity.

But no. He shook his head. Although he didn't know this particular woman, he knew the type. Hard as nails, sharp as glass. Didn't give a shit about anyone, the neighbours said, stuck-up bitch, kept herself to herself, belonged to none of the local community groups, never even contributed to any of the fund-raising events. Webb nodded again; he knew the type all right. And now that she'd finally got her hands on some money, there was no way she was going to let go of it.

Well, maybe he'd keep the possibility of suing her as an option, just in case this story didn't work out.

But it would work out. He knew it would.

Harry Webb had big plans for exploiting the story of Christine Quinn's win; it was the sort of story that came along once in a journalist's lifetime. He'd already sold her name to one of the news agencies for five hundred pounds, the quickest, easiest five hundred notes he ever made. Maybe he should have asked for more.

However, that was only the start.

It was early days yet, but so far no-one had managed to talk to Christine Quinn. An interview with the latest lottery millionaire would be worth something. He could sell it as an exclusive to one of the papers, or maybe talk them into serialising it. There might even be a television interview in it.

But if he was going to do anything about the story, he would have to move fast. Right now, he had all the advantages: she was a neighbour – practically – he knew the district, and the locals knew him. He wasn't some smart-ass city journalist coming in to do a quick story and then vanish again. He was a local man and the locals knew he would treat the neighbourhood sympathetically, and that's why they'd be willing to talk to him. And – his hidden card – he knew Betty Miller, mother of the boy's fiancée. He already had her on tape talking about the forthcoming wedding. He was sure that, once he pointed all this out to Christine Quinn, she would see his point.

And of course there was the book.

Webb grinned. The book was his ace card. He was going to write Christine Quinn's story. Local woman becomes millionaire. It was real Cinderella stuff. It had everything going for it. Ordinary woman wins fortune, it changes her life completely; where does she go from here? There was certainly the possibility of serialisation rights to the book, and probably a television mini-series too … well, maybe not a mini-series, but he could dream, couldn't he?

He'd already made a few gentle inquiries into her past and discovered that she was separated from her husband, a hardened criminal. Armed robbery, grievous bodily harm, something like that. Even better. When he was finished with her, he was going to make Christine Quinn a household name … and his too. Christine Quinn may have won her fortune, but her win was going to make his.

Eight twenty-five.

The door opened.

Webb's rotten teeth flashed as he turned on the ignition and reached for the camera. He knew it. He knew she wouldn't be able to spend time in the house.

Lifting the Nikon, he pointed it through the open window and focused. It was Christine Quinn and the boy, Kevin. The woman's face was hidden behind large sunglasses and she was wearing a light coat over obviously new clothes. The boy was wearing a leather jacket over a white tee-shirt and what looked like new jeans and boots. So, they'd spent some of the money on clothes. He pressed the button and four frames clicked off in rapid succession.

She was younger than he first thought, pretty too, and it was only when he saw the boy walking alongside her that he realised just how small she was.

They were heading for the bus stop, for the half-eight bus. Dragging heavily on the steering wheel, he turned the car and drove down on the wrong side of the road, finally pulling in a little ahead of the couple. He was smiling as he stepped out of the car, tape-recorder in his outstretched hand.

'Mrs Quinn … Christine. We didn't get a chance to talk last night. I'm Harry Webb, your local reporter. I'd like to take this opportunity to congratulate you on your win. I'd like to talk to you,' he added hurriedly as Christine and Kevin brushed past without even looking in his direction.

Webb took half-a-dozen steps after them before he realised that he'd left the keys in the ignition and the car was running. In this neighbourhood, that was tantamount to putting a 'Free' sign on the car. 'Shit,' he hissed, sliding back into the seat and pulling the creaking door closed.

Gunning the engine, he roared down the road after them. 'Mrs

Quinn,' he said through the open window, 'be reasonable. All I want to do is to talk to you. I can do you a lot of good, Mrs Quinn. I want to tell your story. I can make you famous. There's a book and maybe a television movie in it,' he added. 'Lots of money.'

The woman stopped and Webb jammed on the brakes, grinning broadly. Mention of money always got to them.

Christine Quinn approached the car and leaned in through the open window, pushing her sunglasses up onto her head. Webb blinked, eyes watering, as her expensive perfume enveloped him. He mentally added it to the list of things she'd bought and revised the column he was writing:

Lottery winner on spending spree. Ireland's latest instant multi-millionaire today went on a spending spree, splurging ... he'd think of the figure later ... *on the latest fashions and perfumes.*

'I realise you are in a rush, Mrs Quinn. Things to do, money to spend, eh?' he said with a grin. 'Perhaps I could call round later and we could talk over a cup of tea? Better still, why don't you allow me to drive you where you're going now, and we could talk in the car. Maybe make an arrangement for dinner later. My treat,' he added generously. A sprat to catch a mackerel.

Christine Quinn's face was expressionless. 'Mr Webb. Leave me alone. I don't need your money. I've got all the money I can ever want. I want you to stop hassling me. Now, stay away from me and my son!' she snapped, then reached in and twisted the keys in the ignition, turning off the engine. Before Webb could react, she pulled the bundle of keys out of the ignition and tossed them as far as she could back down the road. Then she turned and hurried across the green to where the bus was just pulling into the stop.

By the time Webb had the presence of mind to reach for the

camera, the woman and her son had disappeared into the mêlée of commuters jumping onto the bus.

'Bitch,' Webb swore, climbing out of the car and heading back down the street to look for his keys. Where the hell were they? What the fuck did she think she was playing at? Just because she had a few bob, she thought she was better than anyone else. Well, she'd made a mistake. Harry Webb could have been a very good friend to her, done her a lot of good, even made her a few more bob. You could never have enough money, despite what she said. He'd still do the book, but it would be a very different book to the one he originally envisaged.

Now, where the fuck were those keys?

* * *

'You stay away from that creep, Kevin,' Christine snapped. She twisted around in the seat to look across the green to where Webb could be seen running down the road, obviously looking for his car keys. 'Don't speak to him, not even if he offers you money to talk to you. Say nothing to him. Are you listening to me?' she hissed, glaring at her son. She was trembling with rage.

'Yes, Mum. Absolutely,' Kevin said meekly. He had never seen his mother like this before. She positively radiated anger and aggression ... or was it fear? he suddenly asked himself. Glancing sidelong at his mother, he realised that the lines around her eyes had come back, and that her shoulders were rigid again. As if aware of his scrutiny, she dropped the dark glasses over her eyes.

They passed the forty-minute ride into the city centre in silence, Kevin dozing from the combination of early-morning heat and the lack of sleep the night before. Behind her dark glasses, Christine was scanning the crowded bus as she attempted to master the rage that had gripped her. Webb was a parasite. He was abusing her and intended using her ... but she'd been used too often, first by her father, then by Kevin's father, then by Robert. Well, it wasn't going to happen again.

Directly across from her a man was reading one of the morning tabloid newspapers, the page folded back to reveal one of the headlines:

DUBLIN WOMAN WINS £2.25 MILLION

It was followed by a short paragraph:

> Mrs Christine Quinn (36) is the latest lottery multi-millionaire. Mrs Quinn and her son Kevin (17), who were said to be still in a state of shock by close friends and neighbours, were unavailable for comment.

Christine could guess what the paper said. She took a deep breath, trying to calm nerves frayed by too little sleep and the encounter with the reporter. She needed to get away from the house. Those who didn't know about her win last night would learn about it this morning, either from the other neighbours, or else from the radio or newspapers. The house would be besieged by well-wishers. But how many of them actually meant well, and how many were simply looking for a hand-out? And then there would be the begging letters: they would all be sent to the home address. And that journalist would continue to haunt her at the house.

And then there was Robert, of course.

If Robert learned of her win ... no, *when* Robert learned of her win, he would come to the house. Although she had changed the locks after the last barring order, she had no doubt that he would be able to get in if he wanted to.

So she would have to move out, stay in a hotel ... no, a guest house, far more anonymous. Meanwhile, she'd speak to Simms, the estate agent, and encourage him to get the house together as quickly as possible. She decided she would demand absolute discretion. If news of her new address leaked out, the deal was off. In fact that was the first thing she'd do when she got into town.

And then she'd get her hair done.

Chapter 27

'Mrs Quinn, how marvellous to see you.' Henry Simms stood up and scurried around the desk, hand outstretched, an artificially broad smile on his face. Christine was taken aback by his effusive greeting – for a single moment, she thought he was going to kiss her. 'I didn't expect to see you again so soon. Tea, coffee?'

'Nothing for me, thank you,' she said, as he led her into the same office they'd used yesterday.

Christine observed Simms watching her closely as he settled himself in a chair across the table from her. His snow-white hair was perfect, every strand in place and so thickly coated with hair lacquer that she could actually see the marks of the comb through it. She wondered if he dyed it to keep it that colour.

'I was just putting together the paperwork on Island View,' he said. 'You are still interested?' he continued immediately, keeping his voice carefully neutral.

Christine smiled. 'I am.'

Simms nodded, ducking his head so that she wouldn't see the relief in his eyes. It wasn't unusual for clients to make an offer on a house one day, only to change their minds overnight. It was one of the reasons he never communicated an offer to the seller until he was sure it was genuine.

However, because Mrs Quinn had been so insistent, he had

spoken to the sellers, encouraging them to accept the cash offer. It took all his persuasive powers to convince them that it was indeed an excellent offer. If she pulled out now, he would look like a fool.

Christine wondered if Simms knew about her win yet. He must be living in a vacuum if he didn't, although he looked the type who only bought one of the English newspapers, *The Times* or *The Observer*, and listened to Radio Four. Maybe he hadn't heard yet. 'Have you had the chance to put my offer to your clients?' she asked.

'Indeed I have,' Simms said, surprising her. 'I spoke to them late yesterday afternoon and we discussed it again on the phone last night. They have agreed in principal, but there is a slight problem with the price,' he lied easily. 'Could I ask you to be a little more flexible with your offer? They were looking for two seven-five; you've offered two five.' He smiled and spread his hands. 'You will admit, twenty-five thousand off the asking price is a huge reduction.'

Christine kept her face expressionless. 'How soon can I take possession?' she asked, not answering his question.

Simms shuffled the papers on the desk. 'I understand that you are eager to take up residence. Such a fine property,' he added, 'but there are procedures ...'

'Yesterday, you told me there might be a way to speed things up,' she reminded him.

'That is true. I haven't had the opportunity to look into it yet.'

'But what is the least amount of time I will have to wait before moving in?' she demanded. 'We did talk about two weeks ...'

'We did,' he acknowledged. 'But realistically ...'

Christine stared at him.

'Realistically, between four to six weeks.' He attempted a smile. 'I must confess, I cannot understand the urgency ...' He stopped, and Christine could almost see the gears shifting and moving as things suddenly fell into place for him. When he sat back into the chair with a lazy smile on his fat lips, she knew – even before he spoke – that he *knew*. 'May I ask you an impertinent question?' he said and then, before she could say No, he asked, 'Are you the same Mrs Quinn who won the lottery on Saturday night?'

'I'm not sure how relevant this is, Mr Simms,' Christine said shortly, 'but yes, I am.'

'Congratulations. Now I can understand your urgency. You need to leave your present home. And of course, since your identity has become known, you will be looking for a secret hideaway.'

'Something like that,' she admitted. 'But let me add, Mr Simms, if it becomes public that I am buying a property from your office, then the deal is off.'

Simms sat forward, smooth brow creasing in concern. 'I can assure you of our absolute confidentiality at all times,' he said immediately. He steepled his hands before his face in an attitude of prayer and in that instant looked so like a priest that Christine had to smile. 'I may be able to help you,' he said finally.

Christine stared at him, saying nothing.

'When the present owners of Island View put it on this firm's books, we were given instructions to either sell the property or lease it. That offer is still open, though naturally, if a client is only interested in buying, then that is the only option we would discuss. And likewise, if a client is interested in renting an exceptional property, then obviously, we would never discuss selling.'

'I'm not sure I can see what you're leading up to,' Christine said, genuinely puzzled.

Simms smiled genially. 'Let me put a proposition to you,' he said. 'Suppose you were to rent Island View for an eight- to ten-week period. In the interim, while you're renting the property, the agreement to purchase would go through and at the end of the ten-week period, you would own it.' He saw the smile appear on Christine's lips and hurried on quickly. 'Furthermore, we could add your rent onto the price of the house, which would help sweeten the deal for the present owners.' He spread his hands wide. 'Everyone wins. You can move in tomorrow if you wish, which I think would please you, and the present owners get a better price, which would certainly please them. And, as a bonus,' he added in a conspiratorial whisper, 'no-one knows where you've vanished to.'

'What is the rent?' Christine asked.

'A thousand a week. Ten thousand for the ten weeks. It will bring the price up to two hundred and sixty thousand ... which was the client's reserve,' he added confidentially.

'Do it immediately,' Christine smiled, and then added, 'but on one condition.'

Simms frowned. 'And that is?'

'That I can collect the keys in the morning.'

'You have my guarantee. I will have the papers drawn up today.'

'How much rent do you need in advance?'

'We normally ask for three months' rent in advance ...' Simms began, 'but of course that isn't applicable in this case. Let's say, a month in advance?'

Christine stood up and leaned across the table. 'If I can collect the keys and move in tomorrow, I will pay you the whole ten thousand in advance, by cheque.'

'Consider it done!' Simms beamed.

Chapter 28

With money everything was possible, Christine reflected as she strolled down Grafton Street. Money opened doors. She smiled at the unintentional joke. In her case it had quite literally opened doors. She knew Simms would never have been so understanding and willing to help if he didn't know that she had more than two million pounds behind her.

As she passed HMV, she thought she saw Kevin inside, wandering aimlessly along the aisles of cassettes and CDs. She was about to go in and join him, but then changed her mind. She still found it hard to forgive him for betraying their secret, and besides, she didn't want him hanging around her for the rest of the day. She had a lot to do. She had to look for furniture for the new house, and then she'd have to think about decorations, and of course complete wardrobes of new clothes for both of them. She was determined to take nothing of the old house – nothing of her past – with her.

She thought about telling Helen again. She had meant to tell her this morning, but with all the fuss last night, it went completely out of her head. She'd do it when she got home. She'd ask her around to the house and show her the new clothes and make-up ... and keep the house for a grand finale. Simms had given her the colour photograph off the brochure, so she'd be able to show it to her. She was going to miss Helen. Neighbours were important. She wondered about the neighbours around Island View and how they would react to having a lottery winner in their midst. She hoped they wouldn't be too snooty. Mark Cunningham had seemed pleasant enough and anyway, this was Dublin in the nineteen-nineties; class prejudice was gone, wasn't it?

She paused to look at the display of copper pots and pans in

Switzer's window.

As soon as she was set up in the house, she would have a party for the neighbours, just to get to know them. She'd get someone in to do the catering, make an impression. Maybe Mark Cunningham would be able to help her with the guest list.

But before she did any of this she needed to go to the bank.

She was still slightly bemused with the speed of it all. She'd won the money on Saturday, spent Sunday in an agony of suspense, collected it on Monday and here she was, two days later, just about to move into a quarter-of-a-million pound mansion in Dublin's most exclusive address. Let no-one tell you that winning a huge amount of money didn't change your life – because it did. You just had to try and ensure that the changes were for the better ... and Christine Quinn was determined that her life was going to change for the better. In many ways, it already had.

* * *

'I would like to speak to the manager, please,' Christine said to the young woman sitting behind the desk.

'Certainly. Have you an appointment?'

'No.'

'Is this meeting at Mr Chambers's request?' the young woman continued. The professional fixed smiled never left her lips.

'No.'

'Well, I'm afraid you will have to make an appointment.' She flipped open a book and picked up a pen. 'There is a slot tomorrow afternoon at two-thirty.'

'The day before yesterday, I was able to walk in off the street and see him without any trouble,' Christine said softly. The bank was practically deserted, and she could see the top of the manager's head through a glass partition on the other side of the room.

'I think you probably got a vacant slot. Now, tomorrow afternoon, two-thirty. What name ...?'

'I'm afraid that's not convenient. I really would like to see Mr Chambers now,' Christine said, quietly insistent.

The young woman shook her head. 'That's just not possible ...'

'There's no-one with him at the moment,' Christine said.

'Mr Chambers is only seeing clients by appointment today.'

Christine looked down at the young woman – nineteen, twenty, twenty-one? – and realised that less than a week ago she would have been completely intimidated by the girl's attitude. She would have meekly accepted the appointment for the following day, even though it didn't suit her.

But that was then, and this was now.

'What don't you contact Mr Chambers and tell him that Mrs Quinn wishes to speak to him.'

The woman started shaking her head. 'I really ...'

'I must insist.' Christine was staring across the floor when Chambers looked up and caught her eye. He raised a hand in greeting and stood up immediately. 'Don't bother,' she said to the young assistant as Chambers moved through the maze of desks towards her.

'Mrs Quinn! What a great pleasure to see you.' Joseph Chambers lifted the wooden counter top and stood back to allow Christine to precede him into his office. As he was pushing the door closed, Christine caught a glimpse of the stunned expression on the young assistant's face. She smiled to herself.

'Some tea?' Chambers asked and, before she could say no, he had pressed a button on his intercom. 'Mary, could we have tea for two, please.' He smiled as he sat back into his high-backed leather chair.

'I wasn't sure I was going to get past the young woman at reception. I understand I should have made an appointment to see you.'

'Well yes, that is usually the case. And today is exceptionally busy, so I gave instructions that I was not to be disturbed.'

'Well, I won't take up too much of your time.'

'Oh, no, no. Not at all. You may call at any time. And I will leave word that you are a preferential customer. Preferential customers have access to me at all times.'

'Thank you.'

'Not at all. I'm here to assist you in any way I can,' he added. Then the smile dropped from his lips and he leaned forward. 'And how are you coping, Mrs Quinn, with your great good fortune? Has it sunk in yet?'

'It's started to.'

'I heard your name on the radio this morning. I really am most terribly sorry. I thought you had asked for anonymity,' he said.

'I had. I'm not sure how the news got out,' she lied. 'But some journalist got hold of the story and it spread like wild-fire.'

'This sort of news generally does,' he agreed. 'May I offer you a piece of advice, Mrs Quinn?' he said.

'Please,' Christine murmured.

'Be very careful over the next few days.' He smiled warmly. 'Now, I don't wish to alarm you, but your good fortune will make many people envious, and greedy.'

'I know that.'

'You will get many requests for money, from family, friends and total strangers. My advice to you is to do nothing about them for a few weeks until you get used to the idea of the money and have decided how you want to spend it.'

Christine nodded. 'It's good advice. Thank you.'

There was a tap on the door and a young woman entered carrying a tray. 'Thank you, Mary. That'll be all. I'll pour.' He waited until the young woman had pulled the door closed behind her, and said, 'Now, how can I help you, Mrs Quinn? Have you had a chance to look at those brochures I gave you?'

'I've read them all,' Christine said immediately. She hadn't even taken them out of her bag. 'But that's not why I'm here. I've bought a house,' she said quickly, 'and I just wanted you to clear the cheque when it comes through.'

'Of course. I presume that will not be for some time?' He passed the cup of tea over to Christine, and began pouring tea for himself.

'Well, actually, it should happen very soon. I'm renting the property until the sale goes through. I'll need to write a cheque for ten thousand tomorrow morning, and a cheque for two-hundred-and-fifty thousand within the next six weeks.'

Joseph Chambers poured tea all over his desk.

*　*　*

Which way?

Christine Quinn stood on the steps of the bank and looked up and down the street. Now that she was out of the bank manager's company, she could allow the laughter that had been bubbling up inside her to flow, and she startled a couple coming out of the bank. They gave her a wide berth and went away muttering about a 'madwoman'.

The look on his face when she said she needed to write a cheque for ten thousand in the morning ... and then when she added that she had bought a house for a quarter of a million! He looked as if someone had just kicked him in the stomach. After all his sober advice! To his credit, however, he hadn't complained or questioned, simply assured her that the cheques would clear with no fuss. She left him wiping tea off his desk.

Now, which way?

For once in her life she was slightly lost, even though she had grown up in Dublin. But she was going somewhere she'd never been before in the city centre: she was going to a hair salon. As she turned left and walked down the street towards the quays, she recalled that on Saturday night when she first began to suspect that she won the money, she promised herself that she was going to get her hair done.

Usually she washed her hair herself and allowed it to dry naturally. Once every couple of months she'd get the ends trimmed locally in the little salon above the fish'n chipper. She always imagined she came out smelling of batter and vinegar. She had her hair done a couple of times in the new shopping centre, but it was a unisex salon, and she felt embarrassed sitting there with her head under the drier while men came in, had their hair trimmed and disappeared with the minimum of fuss. And for her it always seemed to take so long. She often sat there for three or more hours. By the time she was through she was intimately acquainted with the various styles of haircuts, including the most popular for boys: a Number Two or Three, when a blade was simply put on a shaver and the boy's head was shaved down to a stubble. A Number One was a skinhead. When she asked Kevin why this was such a popular style – she had counted eight boys and young men getting Number Ones in a single afternoon – he replied that it was because it was a badge of sorts and it was comfortable and lasted for so long. When you were on the dole, you didn't have much money to throw away on a haircut.

Well, whatever salon she chose today, she was determined it was going to be single-sex. But she still wasn't sure which salons were single sex and, suddenly recalling her encounter with the young bank assistant, she wondered if she needed an appointment. Probably.

Crossing the street, Christine slipped into the GPO. She stood beneath the beautiful statue of Cuchulain, while she looked around for the phones. The last time she was in the building, they were to her right, but that area was now converted into a shop for stamp collectors. She finally asked a young woman in a blue uniform who pointed her towards the left where she finally found a row of phone booths opposite the parcel counter.

Standing in the first booth, Christine ran her fingers down the names of the hair salons in the Golden Pages. She was looking for someplace reasonably close by – within walking distance anyway – that wasn't unisex.

She eventually found one just off Grafton Street. Glancing at her watch, she picked up the phone ... and then stopped, looking at the receiver in her hand. Buying a house for a quarter of a million, spending ten grand on rent didn't seem quite real. It was the little things that showed how much her life had changed, like phoning to make an appointment to have her hair done. It wasn't much, but it was a real, tangible proof that her life had changed and, no matter what happened, would never be the same again.

Chapter 29

'The old home looked the same, as he stepped down from the train ...' Wasn't that how the song went, Robert Quinn wondered as he walked slowly through the estate. Engelbert Humperdinck ... or Tom Jones. He was never able to tell them apart anyway. He knew Tom Jones was singing in Las Vegas now, but whatever happened to Engelbert Humperdinck?

The estate hadn't changed much since he last saw it ... except perhaps it had become even shabbier, if that was possible. And the air of gloom that hung over it now was almost palpable. There were fewer cars on the estate – always a sure barometer of wealth. There were more cars in a well-to-do estate, sometimes two cars to a family, and generally the cars were no more than three years old. Here, the few cars were either old bangers or rusted hulks sitting on blocks. Of course, it was the middle of the day; maybe the road and driveways would fill up with new motors after six tonight ... but somehow he didn't think so.

He slipped on a pair of sunglasses as he turned onto Christine's road. He didn't think anyone would recognise him, but he didn't want to take any chances; he didn't want word to get to his ex-wife before he did.

The road was deserted, the pavement shimmering in the noon-day sun, open windows throwing back the light. As he passed the houses, he could hear snatches of radio stations, the blast of a stereo, a woman shouting at children. He smiled grimly. Nothing had changed. In prison, it was those very noises – the sounds of ordinary everyday life – that he missed most.

Robert slowed his pace as he approached the house. He spotted movement in a car parked across the street. Sunlight flickered off a wing mirror as it was adjusted towards him. Someone watching the house?

Police?

Not police. What reason would the police have for watching the house unless they were looking for him ... and they'd no reasons to be looking for him. Yet.

He suddenly smiled. Christ, he was becoming paranoid. But prison did that to you. You spent so much time watching your back that you tended to over-react. It was probably nothing more suspicious that someone waiting for a friend or neighbour to come out of one of the houses.

He was still smiling as he drew abreast of the car – a battered Toyota – and noticed the scattering of cigarette butts on the ground below the driver's window. The smile faded. Someone had been waiting a long time. He knew instinctively that whoever was in the car was watching Christine's house.

He didn't stop as he came up to the house. He walked straight past it without a second glance, although behind his dark glasses his eyes were noting every detail. She had changed the bed-room- and sitting-room curtains, though the venetian blinds, which he had always hated, where still on the downstairs win-dows. Despite the heat, every window in the house, with the exception of one of the bedroom windows, was closed: a sure sign that Christine wasn't home.

Well, he could wait. She'd be back sooner or later. Prison taught you many things: principally, it taught you patience.

At the bottom of the road he turned left, then left again, doubling back on himself. He was also curious to find out who was watching the house – and why.

*　*　*

Well, she was a bitch. That was his considered opinion. Harry Webb pulled hard on the cigarette, holding the smoke in his lungs, resisting the temptation to cough. Reaching over, he dropped the smouldering butt on the ground and pulled the crumpled packet out of his shirt pocket. The last one.

He was going to give these up soon. He was thinking of getting one of those patches that looked like a sticking plaster. They were supposed to be the business. He'd met a guy in the pub, a sixty-a-day man, who used one and gave them up just like that. But the old guy wasn't looking at all well the last time he saw him. Maybe he'd keep up the cigs. Anyway, he only smoked when he was bored.

And he was bored now.

He had been sitting here for the past – he checked his watch, 12:30 – five-and-a-half hours and, with the exception of his brief encounter with Mrs Quinn, it was a complete waste of time. He should have followed the bus into town, tailed her around, seen where she went. He'd have got a bit of a story from that alone. But it took him half an hour just to find the car keys. The bitch threw them into the middle of a bush and he scratched his flesh to pieces reaching in for them. Lifting his arm, he looked at the red scrapes on his pale flesh. Nodding, he added them to the list of things he would sue her for.

The morning wasn't totally wasted though.

Shortly after ten, Betty Miller passed by on her way home from half-nine mass. They chatted for a few minutes, and when she was gone, Webb wrote it up as an 'exclusive interview with the lottery winner's fiancée's mother ...'

He picked up his notebook and looked at it again. 'Lottery winner's fiancée's mother' sounded clumsy. Maybe he'd make her a 'close personal friend' or even a 'best friend'. Webb suddenly straightened. Best friend. Just who was Christine Quinn's best friend? There had to be someone on the estate she was close to. Leaning forward, folding both arms across the steering wheel, he looked at the houses on either side of Quinns'. He knew most of the families: the Keoghs, Batemans, Powers and Whites.

Keogh, he finally decided. Hadn't he seen Christine Quinn with Helen Keogh on a couple of occasions? And they had kids of about the same age – which meant that they had probably gone down to one of the local schools together. He knew that's where a lot of women forged friendships. Maybe he'd call in on Helen Keogh later for a chat. He glanced at his watch; maybe he'd call in there now. He might get a cup of tea, and he needed to get out of the car and stretch his legs. He squirmed around in his seat; he'd never realised just how uncomfortable this seat was. He was saturated in sweat, his shirt was stuck to his back and he felt as if he was sitting in an inch of water.

Christ – all she had to do was to talk to him for five minutes. Then she could have gone her way and he could have gone home.

Bitch!

He caught a flicker of movement from the corner of his eye and turned to look at the passenger wing-mirror, catching the reflection of a bloke walking down the street. Webb was turning away when he realised it was the same bloke who'd walked past the Quinn house less than five minutes earlier. He was turning back for another look when the passenger door was roughly pulled open and the man slid into the seat.

'Hey, what …!'

A large hand fell onto his shoulder, iron-hard fingers tightening painfully, digging into his flesh. He saw himself reflected in the big man's dark glasses.

'Tell me why you're watching that house before I break your fucking arm.'

Webb attempted to pull his arm free. 'Just who the hell do you think …' he began before his voice disappeared to a squeak as the pressure tightened on his shoulder. 'Are you police? You're police,' he answered his own question. He knew now what had happened. Someone had seen the car parked there for hours with him inside, concluded he was casing one of the houses and phoned the police. He didn't recognise this copper though, and he thought he knew all the local lads. 'I'm a reporter. I'm doing a story on Christine Quinn, the lottery winner. You do know she won over two million?'

'So I heard.'

'Well, she lives in that house there. I'm doing a story on her,' he repeated.

'Do you know the woman?'

'Know her? Of course I know her! I know everyone on this estate. I live around here.' He nodded through the grimy windscreen. 'I know Christine well. Why, when she learned she won on Saturday night, I was the first person she phoned. I'm going to turn her story into a book.'

'If you're such good pals, then why are you sitting outside her house waiting for her to come home?'

'I've just driven up,' Webb smiled, beginning to relax. 'I

thought I'd wait for a bit, just to see if she came home for lunch.' He lifted his notepad. 'I was working on my story while I waited.'

The big man plucked the notebook from his hands and flipped the pages. Webb thought about grabbing it back, but, looking at the muscles in the man's bare arms, decided against it. 'What station are you with?' he asked. 'You're not local. I know all the local boys.'

'I never said I was a cop.'

Webb stared at him blankly.

The big man lifted his head, smiling humourlessly. '*You* decided I was a cop.'

'Well, then, who are you?' Webb snatched back his notebook, pages ripping as he pulled it out of the other's grasp. 'And you can fuck off out of my car too – before I call a cop.'

The man laughed coldly. Ignoring Webb's questions, he nodded towards the house. 'Tell me about the woman.'

'I don't have to tell you anything!' Webb snapped. 'Just who are you and what gives you the right …'

The iron-fingered hand fell on his shoulder again, shutting him up. 'I'm Robert Quinn, Christine Quinn's husband. Now, why don't you tell me what you know, eh?'

Chapter 30

Christine picked 'Hair by Maurice' from the Golden Pages because it was right in the city centre, wasn't unisex … and because they could give her an appointment for twelve-thirty.

When she stepped into the small salon, she immediately picked out a slender dark-haired young man, wearing black slacks and a black polo-neck as 'Maurice'. His every gesture was extravagant and overblown. He would be French she decided, and speak English with an accent.

'Can I help you?' The young woman behind the desk looked at her expectantly, pencil-thin eyebrows raised questioningly.

'Yes. I made an appointment by phone. Christine Qu... Christine Doolin.'

'Yes, Ms Doolin. If you will just take a seat, Maurice will be with you in a few moments. Would you like some coffee while you're waiting?'

Christine shook her head. Sinking back into a soft leather-and-shining-chrome chair, she reflected that she had drunk more coffee in the last few days than she had in the previous month. The circles she was mixing with now obviously survived on coffee.

The young man in black swept past, leaving a trace of an exotic spicy cologne in his wake. She followed his progress across the room. Yes, Maurice – probably pronounced Maur-íce – was from Paris. He would fiddle with her hair, and make tut-tutting noises at its condition and would be full of idle show-business gossip as he worked.

Shaking her head at her over-active imagination, Christine rooted through the bundle of bags she had collected so far. When she left the GPO she went into Eason's bookshop, and spent the best part of an hour going through the decorating magazines – *House Beautiful*, *Homes & Gardens*, *Architectural Digest* and *Irish Homes* – looking for ideas for her new home. She was resolved to buy one only, but she kept finding new ideas every time she turned a page, so in the end she bought the lot, delighting in her ability to gather them up into her arms without even thinking of the price. On her way to the hairdresser's, she stopped in Waterstone's and Hodges Figgis on Dawson street and scoured their shelves, before coming away with another sixty pounds' worth of home improvement books and an enormous *Reader's Digest Complete Do-it-Yourself*. She was beginning to regret it now: the books were heavy and the big DIY book weighed a ton.

'You've either just gone into the DIY business or you've bought a house.'

Christine looked up. A tall, broad-shouldered young man in his early twenties stood before her. His deeply tanned skin was highlighted by his cream-coloured linen suit. The light fuzz of hair on his head was a startling white – which had to be dye, she decided, because his thick eyebrows were black.

'I've just bought a house,' she said. 'I'm looking for ideas.'

'I've just taken that plunge myself,' the young man said in an unmistakable Dublin accent. 'I went out and bought all the books too; I threw them away when I decided I wanted the house to be in my style, not some magazine image.' He stretched out a hand. 'You're Christine Doolin. I'm Maurice.'

Christine blinked in surprise. So much for the exotic!

'We haven't seen you here before, have we?'

Christine shook her head as she stood up. The hairdresser's hand was cool, the flesh soft and dry. 'This is my first time,' she said.

'Well, we'll try and make sure it's not your last.'

He led her towards a row of chairs at the back of the salon. 'Now, Heather will wash you hair, and then I'll style it. Did you have anything particular in mind?'

Christine nodded emphatically. 'I want it different.'

'Different?'

She tugged at her hair. 'I want it different. I don't want to look like this anymore.'

Maurice smiled. 'I think we can do that.'

* * *

'You have beautiful bone structure.'

Christine was sitting in a chair, looking at her reflection in a large lighted mirror. Maurice stood behind her, his hands on her shoulders, watching her reflection in the mirror. She found his closeness almost disturbing. It had been a long time since any man had stood so close to her, longer still since any man had paid her a compliment.

Maurice ran his short blunt fingers through her damp hair, pulling it back off her face. 'You're sure you've no style in mind? Nothing you've seen in a magazine?'

She shook her head.

'I always ask,' Maurice said, lowering his voice. 'Some hairdressers like to put their style on a person's hair, but me – I prefer to let the client decide ... after all, they'll have to wear the hair.'

'What if someone wants something completely unsuitable?'

'Well then, naturally, I'll advise them. But if that's what they want, then that's what they get.'

'And what then do you do with someone like me who doesn't know what they want?'

'Well,' Maurice said, running his fingers through her hair again, 'I get to give you what I think suits you. And in your case that's not so difficult. We need something that will frame your face, something soft, sophisticated, flattering. This style doesn't flatter you.'

'I also want something that's easy to maintain. Something simple,' Christine said.

Maurice nodded. 'I can do that.' He lifted a handful of hair. 'I see you're prone to split ends, but we can take care of that.'

'What about colour?' Christine wondered. 'My roots have always been dark, even though my hair is blond. Should I have them toned in?'

Maurice parted Christine's hair to look at her scalp. 'There's nothing wrong with blond hair and dark roots. It's actually quite fashionable. If you don't already use colour – and I can see that you don't – I really wouldn't recommend it, unless you want a drastic change. I can layer your hair slightly and this will blend in the colours. What length will we leave it?' he wondered aloud. 'You've such a beautiful slender neck, I'd be inclined to keep it at shoulder length; frame your face and neck.'

'I'm entirely in your hands,' Christine said. She sat back into the chair and closed her eyes, listening to the liquid snip-snip-snipping of Maurice's scissors.

'Have you been on holidays?' the hairdresser asked.

'Not yet,' Christine said, opening her eyes suddenly. A holiday! She hadn't even thought of a holiday. As soon as they got settled in the new house, she and Kevin would go off on a holiday together, someplace hot and exotic. She'd get some brochures on the way home. 'No, not yet,' she said again, 'I need to get the house sorted out first before I can even think about a holiday.'

'Moving house and getting married are supposed to be the two most stressful times of your life. My fiancée and I have just bought a house in Greystones. It needs quite a lot of work, but that's part of the fun, isn't it, putting your own stamp on the place. Where did you buy yours?' he inquired.

'Skerries,' Christine said quickly, recalling one of the brochures she'd looked at in Simms's office. 'A bungalow overlooking the sea. On a clear day you can see the mountains of Mourne.'

'Is there much work to be done on it?'

'Very little. But like you, I want to put my own stamp on it.'

Maurice nodded. 'There's nothing like having a place of your own, is there?'

'Nothing at all,' she said with feeling.

* * *

It took the best part of three hours.

Christine kept catching glimpses of herself in the mirror, but deliberately tried not to look. She didn't want to see herself until the job was finished.

Initially she was appalled by the amount of hair Maurice seemed to be cutting off her head. She was going to end up bald. After a while she relaxed and realised that this wasn't the local hairdresser, where you were charged for the hot water and gossip. And this wasn't a trim. This was a New Look.

Finally, she closed her eyes, lulled into a light doze by the clicking scissors and Maurice's gentle patter.

She made a list of things that needed to be done before she left the house tomorrow morning. Kevin would have to get the suitcases out of the attic. She would ask Helen to cancel the milk and send on any post ... though that would mean giving her the address. She hoped she could trust Helen. But maybe she wouldn't ask her to do that; she could get her to collect it for her – not that there was ever much post, except bills. Anyway, she would be back to the house during the next few weeks, collecting things.

And what was she going to do with the house? Could she sell it? She wasn't sure what hold Robert still had over the property; did she need his signature if she wanted to sell it? She'd need advice from a solicitor.

But what did she need for tomorrow? She was moving into a completely empty house. It was going to be rough for a few days; they might have to sleep on the floor. She smiled at the irony of it: she was one of the wealthiest women in Ireland and she was going to end up sleeping on the bare floorboards of her new home. She could always stay another night in the old house.

Unconsciously she shook her head. Maurice, snipping away,

held it still.

No, she daren't stay another night in the house. That would be tempting fate. Tonight would be the last night.

'You can look now,' Maurice said, his voice close to her ear. Christine Quinn looked into the mirror ... and a stranger looked back.

Chapter 31

Robert Quinn sat in the car and watched Harry Webb talking to Helen Keogh. From the way the woman folded her arms across her bosom, her large frame blocking the door, Quinn knew that the reporter wasn't getting anywhere with her.

Robert remembered Helen. Christine's friend. She'd faced him down on a couple of occasions and he didn't forgive her for that. But if anyone knew about Christine's win and her whereabouts, then it was Helen.

He watched her step back into her house and slam the door, the sound echoing flatly across the empty street.

Harry Webb dug his hands in his pockets and sauntered back to the car.

Robert closed his big hands into tight fists, resisting the temptation to climb out of the car and drag Webb inside. The reporter might be an arrogant fool ... but he was the fool who had discovered the identity of the lottery winner when the other newspapers had failed. Maybe he was that lethal combination, a lucky fool. Whatever he was, he could still be used; Robert had spent eighteen months in prison using people just like him.

Webb was terrified of Robert, though his fear was tempered with greed. Robert had promised him full co-operation in his proposed biography of the lottery winner, with access to all the correspondence, including his prison correspondence with Christine. There had never been any correspondence, but the reporter wasn't to know that. Right now Robert was telling him what he wanted to hear. Webb had access to resources and contacts that Robert intended using if Christine didn't come back to the house.

And what then?

What was he going to do when he got to her?

Was he going to ask her politely for a share in her winnings? And was she going to give it up meekly? He didn't think so.

He had no legal rights to any of the money ... no, but there were other rights, moral rights, the rights of natural justice. He was merely taking back a little of what he'd given her through the years. She never repaid him ... and she destroyed the only human being he ever really loved, his baby daughter, Margaret. He thought she'd be about ten now, if she'd lived. But she hadn't lived. That bitch had let her die. That's when their marriage had ended. It had died with a three-year old child.

Robert Quinn nodded his head. The bitch owed him – and she was going to pay. Deep down he thought she still loved him. Maybe that was the way to her. Pretend he was still in love with her ...

Webb pulled open the door and got in. 'She knows nothing ...

'She *says* she knows nothing,' Quinn reminded him.

'I believe her. She told me the first she heard about Christine's win was on the radio this morning, and that she hasn't spoken to Christine since last Friday. She sounded almost angry about it.' He grinned. 'Maybe Christine was intent on keeping the news to herself.'

'Well, you've made certain that's not going to happen,' Quinn said mirthlessly.

'Christine Quinn is public property now. She's fair game.'

Robert Quinn nodded in silent agreement. Christine Quinn might be fair game, but she was *his* property. She had been from the moment they'd put those gold rings on their fingers, and sworn those vows.

Separation or no separation, she would always be his.

'What's so funny?' Webb asked.

'I was thinking of our marriage vows.'

Webb stared at him blankly.

'For richer, for poorer,' Robert Quinn said, then threw back his head and laughed aloud.

Chapter 32

'You look amazing,' Kevin repeated. He swivelled around on the back seat of the taxi to look at his mother again. 'I swear, I nearly didn't recognise you.'

Christine smiled, but said nothing. When she'd looked at herself in the salon's mirror she almost hadn't recognised herself. The new hairstyle made her look different. Not younger – no, but more mature, sophisticated. Falling in gentle waves to her shoulders, its simple though elegant look highlighted her blue eyes, her firm mouth and slender neck. With the proper make-up and some jewellery, she would look beautiful.

Maurice had mistaken her silence for disapproval. 'You do like it?' he asked, crouching down beside the chair to look at her reflection in the mirror. 'I mean I can change the style and length if you don't.'

'I love it,' she said softly, reaching over to squeeze his arm. 'It's perfect.'

'It makes you look like a new woman.'

'It makes me feel like a new woman,' she said sincerely.

She had actually walked up to Kevin, who was standing waiting for her at the bottom of Grafton Street beside the Molly

Malone statue, before he recognised her. She laughed aloud at the look of shocked surprise on his face. 'Don't you recognise your own mother?' she teased.

'I know my own mother all right … it's just that I'm not seeing her anymore.'

'A new look for a new beginning, Kevin.' She glanced at the bundle of plastic bags at his feet. 'What did you buy?'

'Some clothes. Jeans, sweatshirt, a lovely black leather waistcoat. What did you get, yourself?'

'Books, magazines. Ideas for the new house.' She lifted the plastic bags. 'And they weigh a ton!'

'If you carry the clothes, I'll get the books.' As Kevin was reaching for a bag, one of the plastic handles stretched and tore. Crouched down on the pavement, he began shifting books from one bag to another, turning them over to look at the titles as he did so. 'This must be some house we're buying.'

'It is.'

The edge of one of the big hardbacks caught and tore a long rent through another bag. Kevin swore silently. 'Did you have to get all these books today?'

'I did. We're moving into the new house tomorrow.' Kevin looked at her blankly. 'First thing in the morning. Now, how about splashing out on a taxi home?'

They caught a taxi in College Green, opposite Trinity College. As they got into the cab, the taxi-driver said, 'We could be in for a slow ride, folks. According to the radio, traffic is backed up all over the place.'

'We're in no particular hurry,' Christine grinned.

'Just thought I'd let you know in case the fare began creeping up.'

'I think we can just about manage it,' Christine said, struggling hard to keep a straight face.

Chapter 33

As soon as the taxi pulled up outside the door, Kevin grabbed the bags and hopped out with the keys in his hands. Christine leaned forward to pay the driver.

'Can I ask you a question, lady?' the driver asked in a light Cork accent.

Christine looked at him, saying nothing.

'Are you the lady who won the lottery on Saturday night?'

For a single moment she was going to deny it, dismiss it with a laugh and a light remark, but instead, she said simply, 'Yes, I am.'

'Well, I'm delighted for you,' the man said sincerely. 'Enjoy it.'

Christine blinked at him in surprise. 'Thank you.'

As she climbed out of the car, he leaned across the passenger seat and rolled down the window. 'And I think the hair is amazing too,' he added.

Looking neither left nor right, Christine strode up the path. She kept expecting Webb to come popping up out of the bushes and stick a microphone in her face, or a crowd of neighbours to come darting out of every doorway. She stopped when she reached the hall door, turned and looked up and down the street. There was a group of women standing outside Mrs White's further down the road. They were all looking in her direction. As the taxi pulled away, their heads moved in unison, following it, then snapped back to look at her. She saw one of the women speaking, then the group began to drift down the road towards her, smiles appearing on their faces.

It gave her a great deal of satisfaction to step back into the hall, push the door closed and slide the bolt across. When she turned around, she found the hall was awash with letters.

'Jesus!'

Kevin nudged at a pile with his boot. 'There must be hundreds here.'

'How did they get our address?' Christine wondered. 'It didn't appear on the news last night.' She remembered the image of a reporter standing before her floodlit house, earnestly speaking into a microphone. But he didn't give the exact address.

'It showed the estate,' Kevin said softly. 'It wouldn't be too hard to get your address once you knew the estate. I'm sure everyone around here knows about the win by now.'

Christine had a sudden image of people wandering around the estate looking for the house of the 'lottery winner'.

There was a knock on the door which made her jump. Kevin took a step towards the door. 'Ignore it,' she snapped.

The letterbox flapped up, framing a pair of eyes. 'Excuse me, Mrs Quinn. You don't know me, but I wonder if I could have a moment of your time.'

'Go away.'

'This won't take a moment. I would just like to discuss a project you might be interested in funding ...'

Christine looked at Kevin in disbelief. 'I said go away.'

'It will only take a moment ...'

Kevin waded through the post and crouched down to stare at the face beyond the letterbox. 'You heard my mother. Now, fuck off!' He snapped the letterbox shut, and held it closed as the person on the other side of the door attempted to shove it open again.

Christine came from the kitchen with a towel which Kevin stuffed into the opening, wedging the letterbox shut.

'I hope we're not in for a night of this,' he muttered.

'I'll go and make some tea,' Christine said. 'Why don't you gather up the letters and we can go through them.'

'You mean you're actually going to read them?' Kevin was astonished.

'There might be a real letter in here,' she reminded him.

'I doubt it,' he muttered, pushing them across the floor with his boot. 'Probably just bills.' He suddenly smiled. But bills didn't matter anymore either.

They divided the letters up into three piles: those with stamps, those without stamps, and finally the few which looked official.

'There's a small crowd outside,' Kevin said, coming in from the sitting room. 'People sitting on the wall, a few of the neighbours, and that guy Webb is out there too. There's also some strange cars on the road.' He had a bundle of letters in his hand. 'These have been slid in under the door just now, would you believe.'

'I would.' The knocking on the door started again, staccato style.

'This is unbelievable. I wonder if the police could move them on. I could hop over the back wall and phone them,' he suggested.

'Don't bother. We'll be gone in the morning, and then they can camp out there all day.'

'You still haven't told me where we're going,' he reminded her.

'Well,' Christine said slowly, 'since you won't be going out tonight, I suppose I can tell you.' Reaching into her bag she pulled out the colour photograph of the house and slid it across the table.

Kevin picked it up and she could see his eyes widening in astonishment.

'It's called Island View,' she said, watching his expression. 'I thought about changing the name, maybe calling it New Beginnings or something like that, but now I've come to like Island View. It's in Killiney. It's Victorian, absolutely enormous inside, with six bedrooms, and you can have any one of them except the master bedroom, which I'm claiming for myself. It's set in half an acre of the most beautiful gardens you've ever seen. There's even an ornamental pool in it. The whole house is surrounded by a seven-foot high wall, and there is private access from the gardens down onto Killiney beach.'

More loud knocking on the door again, and they could hear someone calling her name.

'It looks amazing.'

'It is.'

'How much?' he asked suddenly.

'Two hundred and sixty thousand, but that price includes rent for the next few weeks while the papers are going through.'

He shook his head. 'I'm not sure what you mean.'

'If we were buying the house in the normal way, it would take at least six to eight weeks for all the paperwork to be processed. In the meantime we'd have to live here ...'

Someone hammered persistently on the door.

'... or else we'd have to move out and stay in a hotel for the six weeks. The estate agent gave me the option of renting until the deeds went through. It means we can move in tomorrow.'

There was a sharper rapping as someone tapped on the hall door window with a coin.

'And not a moment too soon.'

A patrol car cruised down the road just after nine, and two officers got out and began moving the people on. By that time quite a crowd had gathered, and Kevin and Christine, standing in the front bedroom upstairs, could see that several of the cars parked on the road bore out-of-town number plates. She found it almost incomprehensible that people would drive up from the country to ask her for money. Did they think she was simply going to give it away? Maybe they did.

Christine and Kevin finally moved away from the window

when most of the crowd had gone. 'Climb up into the attic and get down the suitcases. I want you to pack only the bare essentials, things which you cannot live without. And, Kevin,' she added, 'I don't want us leaving here in the morning with dozens of bags. Remember, what we haven't got – we can buy.'

As Kevin lumbered around the attic, Christine threw open the door of her wardrobe and began pulling out the clothes she would take with her. All the new stuff of course, some old jeans and sweatshirts – she would need these for decorating – a Paul Costello jacket she had bought at a sale of work for a fiver ... and then she stopped. There was nothing else she wanted to bring into the new house. She went through the wardrobe again, pushing back the metal hangers one by one. Clothes which she had been perfectly happy to wear only three days ago, now seemed old and shabby, the material rough and coarse. She pushed the wardrobe door closed: there was nothing else she wanted.

Lifting the box of photographs off the top of the wardrobe, she added it to her pile. From the chest of drawers, she took her new underwear and a baggy jumper she had spent an entire winter knitting. She swept her new make-up off the dressing table into a bag and dropped her jewellery box in on top of that. Then, on impulse, she pulled it out again, opening it to look at the few pieces she'd collected over the years. Her wedding ring and engagement ring sat in one corner of the box. She never wore them anymore; she had taken them off on the day she walked away from Robert, a final acknowledgement that their marriage was at an end. Alongside them was a string of pearls that once belonged to her mother. She didn't know whether they were real or not – and didn't care. Along with a few fading photographs, they were her last links with her mother.

In another little compartment lay a pair of small stud earrings in a Celtic design which Kevin had given her as a present one

Christmas. At the bottom of the box was a St Christopher medal and another of St Jude, Patron of Hopeless Cases. At one time, even after she had abandoned the Church, he had been her favourite saint, and she had completed novena after novena to the saint who was supposed to bring help when all other help failed. She used to pray to him for everything she needed, for money to start a new life, for a husband who loved her, for … for a new beginning. For the chances she had now. Maybe this was an answer to her prayers. And it was ten years too late, maybe twenty? Closing the lid on the box, she dropped it into the bag and then placed the bag on the bed.

Christine folded her arms and looked around the bedroom. But there was nothing else she wanted, except the clock-radio which she would pack in the morning. She turned to the few things laid out on the bed. With the exception of the new clothes she'd just bought, there were pitifully few items she was going to take away. She wondered if it was some sort of symbolic thing: deliberately leaving so much behind, casting off her old life. Suddenly, she shook her head. She could never do that; she still had her memories. She could never let those go.

Thursday, 15 July

Chapter 34

Christine awoke with a start in the early hours of the morning. She sat up slowly and drew her knees up to her chest, folding her arms around her shins, resting her cheek against her knees. Fragments of her dreams fluttered at the edges of her consciousness, gradually dissolving, fading away until only one image remained: she was running down a long corridor, through door after door, each door leading on to another door and then another. As she passed through them the doors slammed solidly shut behind her. And with each door closing, she felt she was losing a little of herself, a little of her past.

Rolling out of bed, Christine tugged her damp tee-shirt from her body. Although the windows were open, the night was completely airless, and she was bathed in perspiration.

She didn't need to be a genius to interpret the dream. The doors represented her present way of life, each one closing behind her now as she moved on – but how then to interpret the sense of loss she felt? There was nothing about her present life she wanted to hang onto, was there?

She shook her head slowly. She didn't think so.

Standing before the bedroom window, she looked up and down the road, realising that this was her last night in the house, her last night in this bed. The sky was brightening to the east, slivers of purple light announcing the dawn. She glanced at the clock. It was three minutes to four. In five hours' time she would walk in to the estate agent's and pay over her money. In six hours' time she would step through the front door of her new home.

Realising that sleep was impossible, she pulled on her dressing-gown and padded silently down to the hall. Their bags – her single suitcase, four of Kevin's – were piled up neatly at the bottom of the stairs. She was going to send Kevin out at around half-seven to phone for a taxi to bring them into town. She planned to have the taxi wait while she signed the papers in Simms's office, and then let it take them on to the new house. But she suddenly realised that the taxi-man would know the address of her new home. No. She'd have the taxi drop them in town, close to the Green. Then they'd get another taxi out to Killiney.

There were more letters in the hall, shoved in under the door, and Christine scooped them up as she went into the kitchen, dropping them onto the enormous pile on the table. As she filled the kettle with water, she realised she didn't know what she was going to do with all the letters. It would be physically impossible to answer them all – in fact, it would probably be better if she didn't answer any of them; maybe it would be better if she didn't even look at them. She supposed she could leave them here. Either she or Kevin would be back to the house over the next few weeks. She'd think about dealing with them then. She had enough on her plate at the moment.

While the kettle boiled, Christine made tea, sat down at the table, and looked at the pile of mail. It was a bit daunting to think that all of this arrived the day after the announcement of her win. Would tomorrow's post bring more? Undoubtedly. When would it stop? Or would she continue to get begging letters for years to come?

She lifted one of the letters, looking at it. There was no stamp, and the envelope bore only four words, *Christina Quinn, lottery winner*. They'd even got her name wrong.

Reaching behind her, she pulled a steak knife out of its wooden block and slit the letter open. What sort of person would write to a complete stranger?

Dear Mrs Quinn,

I was absolutely delighted to read of your good fortune. I know you are a Christian lady and will be willing to help someone less well-off then yourself.

I am married with four children, aged between eight and fifteen. My husband has been unemployed for the past three years and is unable to find work due to ill health.

It is very difficult to make ends meet. If you could see your way to assisting us in any means, I would be eternally grateful and you would remain forever in our prayers.

Christine looked at the letter. It had been written on a page torn from a child's copy-book, in big round handwriting. For an instant, Christine could visualise the writer. It would be a woman like herself, an ordinary woman, who found herself trapped by circumstances in a world where there didn't seem to be any light at the end of the tunnel. Although she had never met the woman, Christine felt she knew her well. She knew dozens of women like her. Smoothening out the page, she put it to one side. She would send her some money.

She opened the next letter in the pile.

Dear Mrs Quinn,

I am desperate. I have not worked for three years. The bank will repossess my house. You have won so much money you would not miss a little. A few pounds would not make a great deal of difference to you, but it would make an enormous difference to me and my family. You don't know what it's like to be in this situation and now you never will.

Christine added it to the first letter. The writer was both wrong and right. Christine did know what it was like to be in that situation, but it was true that she would never be in that situation again. Properly invested the lottery money would last her for the rest of her life.

> *Dear Christine,*
> *You probably don't remember me, but we went to school together. I was really pleased when I learned that you had won the lottery since it gave me the opportunity to discover where you had got to. I'm about to have a baby soon and I would be delighted if you would be the god-mother. When we were in school, we always promised one another that we would be godmother to each other's children.*

Christine stared blankly at the letter. She didn't recognise the name, and then she realised the writer hadn't mentioned the school either. Crumpling the letter into a ball, she dropped it onto the floor.

> *Dear Mrs Quinn,*
> *I have been writing plays for the past ten years, and have even had some success in having them staged. However, I have now written a stageplay which, if I may say so, will rival Les Miserables. I would like to offer you the opportunity of investing ...*

She tore the letter in half.

The next letter had a stamp on it. There was something vaguely familiar about the writing on the envelope, but it was only as she unfolded the thick sheet of cream-coloured paper that she recognised her sister's hand-writing.

Dear Christine,

Nick and I were thrilled to hear about your marvellous good fortune, though I should add that I was disappointed that I had to hear it on the news and not from my own sister.

As it happens the news could not have come at a better time. You know that Daddy has not been well over the past number of years, and while we have tried to give him everything he needs, he has now reached the stage where he requires constant attention. Having him living with us has been an enormous financial drain and now that the children are growing up they need the space. Nick and I have talked it over and we have decided that it would be best for all concerned if you used some of your new wealth to place Daddy in a nursing home where he will be able to receive the best of treatment.

We will call around in the next few days to discuss the details. Also, you do know that Nick has recently gone out on his own. If you wished to invest some of your money in the business, it would be a golden opportunity for you to get in on the ground floor of what is going to be a huge international operation. He could guarantee an excellent return on your investment.

Your loving sister,
Sheila.

Christine read the letter through twice. She wasn't sure whether to be angry or amused. The cheek of the bitch. The last correspondence she had from her sister was a cheap card at Christmas. And the only reason Sheila and Nick had taken her father in to live with them was because they had made him sell the house in Cabra and then invest the money in Nick's new venture. Christine frowned; she wasn't sure if she remembered just what he was doing now: importing American snack foods or something. And now that they had her father's money tied up, they wanted to get rid of him to some nursing home.

She could – almost – understand strangers writing to her for money. She didn't know them, they didn't know her, and she would judge every letter on its own merits. If she said no, then there was no harm done; they might curse her name, and that would be the end of it. But with Sheila it was different. Everything was personal with Sheila. There had never been much love lost between them, and for her sister actually to ask for money outright – which was what she had effectively done – was the ultimate in arrogance. And when Christine refused – there was no way she was giving her a penny – that would only create an even deeper rift between them. When Christine had nothing, when she was living on assistance, Sheila hadn't so much as offered her a pound, even though she herself was well off and knew Christine was really struggling to make ends meet. Her sister and brother-in-law never had any time for her before. But she wasn't a millionaire before. Shaking her head, Christine slowly tore the letter in two. Sheila and Nick were welcome to come calling in a day or two; she took grim satisfaction at the thought of them driving across the city to find an empty house.

She picked up another letter.

Chapter 35

'Now, you know what to do?'

'I know what to do, Mum,' Kevin repeated. 'Straight down to the call box and phone for a taxi ...'

'Have you got the numbers?'

He showed her where he'd written the phone numbers of

three different taxi firms on the palm of his hand in biro. 'I'll order a taxi for half-seven to take us into the city centre.'

'Are you sure you've got change for the phone?'

He rattled his pockets. 'Plenty.'

'Right. Off you go, and remember, Kevin ...'

'I know. Say nothing to no-one.'

'Wait a moment,' Christine said, stepping into the sitting room and parting the blinds to peer out into the street. 'Right. Go.'

'Jesus,' Kevin muttered, as he pulled the hall door closed behind him. He never thought he'd see the day where he'd be sneaking out of his own house. He hurried down the deserted road, head down, hands dug deep into his pockets. But he had only himself to blame. If he hadn't told Sandra Miller, then she wouldn't have told her mother and ... and the news wouldn't have got out. It was his fault they were leaving today. He had really screwed things up.

He looked at the rows of identical houses. It was hard to imagine that this was his last day in the house. He grew up on this estate, went to school here, all his friends were here. He'd spent his whole life here ... his whole life *was* here, although he had always dreamed about leaving, about finding a job and moving out. He had only to look around the estate to see his future: unemployment, an early marriage, and they'd end up living with his mother. But he always swore that he wouldn't end up like that, that he was going to get away and make a life for himself.

And then they won the money.

And the money tied him even more tightly to his mother's apron strings. He'd never be able to get away now.

*   *   *

'That was quick,' Christine said, reaching for the door. Kevin was gone less than five minutes. He probably ran all the way there and back. She pulled open the door ... and found she was facing Helen Keogh. The big woman's face was set in an impassive mask. Christine stared at her speechlessly for a few seconds, feeling her face flame in embarrassment and guilt, before she said, 'It's seven o'clock in the morning, Helen.'

'I know the time, Christine,' Helen said softly, traces of her Cork accent still clearly audible in her voice. 'I saw Kevin running down the road as I let my Tommy out to work, so I guessed you'd be up. Can I come in?'

Christine stepped back. 'Is everything all right?' she asked immediately.

'Everything's fine,' Helen said as she stepped into the hall. 'Your hair looks lovely, it really suits you.' She looked at the suitcases. 'Are you going away?'

Christine nodded. 'You saw what it was like here last night. I couldn't stay another night in the house.' She led the way into the kitchen, kicking through piles of torn and bundled paper, the remains of most of the letters she'd received. She'd kept thirty which she thought deserved some money. 'You'll have to pardon the mess. Everything has been a bit crazy since ... well since ...' Her voice trailed away and she busied herself filling the teapot. She felt embarrassed. She had *meant* to tell Helen, but time and events had moved too quickly. Helen Keogh had been her closest friend for nearly ten years, becoming the big sister she never had. In those ten years they shared so much together, they had no secrets, and yet suddenly Christine felt like a stranger with her ... because she hadn't shared the biggest – and best – secret of all.

'I've been meaning to go around to you,' she said. 'But everything has been such a rush ...' She stopped. The excuse sounded so lame. When she turned around, Helen was staring at her.

'Mrs White told me, and then I heard it on the radio yesterday morning.'

'I wasn't sure on Saturday night that I actually won. And when I got the papers on Sunday, I suppose I went into a state of shock. And then on Monday ... well Monday was a dream. I went into the lottery office with less than a fiver in my bag. I walked out with a cheque for more than two million.' She lowered her voice. 'I think I spent about three hundred pounds that day. It was lovely, Helen, being able to spend so much without even thinking about it! And then on Monday night, I was just so exhausted.'

The kettle whistled and she turned around, busying herself filling the teapot. When she turned back to the table, Helen was sitting leafing through the small pile of begging letters Christine had kept. 'They're the ones I thought were deserving. Some of the others though ...' She shook her head. 'You wouldn't believe some of the others.'

'Oh, I would. Money does strange things to people,' she added, and Christine wasn't sure if it was a dig at her or not.

'On Monday night Kevin went out with Betty Miller's youngest girl ...'

'Sandra.'

'That's the one. He told her about the win, though I begged him not to tell a soul. She told her mother, and the next day everyone knew.' She poured tea into two mismatched cups. 'I was going to tell you on Tuesday night when I came home ... but the news had got out by then and the reporters were here. I spent the day in town yesterday. And you saw what it was like last night.' She reached over and squeezed her friend's hand. 'I'm sorry I wasn't the one to tell you ... things have just been so crazy. I haven't been thinking straight.'

'I'm sure I'd have been the same if I was in your position,' Helen said quietly.

Christine immediately felt even more guilty, because she knew Helen would have shared the news immediately.

'I just came around to congratulate you, and tell you if there's anything I can do, or if there's anything you need ...'

Christine smiled. 'You're the first one who's offered to give me something. Everyone else wants to take something.' She pushed the cup of tea across the table. 'I even got a letter from Sheila. She wants me to pay to put Daddy in a nursing home, and she wants me to invest in Nick's new business.'

'Cheeky bitch,' Helen sipped her tea. 'Have you made any decisions yet?'

Christine lowered her eyes, staring into her tea. 'Not yet. Not really,' she added. 'I bought some new clothes,' she said suddenly, perking up. 'You have to see them ...' Her voice trailed away as she realised they were packed away in the suitcase. 'They're all packed up.'

'How long are you going for?' Helen asked.

'For a few days,' Christine said quickly. She was about to say: to a hotel, but she still felt guilty because she had treated Helen so badly. 'Not a word about this to anyone,' she said suddenly, reaching into her handbag which was hanging on the back of the chair. She pulled out the picture of Island View. 'I'm buying this. It's got six bedrooms and half an acre of the most beautiful gardens. Oh, it's so lovely, Helen. You'll have to come and see it. And you can help me with the decorating too. You know all about colour schemes.'

Helen nodded unenthusiastically. 'So you'll be moving away,' she stated flatly. 'When are you moving into the new house?'

'Well ... soon. Today in fact. I can't stay here, you know that,' she said earnestly. 'And you know why.'

'Robert,' Helen said.

Christine nodded. 'Robert. If he's out of jail, then he'll have heard the news, and I'm sure he'll come looking for a share.' She nodded to the paper-strewn floor. 'If total strangers can demand some of it, you can be sure he will.'

'He has no legal right to any of your money,' Helen reminded her.

'Robert never paid too much attention to the law. He ignored the barring order, remember. But do you know what's even more frightening?' Christine added. 'If he did come demanding money, I know I'd give it, just to get rid of him. He still frightens me.'

'If you give him so much as a penny, he'll come back wanting more, you know that. It would never end. He'd want it all.'

Christine nodded.

'You're right to go. Just make sure no-one has your new address.'

'It's Island View, Killiney Hill,' Christine blurted out, wanting to make up to her friend and give her something which no-one else had. 'Not a word to anyone. Even Kevin doesn't know the exact address yet.'

Helen stood up and carried the two empty cups to the sink, rinsing them out quickly. Christine stood beside her, drying them on an old teacloth.

'I'm going to miss you,' Helen said abruptly. She turned and hugged Christine close. 'I'm so happy for you. You've had so much sadness in your life, you deserve this chance at happiness. And yet I'm almost sorry you won the money, because I'm losing a good friend. And all the money in the world can't buy friendship.'

'You're not losing me,' Christine said, patting Helen's back.

'Yes, I am.' The older woman pushed her away, holding her at arm's length. 'Things will never be the same again. You're moving away, starting again. You'll come back here a few times, call around and visit and maybe I'll even come and visit you in your new home in Killiney. If you get a phone we'll talk for a while every couple of weeks, then the calls will taper off. We'll send each other Christmas cards, but eventually that'll stop. How many times have you seen it happen?' she continued as Christine shook her head. 'Sure, I've done it myself.'

'It won't happen,' Christine promised fiercely. 'It won't.'

'It has happened already. Last week, I saw you every day. But today is the first time I've got to speak to you this week. Our lives are moving in different directions. Oh, I'm so happy you won … and yet I wish you hadn't. I'm sorry, that's selfish, I know.'

Christine shook her head. 'Don't say that. The money won't make any difference to me, to us. There's enough for both of us. I want you to share in my good fortune.'

Helen shook her head, tears sparkling in her eyes.

'I'm not offering you charity … I'm only giving back a little of what you've given me over the years. You were always there when I needed you; that's something I can never repay. But you'll let me help you. If you want anything – *anything* – just ask.' But even as she was saying it, she knew Helen would never ask. And what Helen said was true: things would never be the same again: she was moving on, moving away. In normal circumstances, maybe the close bond she had forged with the older woman would have survived, but these weren't normal circumstances. She wasn't just moving out of the estate into a new house, she was moving out of an entire way of life.

'I'll keep in touch,' she whispered. 'I swear it.'

Helen hugged her fiercely and nodded. They both knew that at that moment she meant it, and it was a promise she would try and keep. But Helen Keogh represented her past, and Christine Quinn was turning her back on her past.

Chapter 36

Harry Webb saw a flicker of movement in the rear-view mirror. He twisted quickly, groaning aloud as stiffened neck muscles protested, popping audibly. Pressing his hand to the back of his neck, he turned to look out through the rear window, and mentally added whip-lash to the list of injuries for which he would sue Christine Quinn.

It was the boy, Kevin Quinn.

Now where was he going at this hour of the morning?

Moments later another door opened – the Keoghs – and the reporter watched a small stout man hurry down the garden path, checking his watch, obviously rushing for the seven o'clock bus. Helen Keogh waited until her husband turned the corner at the bottom of the road, waved, then pulled her hall door closed and walked slowly and deliberately to Christine Quinn's house. She knocked once and the door was opened immediately. Webb nodded slowly: Christine was obviously waiting for her. The woman disappeared into the hall and the door closed behind her. Webb checked his watch – two minutes past seven – as he jotted down the details in his notebook.

So, Robert Quinn was right: Helen Keogh had known about Christine. He should have guessed that her vehement denial of any knowledge of the lottery win was a lie.

*   *   *

Kevin Quinn came running back to the house some time later, and the taxi arrived at twenty to eight.

Harry Webb turned the key in the ignition as soon as he saw the car turn into the estate, slowing to a crawl as the driver checked the house numbers. He could think of no one else who'd be using a taxi at this hour of the morning.

Lifting his camera, he pointed it at the Quinns' door. He had already checked the focus and settings. Any moment now. He pressed the button as the door opened, four shots clicking off in quick succession:

First, Kevin Quinn, laden down with bags, hurrying down the path, looking anxiously up and down the road ...

Then Christine Quinn and Helen Keogh standing in the doorway ...

The older woman hugging Christine ...

And finally, Kevin going back into the house, obviously for more bags.

Webb scribbled down the name of the cab company and the taxi's registration; if necessary he could trace the owner of the cab, maybe slip him a few bob for information on where he had dropped Christine and the boy. Lifting the camera he fired off another round of shots:

Christine pulling the door closed, turning to look up at the house ...

Kevin and the taxi-driver slamming the boot on the bags ...

Christine hugging Helen by the side of the road, both looking forlorn ...

Christine and Kevin in the cab, Christine leaning out to wave to Helen.

As the taxi pulled away, Webb took a single shot of Helen Keogh standing by the side of the road, one hand raised in farewell. It was the perfect image for his book. The lottery winner turning her back on her past, her friends.

Dropping the camera onto the seat, he ducked down as the taxi drove past. When it turned at the bottom of the road, he pulled out after it. What he needed now was one of those portable phones so that he could phone Robert Quinn and tell him that he was following Christine. He swore briefly as they pulled out of the estate onto the main road. The early morning rush was building up and he couldn't afford to lose them; they had several heavy bags which meant they wouldn't be coming back to the house. If they managed to get away, he might not be able to trace them and his exclusive story would become stale, and stale news was unsaleable. And on top of that Robert Quinn would be very annoyed.

Chapter 37

She signed her name eight times, her large rounded signature becoming increasingly scribbled with each sheet of paper that Simms passed across the desk.

'A short-term lease ... sign here and here. A contract ... sign here and here. And this agreement ... sign here. I will also need your signature here, here and here.'

Christine put down the fat fountain-pen Simms had given her and flexed her fingers. 'I don't think I've ever signed my name so often.'

Simms smiled. He rubbed his hands together briskly. 'Well, Mrs Quinn, I'm afraid you have only started. We should have contracts through before long for the sale of the house and they too will require your signature, of course. I took the liberty of arranging a solicitor for you.' He stopped. 'I trust that was in order?'

'Yes, thank you. I hadn't even thought of it.'

'And there is still one final signature I need ...'

Christine looked at him blankly.

'The cheque.'

'Of course!' Digging in her bag, Christine took out the new chequebook and folded it open. It was a while since she had written a cheque. Robert had taken her last cheque book – and used it. Taking her time now, she filled in the date, Thursday, 15

July, the estate agent's name and finally the amount: ten thousand pounds.

When she came to fill in the amount in figures, she panicked briefly, not able to remember how many noughts were in ten thousand – three or four? Smiling at her sudden fright, she drew four perfect noughts after the one and signed her name with a flourish. She took a moment to look the cheque over. It was the largest cheque she had ever written. Holding it in her hand, she suddenly realised that she was handing across more money than she'd ever possessed up to now. And it didn't even make a dent in her winnings. It was about ten days' interest on the two-and-a-quarter-million.

Christine pushed the cheque across the table. 'I have spoken to the bank, Mr Simms, so the cheque will clear without a problem. When will you need a deposit on the house?'

'When the contracts have been drawn up. Another ten days or so,' he said. He pulled open a drawer, lifted out a small brown envelope and shook out a set of keys. Holding them across the table in his left hand, he stretched out his right towards Christine. It took her a moment to realise that she was meant to shake hands. Again she wanted desperately to laugh out loud.

'Congratulations, Mrs Quinn. You are now in possession of Island View. I hope you will be very happy there.'

'We will,' she said, closing her hand into a fist, squeezing the keys so tightly that the metal cut into her palm. 'We will,' she said, fiercely.

Chapter 38

'And here we are,' Simms said, slowing the big car while he pointed the electronic remote control at the iron gates. As they swung inwards, he passed the control over to Christine. 'You should have this now.'

She twisted around in the front seat to look at Kevin, who was staring open-mouthed at the house that loomed up through the lush greenery. 'What do you think?' she asked, anxiously.

Kevin nodded, then licked dry lips and said, 'It looks ... amazing.'

'And just wait till you see inside.'

Simms pulled up in front of the house, turned off the engine and tugged a lever at the side of his seat which caused the boot to pop open. He glanced at Christine. 'Well, it's all yours now. Welcome to your new home, Mrs Quinn. And you too, Kevin.'

Christine turned to look at the house. This day last week she'd been living in a small three-bedroomed house on the outskirts of Dublin. If people had told her then that less than a week later she would be moving into a six-bedroomed mansion, she would have laughed at them. Slowly – no, not so slowly – the changes the money had brought with it were taking effect, irrevocably altering her life.

'I'll get your bags,' Simms said, stepping out of the car.

Christine had originally planned on getting a taxi out to the house, but it had become obvious that Simms would have to drive them, to take them through the security system and show them how everything worked. She breathed deeply as she stepped out of the car. The morning air was warm and dry, scented with the smells of the garden and the salt of the sea. It smelt clean, she decided. Fresh.

Standing beside her son, she rested a hand lightly on his

shoulder. 'What do you think?' she asked him again.

'It's enormous.'

'I told you it was big.'

'I know. But I had a different image in my head. I didn't realise half an acre was so big ...'

'Kevin,' Christine said gently, 'this is only the front garden. The back is three times the size of this!'

'Who's going to cut the grass?' he asked immediately.

'You are. I'll get you one of those lawn-mowers you can sit on.'

Simms had piled their bags on the steps and was waiting patiently, keys in hand. 'This property is protected by a sophisticated alarm system, and it's important that one of you knows how to work it.'

'You'd better show the two of us,' Christine said.

The estate agent turned the key in the lock and pushed the door open. A buzzer immediately started whining. Simms stepped into the hall and tapped a code into a small pad behind the door. The whining stopped and a green light appeared on the pad. 'The code is one, nine, three, zero. 1930. I believe it was the year one of the present owners was born. I'll arrange for the alarm company to come out and change the code. Now, the main control panel is in the cupboard under the stairs ...'

Simms spent the next ten minutes demonstrating how to turn on and off the electronic alarm. Christine was initially daunted by the ornate grid of lights set into a black box in the small cupboard. Simms explained that each light was linked to a room in the house. If the light showed green, then the room was not alarmed; if it was red, then it was alarmed. If it was green and blinking, that meant there was a problem such as an open window, a door ajar; and if it was red and blinking, then the room had been interfered with. Alongside the box was a tiny television monitor which flickered madly when Simms first turned it on before settling to show an overhead view of the front gates.

'If the gates are locked, visitors can speak into that little box set into the wall nearby.' He lifted a small white phone. 'You will find these intercom phones in the kitchen, sitting room and master bedroom. They will allow you to speak to the person at the gates. If you want to check first, simply turn on the monitor and you will actually see who is there. Of course you can always refuse entry by simply not opening the gates. If you have any problems, press this button here: it's a panic-button connected directly to the local garda station. They can have a car around here in a matter of minutes.'

'It's like Fort Knox,' Kevin muttered.

'This is a rather exclusive area,' Simms reminded him. 'More millionaires live on this hill than in any other part of Ireland. Security is an integral, and necessary, part of every house here. But of course,' he added hastily, watching Christine's eyes widen, 'the very fact that the house – and every other house on the hill – is so well protected, ensures that the crime rate is low. You will be perfectly safe here, I assure you. No-one can get in unless you let them.'

The estate agent took them through the rooms, showing the power points, the phone and television sockets and the sensors for the alarm.

'Technically, of course, you can do nothing to the house until you actually buy it,' Simms explained, as they walked back to the hall. 'So, I'm afraid no major alterations for the moment,' he smiled.

'I think we can live with it as it is,' Christine said.

Simms turned at the door. 'You have my card. If there is anything you need, please don't hesitate to contact me.' He opened the door and stepped out onto the drive. In the distance, churchbells were tolling noon. He turned and shook hands with Christine and, after a moment's hesitation, with Kevin. 'Once again, my congratulations and best wishes. I'm sure you will be happy here.'

'Thank you for everything, Mr Simms. You have been more than helpful.'

'My pleasure. I'll be in touch,' he said, pulling out his keys and heading for his car. 'Perhaps you would be good enough to open the gates for me?'

'I'll do it,' Kevin said quickly, glad of the opportunity to play with the sophisticated system.

Christine stood at the door, watching Simms turn his car in the driveway – *her* driveway – then move off, gravel crunching under his thick tyres. She raised her hand as he disappeared around the bank of foliage.

'I can see him on the TV,' Kevin called. 'He's just passed through the gates. I'm locking them now …'

Closing the door, Christine wrapped her arms tightly around her body, leaned back against the cool wood, and allowed her eyes to move across the marble hallway and up the polished banisters.

It was hers.

This house, this beautiful house, was hers.

She had been raised in a tiny two-up, two-down in Cabra; she had lived in a succession of one- and two-bedroomed flats as a teenager and young woman, and shortly after she married, she had moved into a soul-less housing estate. She never thought she'd leave it, and when she split up from Robert, she knew she never would. She'd imagined that her life had ended there, that it had nothing more to offer.

She had been wrong.

She felt young again, like a teenager.

She was starting again.

And she was going to start by making this beautiful house into a home.

Kevin emerged from beneath the stairs.

'Now, tell me honestly,' Christine said, 'what do you think?'

The young man shook his head. 'I can't believe it. I mean, it's huge. It looks amazing.'

'Honestly?'

'Honest, Mum.'

'Well, just wait till we decorate it. Now, tell me, which bedroom are you going to choose?' She picked up two of the bags and started up the stairs, adding, 'the big room is mine.'

'I thought as much.' He tucked one of the smaller bags under his arm and then lifted one in each hand. 'I rather like the white one ... or the green one,' he said, following her. 'What are we going to do for furniture?'

'Buy it.' She dropped one of the bags at the top of the stairs and carried her own down the corridor. 'Everything we need, we're going to buy.'

'Everything?'

'Everything!'

'But what about the things at home?'

Christine pushed open the door of the large bedroom and dropped her bag on the white carpet. 'Kevin, this is our home now. Everything in it is going to be the best. Nothing second-hand, nothing broken.'

He nodded uncertainly. 'But there's nothing here. No beds even.'

'So, we'll sleep on the floor tonight.'

'Maybe I could get us some sleeping bags.'

'That would be a good idea.'

'I could head into town and pick us up a couple of bags in one of the camping shops.'

'Do it later. First, I want you to help me open every window and door in the house. Let's get some air moving through the place.'

They spent the next hour exploring the house, walking around every room, opening doors and windows, peering into cupboards, climbing up into the enormous attic which was accessible by a narrow stairway set into what looked like a press, discovering a cellar which smelt faintly of onions and had a dozen dusty wine bottles on a rack in the corner. With a hoot of delight Kevin pulled one out ... only to discover that it was empty, as were all the others.

In the dining room, Christine threw open the glass doors and stepped out onto the patio. The garden shimmered in the early afternoon sunshine and the air was so still she could hear the nearby droning of bees as they moved through the fuchsia and the explosion of honeysuckle which crawled up the walls to curl around the metal balcony of her bedroom above.

She was going to furnish the patio with earthenware pots of different shapes and sizes, and fill them with aromatic herbs and scented flowers. She'd get some of those flowers which only released their fragrance at night. Helen had them under her bedroom window, and at night the room had a wonderful scent. She would make sure that they ate their evening meal in the dining room, with the doors open when the weather was right, and the room would fill with the delicate fragrance of all the flowers.

In fact, Christine decided, she was going to fill the whole house with flowers. Flowers reminded her of her childhood, when her mother was alive. Her mother had loved flowers. 'Oh, Mama, why aren't you alive to see this now?' she whispered, brushing away sudden tears. Her mother would have been so proud, not envious like Sheila or so many others, but just proud and pleased. Her mother would have wanted flowers.

This room, the dining room, would be filled with dried flowers. She had seen pictures of dramatic displays in one of the magazines. But nothing scented: she wanted the real smells from the gardens to percolate into the room.

The hall ... now the hallway needed something simple and dramatic. Maybe a yucca or a palm tree, something elegant ...

She stopped. She could hear Kevin singing in the distance, not one of the incomprehensible, harsh songs he usually roared out, but something softer, gentler. This house was going to be good for him. They would both be happy here.

She wandered into the sitting room. More dried flowers here ...

'What are you doing, Mum?'

Christine turned suddenly. Kevin was standing in the doorway, hands dug into the pockets of his jeans. 'Planning,' she said quietly. 'Just trying to decide how I'm going to decorate each room. Have you settled on a bedroom?' she asked.

'The white one. At the top of the stairs on the right. Furthest away from yours,' he added. 'Then you won't be able to hear my radio.'

'Nor will I be able to hear you sneaking in at night,' she added, shrewdly.

'Which reminds me: what are we going to do about keys? Should we get the locks changed?'

Christine shook her head. 'I'm not sure. I don't think we can until we actually own the house. Remember, we're renting this place until the sale goes through. How many keys have we got?' she asked.

'Two front-door keys, and one for the back door. There are bunches of keys in the cupboard under the stairs beside the alarm, but they look like duplicate room keys.'

'That should be enough.' Tilting her head back, she looked up at the ceiling. A naked bulb dangled forlornly on a single wire. She wanted a chandelier for this room, a Waterford Crystal chandelier. It would throw multi-coloured flashes of light across the ceiling.

'We really should get new locks,' Kevin said. He fidgeted.

'What's wrong?' Christine wondered.

'I'm hungry. Aren't you?'

She shook her head. She was too excited to be hungry. When she glanced at her watch she was astonished to discover that it was after two. No wonder Kevin was hungry; they'd had breakfast at six-thirty and nothing to eat since.

'I was going to go into town and get us a pair of sleeping bags.'

'Do that. Take some money out of my bag. How much do you think you'll need?'

He shrugged. 'The good ones are expensive.'

'Well then, you get the best you can. Get something to eat in town. I'll go down to the local shops while you're gone and get us some bread and salads for tea. And Kevin,' she called as he turned away, 'you do know how to get back here?'

'I'll find my way. I know the DART runs by Killiney.'

'Well, take care then.' She turned back to the marble fireplace. She would need something on both sides to take the bare look off it. Maybe statues.

Christine's handbag was hanging on the banisters at the bottom of the stairs. Kevin opened it and found the thick envelope of money in the zip section at the back.

'I'm taking two hundred for the sleeping bags,' he shouted.

'That's fine,' his mother called from the distance.

Carefully pulling six fifties from the bundle of notes, Kevin pushed them into the back pocket of his jeans.

Chapter 39

'You lost them,' Robert Quinn said bitterly. He stared down into the half-finished pint of Murphy's, his knuckles whitening around the glass and for an instant, Harry Webb was convinced he was going to throw it in his face.

'I couldn't find a parking spot around the Green,' Webb said defensively. He raised his voice above the lunch-time hum of the city-centre pub. 'Look, following them all the way into the city without being spotted isn't bad. They got out of the taxi before the Stephen's Green Centre at the top of Grafton Street. I double-parked while they paid off the driver, but then I was moved on by a parking attendant.'

Quinn raised his head. His expression was fixed, eyes cold and angry. 'You're telling me you allowed a traffic warden to move you on?'

'She was going to give me a ticket.'

'How much is a ticket?'

'Fifteen or twenty pounds.'

Robert Quinn's expression was icy. 'How much do you think you'll make from this book of yours?' he snapped. 'How much? Ten grand? Twenty? More? And then there's the money I was going to pay you for information. But you're prepared to throw all that away because you didn't want to get a fifteen-pound fine! You're an amateur, you know that. Nothing but a fucking amateur.'

'I'll find them again, don't worry.'

'I won't worry. But you should.' He raised his glass and finished the drink in one long swallow.

'Let me get you another,' Webb said, hopping to his feet, glad to be away from the big man's gaze.

Robert watched the reporter standing at the bar, desperately attempting to get the barman's attention. He shook his head slightly. He initially thought Webb might be useful. That was why he had offered to do a deal: tell Webb his side of the story, an exclusive interview, in return for information on Christine. But he was beginning to doubt if the fool had any usefulness at all.

Webb returned with two pints.

'However,' he said, sliding into his seat and lowering his voice, 'I do have these.' He pushed a large brown envelope across the round table.

Robert Quinn glanced at him before he tore open the envelope and shook nine glossy black-and-white photographs onto the beer-stained table.

'Here, careful with those,' Webb said, wiping at the table with a tissue. 'I want to use them in my book.'

Robert hardly recognised Kevin, the boy had grown so tall. Give him another year or two and he'd be handsome. The photo showed him struggling down the path with a bag in each hand and another under his arm.

'At what time were these taken?'

'Twenty to eight this morning,' Webb said quickly. 'I slipped a guy I know a few bob to develop them quickly for me.' He paused, waiting for Robert's offer to pay for the prints.

Robert looked at the next photograph.

Christine.

He hadn't seen her for ... how long? Must be nearly three years now. If he hadn't known she was the woman in the picture, he would never have recognised her. He stared intently at the grainy photograph, memorising her features. He saw only a vague image of the young woman he had married ten years ago. She had been pretty then, but the years had added a layer of lines and worry to her face, making her pinch-featured, bitter. The image he had carried with him until now was of an angry, sullen face, with tightly-closed lips and squinting eyes. But with the new clothes, new hair style, a little more weight on her face filling out her cheeks, wiping away the lines, she was actually beautiful.

'Who's the woman standing in the background with Christine?' Robert asked. 'I can't quite make her out ...'

'Next picture,' Webb said glumly. Robert Quinn wasn't going to pay for the photographs; which meant that he, Webb, was going to be personally out of pocket for them.

Robert picked up the next picture. Christine and Helen Keogh were standing together in the doorway, and in the next picture they were hugging. He nodded. That bitch had known about Christine's win. He lifted the picture to look at his wife, ex-wife – well, she was still legally his wife even if they *were* separated, he reminded himself. It was she who had separated from him; he had never wanted a separation, and if he'd had his way they would still be together.

For better, for worse, for richer, for poorer ... wasn't that how it went?

He picked up another photograph. 'How many bags did they carry out?' he asked Webb, not looking at him.

'Four ... five, something like that.'

A hotel or guest-house, then, that's where they were staying. Her sister's maybe: but no, Christine had never got on with Sheila.

'What do we do now?' Webb asked.

Robert looked surprised. 'We? *We* do nothing. You try and find out as much as you can. Talk to the neighbours. Talk to that woman who claims Kevin is engaged to her girl. Maybe the boy told her where they were going.'

'I'll do that. And what are you going to do?' he asked.

'I'll meet you here at the same time tomorrow,' Quinn said, ignoring the question. He turned the photographs over, one by one, until he came to the last shot of Helen Keogh standing by the side of the road, one hand raised in farewell. If all else failed, then *she* would know where Christine had gone. He glanced at his watch. It was doubtful if Christine was coming back to the house today; maybe he should pay it a visit, just in case she had left anything behind.

Chapter 40

Christine eventually gave up making lists in her head, and dug a piece of paper and a pen out of her bag. Wandering from room to room, she jotted down whatever came to mind, colour schemes, essentials she'd need, furniture for the rooms.

She knew she'd have to get the kitchen, her bedroom, and Kevin's bedroom done first; all the other rooms could come later. She'd start with the kitchen, since they'd be using it all the time.

Wandering in there, running her fingertips across the polished wooden cabinets, she looked around, thinking out what she would need.

The present owners had left their washing machine, tumble-drier and chest freezer in the utility room, but she remembered Simms had said they would take them away. She made a note to herself to phone Simms and ask him to take care of them for her. Which reminded her ... in big letters across the top of the page, she wrote PHONE. Tomorrow morning, she'd make arrangements to have a phone installed.

So, she was going to need a fridge and a dish-washer ... though maybe a dish-washer was an extravagance, after all, there were only the two of them ...

Christine suddenly burst out laughing, the sound echoing

around the empty kitchen. What was she doing? She was thinking like the old Christine Quinn.

She was having a dish-washer, even if it was only for herself – and damn the expense. Also, a fridge, a deep chest freezer, a washing machine, a tumble drier, a food mixer, a liquidiser, a juice extractor, rows of copper pots, blocks of kitchen knives and just about every other kitchen utensil she could think of.

A dinner service.

She had always wanted a dinner service, with plates and cups and saucers and side-plates that matched. All her life she had lived with mis-matched plates, bits and pieces she picked up over the years, oddments she collected in sales. Well, now she was buying herself a set that matched. Something delicate and beautiful in the finest bone china. She had a sudden image of Kevin breaking a piece and immediately decided that she would get two sets. One for special use and one for ordinary everyday wear.

And a canteen of cutlery. King's cutlery.

She'd seen them in Switzer's windows, enormous wooden boxes of heavy gleaming cutlery, not like the cheap metal forks and spoons she was used to, and knives which bent when you tried to cut anything thicker than bread with them.

She added cutlery to her list.

When she discovered the television socket in the kitchen, on a shelf above the counter, she decided that she'd get a small portable television for that corner. One of the little black cubes which held a clock and a radio as well. She'd seen them in Harry Moore's in Henry Street.

Of course Kevin would want a TV and video. They'd never had enough money for a video, and she always resisted the attractive 'interest-free credit' deals that were advertised everywhere. They could afford a video and a good TV now. But she'd leave all that to Kevin.

As she came out into the hall, she kicked off her shoes,

pressing her feet to the cool marble. Barefoot now, she wandered into the dining room.

She'd need a dining room suite, a long narrow table and six chairs, and a matching cabinet, something tall and dark and elegant to hold her glassware. That's all she was putting in this room. Well, maybe a standard lamp in that corner, and a small table holding a huge display of flowers.

By the time she reached the sitting room, she realised she was rushing things. It would be far better if she took it easy for a few days, got used to the feel of the house, tried out different colour schemes, before she settled on anything or bought furniture. Some rooms were going to be easier than others, of course. The dining room was simple, because it needed no decoration and all she had to do was decide upon the type of furniture she wanted there. But the sitting room was a different matter altogether: she was going to decorate it from scratch.

She padded up the stairs – she would put a plant just here where the stairs turned – and then walked down the landing to her bedroom.

Maybe it *was* a dream. Maybe she was going to wake up any moment now and discover that the last six days had not really happened, had been nothing more than a beautiful fantasy.

But the musty dry smell of the house, the prickling of sweat on her forehead, the tickling of the carpet under her bare feet: all of these were real.

Christine pushed open the french windows in her bedroom and stepped out onto the iron balcony. The metal was chilly, hard and uncomfortable under her feet; the scent of the honeysuckle that wrapped itself around the balcony was rich and strong in her nostrils; the colours of the garden, green and brown and gold, were shot through with splashes of vibrant colour. Christine noticed all these things. They were real enough too.

Stepping back into the bedroom she closed the windows. This was not a dream. She was not going to wake up. Last Saturday night, when her numbers had come up, the life she had been living had ended and this new life had begun.

She looked into the small en-suite bathroom. The walls above the sink were covered with mirror tiles and, as she stared at her reflection, she realised how hot and grubby she looked. She rubbed at a speckling of dust on her forehead, smearing it into long lines. Her hands were filthy.

She wondered if there was any hot water. She had told Kevin to turn on the immersion, but he'd probably forgotten ... Christine spun the hot tap. It chugged and spat, then steaming hot water splashed into the small sink.

Returning to the bedroom, she pulled out the small bag of toiletries she'd bought on Monday and carried the lot into the bathroom and laid them out on the shelf above the sink. Shampoo, conditioner, soaps, shower gels ...

Christine glanced over her shoulder at the shower stall. Kevin was out and wouldn't be back for ages ...

Quickly stripping naked, she stepped into the shower and stared at the controls, trying to work out just what they did. She turned a lever ... and a spray of ice-cold water stung her skin, making her squeal with fright. Gradually mixing the water first to tepid, then warm, then bringing it as hot as she could bear, she stepped into the shower and pulled the glass door closed.

Christine turned her face to the spray as she lathered shower gel into her skin. The gel smelt of exotic spices, of far-away places. When everything settled down she'd book a holiday; someplace hot. She squeezed more of the gel into her hand, relishing the feel of the thick soap.

She turned her back on the water, allowing it to splash down her back and across her buttocks. She rubbed her soapy hands across her shoulders, beneath her arms then down over her breasts, feeling her nipples harden beneath her touch, her sudden arousal startling her, catching her unawares.

She hadn't felt like this for a long time.

Her hands slid across her belly and as she lifted a leg to soap her thigh, the edge of her hand brushed her groin. The featherlight touch was electric, shocking in its intensity.

Christine stood in the shower, feeling her heart pounding, her breath coming in great heaving gasps. She was aware of the water beating against her flesh, the droplets spattering against her skin, water coiling around her breasts, dripping from almost painfully hard nipples, the heat in her groin.

It was the excitement of the money and the house ... nothing more.

She felt ... she felt ...

So alive.

Snapping off the water, she stepped from the shower, aware that her legs were trembling. Wrapping herself in a thick bathtowel, she stepped into the bedroom.

When she'd first seen the room she hadn't been able to imagine a reason for a shower in the bedroom, but now ...

There hadn't been men in her life in the last few years, but that didn't mean there wouldn't be now. She had a sudden vivid image of herself making love in this room. Hot, passionate love. And when they were finished, they would shower together in the bathroom, their hands on each other's bodies, touching, pressing ...

Enough! Taking a deep breath, Christine concentrated on drying herself. She looked around the room, mentally filling it with furniture.

A bed, the biggest, widest bed she could find, with silk sheets and a duvet that would match the white-and-gold colour scheme of the room. She'd also need a bedside table, and a wicker chair that she could pull out onto the balcony. She'd have to get a dressing table too, but other than that she couldn't think of anything else for the room. She might get a picture for the wall – no, not a picture, a wall-hanging, one of those big woven hangings, something dramatic, with loud strong colours.

Leaving the door open, she wandered down the hall to the room Kevin had chosen. She pushed open the door, and stopped, smiling at the mess he'd managed to make of it already – and all he'd done so far was open his suitcases. Clothes were strewn across the floor, cassettes which had been piled up against a wall had fallen over, and the latest issue of *In Dublin* lay folded over across the radiators.

The room was off-white, blue-white walls with a drab cream-coloured carpet. If they were going to change the colours – and she was sure Kevin wouldn't want to live with the present colour scheme – it might be better to do it before he moved in permanently. He could sleep in one of the other bedrooms while it was being decorated. She'd talk to him about it when he came home.

She went back down the corridor, looking into each room, making sure Kevin had opened all the windows. Stopping in the doorway of the last room, she looked in, and felt something catch at the back of her throat. The pink bedroom was next to the blue room, which had been the nursery. The combination of images, the child's nursery and a girl's bedroom, opened up afresh for her a wound that would never heal. She knew that she should be sharing this day with another, her own precious baby. The child would love this house. She would be just at the right age to enjoy it in a way that Kevin couldn't, and if Margaret were alive, then maybe she and Robert would still be together, and they'd be moving in here as a family.

Standing in the doorway of the girl's bedroom, Christine Quinn wept silently.

The winning numbers –

T H R E E

Chapter 41

The migraine had started even before Robert arrived home on the Friday night.

Christine had asked him to come home early, because she was to go to a parent-teacher meeting in Kevin's school, and she wanted to have both children settled in bed before she left. She could have left them with neighbours, but that would mean having to wake them up again when she returned from the meeting, and getting two lively youngsters to sleep again would be almost impossible.

Robert was usually home by six-thirty or seven at the very latest, if traffic was bad, but when it turned seven-thirty, she knew he was going to be late again. This would be the fourth Friday in a row ... and she knew that when he eventually rolled in, he'd be reeking of drink, having spent a sizeable amount of his pay in the pub close to the bookshop where he now worked.

Maybe getting him the job had been a mistake. But the repping job he'd had when they first married simply hadn't worked out. It was a fine job for a single man with no obligations, and it suited Robert when he was single. But he was married now, and away from home too often, leaving her alone in the new housing estate for up to a week at a time while he travelled around to the bookshops in the thirty-two counties. She worried constantly about him, thinking of him driving all over the country in all sorts of weather. It wasn't too bad during the summer months, but during the winter she would watch him go out in the mornings and not know what time he'd get back in the evening, or indeed, if he'd get back at all. And if he was forced to stay over because of the weather, then that was more expense. Also, the uncertainty of their income made managing a budget almost impossible. Robert was paid a commission on everything he sold, and his basic salary was slim. So the income was meagre enough, especially in winter, when his stock of gardening, poetry and specialist DIY titles were in poor demand.

When Christine became pregnant with Margaret, she started putting pressure on him until eventually he caved in and agreed to give up the job and look for something else. She contacted all the bookshops on his behalf and he eventually got a job in the same bookshop she'd been working in when they first met. The pay still wasn't great, but the hours were regular, the work was light and at least she knew where he was during the day.

Although he'd been pleased with the job for the first year or so, she knew he was depressed lately. The staff had changed, the old man who had run the shop for forty years retired and the new staff were a young lot. He wouldn't talk to her about how he felt, and she sensed that the job wasn't going well. Robert had always had a problem with authority; he'd been his own boss for too long, and she thought he resented being told what to do. He started coming home irritable and sullen in the evenings. Often he ignored the three of them and sat in front of the television after tea for the rest of the night, answering her questions in monosyllables. Even Baby Margaret, whom he adored, failed to brighten his dark moods.

And then the drinking started.

Christine had a horror of drinking, vivid memories coming back to haunt her, of what her father had done to her when he was drunk.

She'd talk to him, as soon as she came back from the school meeting ... if she ever managed to get away.

Helen Keogh called at a quarter to eight. 'Are you ready?' she asked.

'I can't go just yet, Helen. Robert isn't home.'

'Is he working late?'

'I don't know. He didn't say anything to me, but maybe

something came up at the last minute. You go on and I'll follow you down.'

'You can always leave the children over at my place. My Tommy'll look after them.'

'I've just got them down, and if I take Margaret up again, she'll be awake for the rest of the night.'

'I'll head on then. I'll keep a place for you.'

Christine stood on the doorstep and watched the big Cork-woman disappear to the left at the bottom of the road. She remained standing at the door for the next twenty minutes, hoping she'd see Robert's tall shape round the corner. His dinner was in the oven; she could have it on the table before he reached the door. It would only take her five minutes to get down to the school.

But Robert didn't arrive.

Helen stopped by at nine-thirty on her way back home.

'I'm worried sick, Helen,' Christine said, standing at the door with a glass of water in her hand. She quickly swallowed two aspirin to try and ease her throbbing head.

'He probably stopped off somewhere for a drink with a few of the lads,' Helen said, trying to calm her. 'Is he often home late?'

'Sometimes. On the last couple of Fridays,' she finally admitted.

'Well, there you are, then. He stopped in for a drink. He just forgot about the school meeting and didn't notice the time slipping away. He'll be in soon, all embarrassed and sorry. Well, you just make it plain to him that you're annoyed. There's no point in letting it go as if it doesn't matter.'

Christine nodded.

'I'd better head on home.' Helen was about to say more, to tell Christine to call over if Robert wasn't in by midnight, but she knew that would only scare the younger woman. Instead, she said, 'You know where I am if you need me.'

By the time Robert arrived in at twelve o'clock, Christine was frantic. She was sick in her stomach and her head was pounding so hard she could barely see.

She raced into the hall as soon as she heard his key in the door. 'And just where the hell have you been?' Although she felt like screaming, she kept her voice down to a hoarse whisper so as not to waken the children.

Robert turned and stared at her, and she could smell the drink off him from across the hall.

'Do you know what time it is? And I asked you to come home early tonight so that I could go down to the school for a parent-teacher meeting.'

'I stopped off for a drink.'

'Jesus, Robert,' she said, disgusted.

'Ah, don't take that fucking attitude with me. There's no harm done.'

'I've been waiting here worried sick about you.'

'I'm going to bed.'

'Is that all you have to say?' she demanded.

'It's not the end of the fucking world,' he snapped. Turning on his heel, he clumped heavily up the stairs, and then the bedroom door slammed.

Moments later Margaret started wailing. It took her the best part of an hour to get the child back to sleep. When she finally stepped into the bedroom, her head throbbing, she found Robert stretched out on the bed, still fully clothed. The room stank of alcohol. Crossing to the window, she pushed it open, allowing a little of the cool night air to waft into the room and dispel the sickening odour. Then, that as she sat on the edge of the bed, she noticed that he had opened his eyes. He was awake.

'We need to talk,' she said quietly.

Robert blinked at her sleepily. 'Tomorrow,' he mumbled.

'Tonight. What you did tonight was unforgivable. You knew I

needed to go down to the school ...'

Robert raised both hands, silencing her. 'Look, just shut up! Right now I feel like shit. And I've got to get up for work in the morning, remember, because I now work in a bookshop that opens on bloody Saturdays!'

'It's the job, isn't it? You're having problems in work.'

'Leave it,' he snapped.

'No, I won't leave it. Talk to me. Tell me what's wrong!'

Sitting up, he suddenly caught her shoulders and jerked her forward until her face was inches from his. His breath was foul on her face. 'Look, I said leave it,' he hissed. 'Now just ... just fuck off and leave me alone!'

She recoiled at the vehemence in his voice. He had never spoken to her like that before. Rolling off the bed, he stamped out onto the landing and slammed the bathroom door behind him. Margaret was screaming again before the toiled flushed.

Christine finally dozed off just as the sky was lightening towards dawn. Margaret had been awake on and off through the night, and her own headache had settled down to a pulsing migraine and sick stomach. She knew from experience that what she needed to do now was spend a day in a darkened room with a cold compress on her forehead. But with Robert heading out to work there was no possibility of doing that. Maybe she'd ask Helen to take the children. That would give her a chance to lie down and rest for awhile, and try and shake this off before Robert returned in the evening.

The alarm-clock rang out, jerking her awake. Christine sat up ... and felt the pain flow up into her head and explode there. Her stomach churned.

Robert glanced curiously at her as he rolled out of bed. He washed and shaved, made his own quick breakfast – tea and toast – without offering her any, and dashed off for the ten-past-eight bus, and all without saying a single word to her.

When she heard the front door slam, she gently rested her head on the pillow hoping to get a few minutes' rest ... but Robert's departure woke Margaret, who started screaming, and then Kevin climbed into bed beside her and started nattering. She knew she'd get no sleep.

Christine crept around the house for the rest of the morning, eyes half closed against the brilliant sunshine, desperately trying to make no sudden movements. She drew all the curtains to keep down the light, and tried to avoid the front of the house which was washed in morning sunlight. She took four aspirin and, an hour later, another two, but she knew she was wasting her time: the sickening migraine had settled like a metal cap over her head, squeezing tighter with every movement, lancing pain into her eyeballs.

She made the children's lunch around one, the smells of cooking – beans on toast – turning her stomach, making her throw up. As she lay crouched over the toilet she wondered if she was pregnant. The last time she'd been like this had been shortly after Margaret had been conceived, the hormonal imbalance upsetting her entire system. But when she worked out when they'd last made love – and she realised that they hadn't for quite a while – she decided she couldn't possibly be pregnant.

When she returned to the kitchen, Margaret had upset her plate of beans and Kevin had disappeared, leaving his lunch unfinished. She cried tears of frustration and by the time she cleaned up the child and the floor, she was ill again.

Realising that she desperately needed to lie down, Christine put Margaret in the front garden after first locking the gate and tying a piece of string around it so that she wouldn't be able to get out. She called Kevin, warned him not to undo the string and to keep an eye on his sister. She told him to come and get her if anything happened.

It was three o'clock when Christine lay down in the darkened bedroom with a cold cloth over her forehead and eyes. She set the alarm for five, just in case she dozed off. As she drifted into a troubled sleep the last sounds she heard were Margaret's happy chuckles from the garden below.

Perhaps someone opened the gate. Maybe Margaret did it herself; her little fingers were always busy. Possibly Kevin did it, though he usually climbed over the gate, even when it wasn't tied up.

When Robert turned into the estate at half-past six that evening, he spotted Kevin playing with a group of his friends in a nearby garden. He paused to talk to the boy, then continued on up the road to the house. He stopped in shock when he saw Margaret playing on the pavement. He looked around, expecting to see Christine chatting to one of the neighbours ...

Margaret lifted her head, sunlight shimmering off her jet black curls, spotted her father and immediately got to her feet and raced squealing towards him.

She didn't see the car reversing out of the drive, and the driver didn't even register the thump against the back of the car.

And Robert Quinn never forgave Christine because, later, when someone realised that the mother was missing and he went into the house to look for her, he found her sleeping peacefully in bed. He knew that if the lazy bitch hadn't been in bed, his daughter would still be alive.

Chapter 42

It took him an hour to get the sleeping bags.

Kevin started with the Scout Shop, then checked out the shops in Liffey Street and Capel Street which sold camping gear. He had thought it would be a simple matter of walking into one of the shops and picking two decent-looking sleeping bags. He was astonished at the range available – some came with hoods, others were padded or quilted, others even had mattresses. He eventually settled for two padded bags that looked warm and comfortable. He also bought two inflatable pillows. As he struggled down Capel Street carrying them in a bulky plastic bag, he wasn't sure whether to be angry or amused by the thought that he'd spent nearly a hundred and fifty notes for something which they would use for one or two nights at the most.

Moving into a house with no beds – no furniture at all – was craziness. And that house was something else. Ugly, old-fashioned and uncomfortable. He hated it.

Oh, he'd never admit that to his mother of course, but he didn't like it, hadn't liked it from the moment he'd seen it through the trees. It looked like something from a television drama. It was too big, too empty and, even though it was surrounded by neighbouring houses, it was isolated. He'd wandered down the road from the house looking for a bus-stop or a dart station and all he saw were similar houses set behind high walls, with locked gates.

He hated the posh address and he particularly disliked the stupid name. Island View. What island? He could see no island from any of the rooms. All he could see were the trees that surrounded the house and made it look as if they were now living in the heart of the country.

And what did they want six bedrooms for? Six! They'd lived in a three-bedroomed house up to now; they used two of the bedrooms and the third was a store-room. The house was way too big for their needs, and it was soul-less. It looked like something from a magazine, the home of a rock star. But he and his mother weren't rock stars. They were ordinary people, who'd lived ordinary lives right up until last Saturday night.

And then they became millionaires.

Maybe the glamour had gone to his mother's head, maybe that's why she bought herself a mansion with a garden that was one half jungle and the other half bigger than a football pitch. Oh sure, it looked fine now, but what was it going to look like in a couple of weeks' time when the garden needed tending and the grass needed mowing? It'd be a full-time job just keeping up with it. And *he'd* probably be stuck with the gardening.

The house hadn't come cheap and the upkeep would be ferocious. It would eat into the money. And what about all the hidden costs of a house like that? The heating bill alone in the winter would be enormous. Just decorating it was going to cost a fortune. He'd looked through some of the books and magazines his mother had bought yesterday. He realised now why she picked them: there were similarities between some of the pictures and the house she'd bought. She was going to make it look like something out of those magazines.

He nodded: it was going to cost a fortune.

Maybe that's what he was really worried about. The money. If his mother continued to spend as she'd started, then, when it was time for him to get his share, there wasn't going to be very much left. Maybe he could talk some sense into her, slow her down. As he crossed Capel Street Bridge, he wondered if it would be possible to get her to sell the house. No, not yet. Maybe in a year or two though. He could work on her, point out how an apartment in the city centre would be much more suitable, safer too, and easier to keep and clean. He might be able to convince her to sell the house and put the money back into the account. You never know, they might make a profit on the deal.

He was sorry she hadn't spoken to him about it first. He would have talked her out of it. She usually discussed everything with him, asking his advice, actually listening to him. He knew his relationship with his mother was an unusual one; most of his friends had a distant and often cold relationship with their parents, but he was actually very close to his mother. And he knew that the reason she didn't confide in him about the buying of the house was because he'd told Sandra Miller about their win.

If only that bitch had kept her mouth shut.

Well, maybe he should have kept his mouth shut too. If he had, then they'd still be living at home, and he'd be going out tonight, instead of heading back to an empty house, with nothing to do, not even a TV to keep him going.

He glanced at his watch. Just gone three. Maybe he'd get himself a little something to help pass away the long evening.

Kevin had first experimented with drugs when he was thirteen. Together with one of his friends, Dave Little, he sniffed glue from a plastic bag. It gave him a pounding headache and made him violently sick ... in fact they'd both been sick, especially Dave who threw up all down the front of his jumper.

Kevin smiled at the memory. They eventually burned the jumper in the field at the back of the house and Dave swore to his mother that he'd lost it.

It was Dave who had introduced him to magic mushrooms some time later. He had a bag of about two hundred of the small shrivelled buttons which he'd picked on a camping trip in the Dublin mountains. They waited until Dave's mother had gone out to work, then they spent the morning cleaning the mushrooms and washing off the muck and cow shit. They tried a few raw, but found them dry and unpalatable. Then Kevin had the idea of cooking them in butter, the way his mother cooked mushrooms. They each ate about a hundred before Kevin realised that the room was changing shape and the colours were bleeding, shifting into one another. Lifting his hand before his face, he was able to see through it, right down to the bones.

Kevin loved the buzz, the feeling of power, the sense that he was someone special, someone in control.

He did mushrooms with Dave on and off for a year, but after a while they discovered that they were having to eat more and more in order to get close to that first great buzz. And often, a few hours after eating the mushrooms, they were violently sick. Kevin suspected that it was because some other type of wild mushroom had become mixed in with the magic mushrooms.

Dave then went on to experiment with tablets – uppers and downers – and lately with acid. Kevin didn't go that road; instead he'd tried some Ecstasy at a party. He loved the sensations the small white tablets aroused in him: a sudden burst of intense good feeling, then a long slow slide while the drug wore off, during which time he felt completely at peace with the world. If he was going to survive the next few days while his mother ran around the place like a mad thing, then he reckoned he was going to need something to keep him cool.

Kevin struggled through the late afternoon crowd in Grafton Street. The sleeping bags were awkward; he should have got them last on his way home ... on his way back to the new house. It would never be a home, he decided; it was going to be a showcase. But some E would make it just a little more acceptable.

He found Skinny at his usual seat just inside the gate at Stephen's Green. The tall gangling young man in the worn army fatigues lived up to his nickname; he was all jutting bone and stretched skin, his long dirty blond hair hanging lank to his shoulders, mingling with his scrawny beard. Skinny supplied some of the best drugs in the city. He only did the soft drugs, refusing to handle the heavier stuff. Rumour had it that he had once been a heroin addict, but Kevin wasn't sure he believed that, though every time he saw him, he thought Skinny looked thinner and sicker. He suspected it might be AIDS.

'Skinny! How's it going?' he said, sitting close to the young man, though not looking at him. They were both scanning the crowd. If they saw anyone looking their way, they'd get up and walk off in different directions, and meet again at the bottom of Grafton Street.

'I heard a story about you,' Skinny said. He drew hard on a cigarette, the paper crackling audibly. Holding the smoke in his lungs for a count of five, he let it out long and slow.

'That must be some tobacco,' Kevin said, ignoring the question.

'John Player, Extra Mild. You know I don't do this shit anymore.'

'Someone told me that, but I wasn't sure whether to believe it.'

'Believe it.'

'I'm looking to score some E.'

'A story that you'd come into a lot of money. And I mean a lot,' Skinny continued. 'Is it true?'

'Maybe.'

'Maybe it's true, or maybe it isn't?' he asked.

'It's true. News gets around,' Kevin said shortly.

'That sort travels fast. Three people – no, four – told me the same story today. Also told me you were engaged to some female.'

'That bit is not true. I know the girl, that's all. But when her mother heard we won the money, she immediately decided I was getting married to Sandra.'

'Do I know her?'

'She was at Tony's party on Saturday night.'

'Blond bimbo?'

'That's the one.'

Skinny laughed silently. 'Didn't see you as the marrying type.'

'I'm not. Jesus, I need some E just to stay calm.'

'What do you want?'

'Give me three ... no, five. I think it's going to be one of those weeks.'

'I won't ask if you've got the cash.'

Kevin pulled out the hundred pounds, keeping it cupped in the palm of his hand. 'I've got it.'

Skinny smiled mirthlessly. 'Whatever happened to the good old days when you used to buy one measly tab?'

'Long gone,' Kevin grinned. 'Long gone.'

Chapter 43

Christine was standing in the dining room, arms folded across her breasts, quietly enjoying the atmosphere of peace and calm, listening to the sounds of the birds and insects through the open patio doors. In her old house at this time, she'd be hearing the sounds of children playing in the street, people shouting, a dozen radios blaring, the constant hum from the new motorway.

Noise, just noise. She used to put on her own radio just to drown it out.

It was so quiet here, though if she listened very carefully, she thought she could hear the distant hissing of the sea. She'd go down onto the beach tonight, she decided.

She was turning away when she became aware of a flicker of movement through the open patio doors. Her heart lurched when she saw the figure of a man moving through the bushes. Holding her breath, she took a step back into the dining room, frantically trying to remember where the nearest panic button was situated. Under the stairs, beside the front door? Yes.

The figure stopped, and she saw the white blur of a face turn towards the house. She squinted short-sightedly, trying to make out the features. Glasses – she was going to have her eyes tested and get herself a pair of glasses, or maybe contact lenses.

This side of the house was in shadow and she was well back in the room, so she wasn't sure if the person standing in the bushes could see her. All she had to do was take a step backwards through the open door into the hall, then dart around to the cupboard under the stairs and press the button.

Christine took another step backwards as the figure moved into the sunlight and then she suddenly recognised Mark Cunningham. She stopped, feeling a wave of relief wash over her. She took a step towards the open patio doors, then stopped again, watching him through the window as he walked across the lawn towards the house.

Mark Cunningham was dressed in white today, as if he'd just stepped off a tennis court, a white tee-shirt over white shorts with white socks and runners. The sparkling white accentuated his deep tan, though it highlighted the grey in his thick black hair. As he came closer and his features swam into focus, she saw that he was as handsome as she remembered him, with his deep intense blue eyes.

He stopped at the foot of the patio. 'Hello? Is anyone there?'

Christine hesitated, suddenly shy, almost embarrassed ... then abruptly realised that this was *her* house, *her* patio, *her* garden! Taking a deep breath, she stepped out from behind the doors into the light.

'Hello, Mr Cunningham.'

'I saw the open doors ...' He stared at her blankly for a

moment, then he suddenly smiled. 'Christine Quinn! You were here on Tuesday.'

She walked out onto the patio, wondering what on earth she must look like, having spent the day grubbing around the house, poking into all its dusty corners.

'You've a great memory for names.'

'It's an occupational hazard, I guess.' He stopped, eyes narrowing as he thought of something. 'You wouldn't be the same Christine Quinn I heard about on the ...'

She nodded silently.

'You are! Well, congratulations. Well done. I'm delighted for you. What a stroke of luck, eh?' Lifting one leg onto the low wall that surrounded the patio, he rested an arm on his knee, and gestured at the house. 'Back for another look?'

Christine shook her head. 'I've bought it,' she said simply. 'I moved in this morning,' she added, face breaking into a broad smile.

'That was quick.'

'There didn't seem to be any point in hanging around. I saw it, I liked it – so I bought it,' she finished.

'You're decisive. I admire that.' He gestured over his shoulder at the pond. 'I just popped in to drag some more weed out of your pool. If you don't keep it clear, it will kill everything in it, and there are some really nice lilies there that I don't want to see choked to death. You don't mind, do you?' he asked suddenly.

'No, not at all,' she smiled. 'Feel free to come and go as you please. If you'll show me what to do, I can help.' She fell into step beside him as they strolled down the garden and she realised just how tall he was. Her head came level with his shoulders. 'How did you get into the garden?' she asked.

He nodded through the trees, grinning like an overgrown schoolboy. 'Your garden backs onto mine. I've an incredibly ancient oak tree with branches that lean out over your wall. I simply climb up the tree, shin out along the branch and drop in here.' He looked down at Christine. 'It's quicker that way. My house is up the road to the left,' he added. 'I have a key which the previous owners asked me to hold for them. I'll give it back to you, though I don't suppose it's much use now.'

'Well, it still is, actually. I haven't got around to changing the locks yet. And I'm not sure if I can,' she said. 'I'm renting the place, you see, until the sale goes through.'

He nodded quickly, squinting into the sunlight and she could see how the lines deepened around his eyes. 'I see. I was wondering how you managed to take possession so quickly. But I'm sure there's no problem about changing the locks.'

'Do you know someone locally who'd do it for me?'

'Oh, I can do that for you. It's straightforward; all I need is a screwdriver.'

'Oh, I couldn't ...' she began.

'It would be my pleasure. Now, look here,' he said, crouching down at the edge of the pond and picking up a stick he'd left there, 'd'you see that weed ... that's the stuff you have to get rid of. Just hook it out and dump it into a bucketful of water.'

'Why into a bucket?'

'That's just in case you've caught up any little pond life with the weed. Once it settles in the bucket, you can dispose of the weed, and the frogspawn or whatever else goes back into the pond.'

'We don't have a bucket,' Christine said.

'I've left one round at the side of the house, just under the outside tap.'

'I didn't realise I had an outside tap,' she confessed. 'We got here about noon, and we've spent the day simply wandering through the house, looking around, getting the feel of the place.'

'We?' Mark asked casually.

'My son Kevin,' she explained. 'I'm separated from my husband.' She was about to say more, but simply added, 'I'll get the bucket.'

'Let me,' Mark said, straightening. 'I haven't seen Kevin around,' he said as they strolled up the garden.

'He went into town earlier this afternoon. He had to get a few things. We came with nothing. But I've plans to go into the city tomorrow to buy a few essentials.'

'I think you will enjoy it here. It's quiet, peaceful, and private,' he added.

'That's good, I want peace and quiet. And privacy.'

He grinned. 'Yes. I'm sure you made lots of friends when your good fortune became known.'

'A local newspaper reporter discovered I'd won; that's how the news got out.'

'What bad luck!'

Christine shrugged philosophically. 'Yes. It made me make some rather quick decisions, but on the plus side, I'm not sure I'd have found this place if I hadn't been under pressure.'

Mark pointed to the tap set into the wall. There was a red plastic bucket on the ground under it, catching the water that dripped down every few seconds. He spun the tap, water thundering into the bucket. 'Oh, I'm sure you would,' he said suddenly.

She looked at him in surprise.

'Find this place, I mean. If it was meant for you, you would find it.'

When they finished clearing the pond, Mark went back into the house with Christine. He examined the lock on the kitchen door and front door.

'I can do nothing with the back door; you'll need a professional for that. But the front is fairly straightforward. When you're in town tomorrow, if you pick up some locks of the same name and design and measurements – that's very important –

I'll fit them for you.'

'That's very kind. But …'

'No buts,' he said with a smile. 'I'm delighted to do it.' Standing at the front door he breathed deeply, his broad chest stretching the thin material of his tennis shirt.

'This is a really lovely house. Beautiful gardens. Far nicer than mine,' he confided.

'I fell in love with it the moment I saw it.'

'It's that sort of place.'

He glanced at his watch. 'I'd better go, and let you get back to your unpacking.'

Christine laughed. 'I've nothing to unpack. We travelled very light. And I can't even offer you a drink – I've absolutely nothing in the house. I'll be going down soon to the local shops to get something for tea.'

'Don't tell me you've been here all day with nothing to eat?' he asked sharply.

'I wasn't hungry.'

'I'll bet you are now! I'll be back in five minutes,' he said suddenly and trotted off around the side of the house.

Christine stared after him, wondering where he'd gone and what he was coming back for. Finally, she stepped back into the hall and closed the door. He was a nice man, she decided, he seemed warm and genuine, but …

There was always a 'but'. Experience had taught her caution, made her cynical. They rarely did something for nothing. Why was Mark Cunningham offering his help; what were his reasons?

* * *

When Kevin returned an hour later, he found his mother sitting on the patio steps with a tall handsome stranger dressed in tennis clothes. The remains of a salad were spread out in bowls and plates on the stones, alongside small green bottles of Bally-gowan water.

Kevin dumped the sleeping bags in the kitchen and came forward warily as his mother and the stranger stood up. The tall man wiped his hand on his shorts before stretching it out.

'Kevin, this is Dr Mark Cunningham, our neighbour,' Christine said, introducing them. 'And this is my son Kevin.'

'Pleased to meet you,' Mark said, shaking Kevin's hand firmly.

The young man nodded.

'When Mark discovered we'd nothing to eat in the house, he brought over some things for supper. We've kept yours,' she added.

'I'm not hungry,' Kevin said sullenly. 'I had a burger in town.'

Embarrassed by Kevin's behaviour, Christine turned to Mark. 'It really was very kind of you to go to all this trouble.'

'It was no trouble, I assure you,' he said standing up. 'And as a doctor I really must insist that you eat regularly. I'll be off now.'

'Your plates ...'

'I can collect them tomorrow.'

'I'll drop them round.'

'Perhaps you and Kevin would like to come over for dinner tomorrow night?' he asked suddenly, looking at each of them.

Confused, Christine looked at Kevin, then back to Mark.

'That's if you've no other plans,' he added.

'No,' she said.

'Then come around eight.'

She nodded dumbly.

'You can meet my mother,' he said with a smile.

'Your mother?'

He spread his hands to encompass the salads. 'You didn't think I made all this myself, did you!'

Chapter 44

Robert Quinn lay with one arm behind his head, the other wrapped around Rachel Farmer's shoulder, hand resting on her breast. She was sleeping deeply now, exhausted after a bout of energetic lovemaking.

Robert tried to sleep, but his thoughts kept returning, again and again, to Christine. Even as he'd been making love to Rachel, he found himself thinking of his ex-wife, and strangely, her image aroused him even more than Rachel did.

Where was she now? he wondered. Where was she sleeping? And was there a man in her life? Until this afternoon he would never have even considered the possibility. Once the first excitement of marriage had passed, he thought of her as a drab, sexless creature. But now, having seen Webb's photographs, he realised she would have no problem finding herself a man. And of course the money was an added incentive to any man. Two-and-a-quarter million very good reasons to be nice to her.

How much would he look for?

As her husband, he was entitled to half. He'd supported her while their marriage lasted, even bought the house that she had him barred from. Barred from his own home: he'd never forgiven her for that.

She'd cost him in other ways too. She made him give up his good rep's job and work in that stupid bookshop. If he'd stuck at the repping, he would have made a success of it. Sooner or later he would have picked up one of the companies with the big-name authors; he would have made his fortune then. But oh no, Christine wouldn't wait. She made him throw it all away to become a shop assistant, trapped in a poky little bookshop all day, every day, being ordered around by a spotty-faced kid who called himself the assistant manager. Later, when he lost that job – sacked because he eventually lost his temper and punched the little shit in the face – and had no other way to support the family, he turned to thieving.

That was her fault too. She'd made him a thief. He nodded slowly and Rachel turned and mumbled in her sleep.

And once he'd started out on that road, he eventually ended up in prison. All the opportunities he'd lost because of her, the money he never made because of her, and the time he spent in prison: she owed him for all that.

So, he would ask her to pay him back, to give him a little of what he'd given her. It was a reasonable request. She wouldn't refuse. And he wasn't greedy. He would only ask for a million. He reckoned all the pain and hurt she'd put him through was worth a million.

And this wasn't a request she was going to refuse.

Chapter 45

Christine Quinn lay on the floor of the white-and-gold bedroom in the padded sleeping bag and stared at the ceiling. The room was in almost total darkness, and after too many years of living in a house with a street light just outside her bedroom, she found the darkness – and the silence – disconcerting.

Although it was after midnight and she'd been up since before six, she was too excited to sleep. So many things had happened today, so many new images, so many new experiences! Everything was moving so quickly now. The whole pace of her life had stepped up. Winning the money had put her on a rollercoaster … and it was only now picking up speed. Suddenly she had things to do, she had a purpose, a reason to look forward to the morning … a reason to look forward to tomorrow night.

Eight o'clock, Mark had said. She wondered how she would dress, and what should she bring ... food, wine, maybe a small present for Mark's mother? Or would that be too much? Probably.

And Mark.

What did he want?

Did he want anything, or was he just being neighbourly? She was moving in a different class of society now, she reminded herself. She had entered the world of the rich. Rich people acted differently, had different motives, goals, attitudes.

But people were still people, and she sensed that Mark was just a genuinely nice person. She hoped he was; it would be nice to have a neighbour like him.

Unzipping the sleeping bag, she got to her feet and opened the doors that led out onto the balcony. The stars were hard and brilliant over her head, the fragrance of the plants rich and strong, the low rumble of the sea clearly audible now. Gooseflesh rippled on her bare arms and she felt her nipples harden with the chill under her thin cotton tee-shirt. But she didn't mind; she revelled in these sensations, because they each reinforced the point that she was living a new life, in a new world. There were stars in her old world, but they weren't as clear; there were fragrances, but they were different, not as strong, not as pleasant; and the sounds of a rumbling motorway had been replaced by the gentle murmur of the sea.

Taking a deep breath of the fragrant air, she wondered what tomorrow would bring.

Friday, 16 July

Chapter 46

They had breakfast in Bewley's in Westmoreland Street. The early-morning crowd had thinned out and they managed to get one of the small private booths. Kevin wolfed down his breakfast of egg, sausage and black pudding, while Christine only picked at hers, idly skimming through a copy of *The Irish Times* she'd found on the seat. A paragraph entitled, LOTTERY TO REACH £1m, caught her attention:

> *Saturday night's lottery is due to break the million pound mark. Wednesday night's lottery draw was not won and the pot was carried forward. Last week Mrs Christine Quinn of Dublin beat odds of 3,262,622 to 1 to win more than two million pounds. The odds against five numbers coming up are 16,477 to 1, and 411 to one for four numbers.*

Three million, two hundred and sixty-two thousand, six hundred and twenty-two, to one against. Hopeless odds. And yet she'd beaten them. Shaking her head in astonishment, Christine folded away the newspaper.

'Did you sleep well last night?' Kevin asked.

'I did. The sleeping bag was very comfortable. Did you?'

'On and off,' he shrugged. 'The place was just a bit too quiet for my liking. I suppose I'll get used to it.'

Christine sipped her tea. 'You will.'

'I was thinking, Mum,' he continued, staring at his plate, his voice casual enough to alert her, 'I was thinking that the house is very big, just for the two of us, I mean.'

She looked at him across the rim of her teacup, saying nothing.

'I mean, it's lovely and all that, but we're never going to use half the bedrooms.' He raised his head and looked at his mother's plate. 'Are you going to finish that?' When she shook her head, he reached over and swapped their plates. 'I was thinking,' he continued, 'that you've probably bought a lot of rooms we're never going to use.'

'We didn't use all the rooms at home. We hardly ever used the sitting room,' she reminded him. 'And the small bedroom was only ever used as a dump.'

The small bedroom had been Baby Margaret's; Christine rarely entered it, the teddy-bear-and-rainbow wallpaper a pathetic reminder of the dead child.

'Well, I'm seventeen now; I'll be eighteen soon. I might think about getting a flat closer to the city centre. That would mean you'd be alone in that big house, all by yourself.'

Christine ran her hand through her hair, pushing it back off her face. 'But you have no need to move into a flat; there's plenty of space in the new house; you said so yourself. You could come and go as you pleased, you know that.'

'I know that. It's just ...'

'Just what?' she asked.

'I was just wondering if we shouldn't think of a smaller place.'

'Why?' she demanded, fiercely. 'I don't want a smaller place, Kevin. I've dreamt about owning a house like Island View since I was a little girl. This house is a dream come true for me.'

He nodded, unsure of what to say.

'Tell me the truth: do you like the house?'

'I do. Of course I do. I mean ... it's really great. I was just thinking of you in a couple of years' time when I'm gone. You'll be all alone there.'

Christine smiled almost sadly. 'I've just turned thirty-four, Kevin. I know that may sound positively geriatric to you, but

I'm still a young woman. It's not outside the bounds of possibility that I might meet someone again.' She blinked away a sudden image of Mark Cunningham as she said it.

Kevin looked at her in astonishment. He had never heard his mother speak like this before. Lifting his cup of tea, he sat back into the high leather seat, and looked at her critically, trying to see her as a woman and not as his mother. He had to admit that she was pretty, maybe even beautiful.

'Trapped at home in a housing estate with nothing to do and no money to do it with, I'd very few chances of meeting anyone. But I've got the money now. I'm going to start living, Kevin,' she said, seriously.

He nodded slowly. 'You should.' Then he grinned. 'So long as you don't turn into one of those mothers who start dressing like teenagers ... and then start dating them.'

'I'll try not to do that,' she said, standing up. 'But I can't promise!'

They turned to the left as they came out of the café and crossed O'Connell Bridge. Christine dropped her sunglasses over her eyes, enjoying the anonymity they gave. She was sure no picture of her had been published in the paper; still, she didn't want to run the risk of being recognised.

'Where to now?' Kevin asked.

'Bank first. I want to get some cash.' She lowered her voice. 'We've gone through the best part of a thousand since last Monday ... and, you know, for the life of me I don't know where it's all gone.'

'Easy come, easy go,' Kevin quipped.

'Last week, I could tell you to the penny exactly how much I had in my purse.'

'Last week you hadn't got a thousand notes in your purse, and more than two million in the bank,' Kevin reminded her.

* * *

Christine took two thousand in cash out of the bank. As the teller was counting out the second thousand, Joseph Chambers appeared out of his office. Spotting Christine, the bank manager raised his hand in greeting and came hurrying over. 'And how are you today, Mrs Quinn?'

'Very good. And you, Mr Chambers?'

'Good. Good. Have your credit cards arrived yet?'

'Not yet.' She suddenly realised they would have gone to the old address. She would have to have her post re-directed.

'I put a priority tag on them,' the bank manager assured her. 'They should be through either today or tomorrow. But your cheque cards came in this morning.'

Crouching down, and giving Christine a clear view of his bald spot, he rooted under the desk and pulled out two plastic cheque cards. 'I'll need your signatures here,' he said, passing them a felt-tipped pen.

'I trust everything is going well, Mrs Quinn. I cleared that cheque for ten thousand. It was presented yesterday afternoon.'

'That was quick. I only wrote it yesterday morning.'

'So I noticed.' Christine wondered if he'd ask what she had spent ten grand on. 'Have you decided on a property yet?' he asked.

'Yes, I have. I'll speak to you about that soon. And we must talk about investments,' she added.

'Any time. Just give me a ring to let me know when you're coming in. Perhaps we could discuss it over lunch?'

Caught off guard, unsure how to respond, she finally nodded. 'Yes, that would be nice.'

'Well, give me a ring as soon as you're free.'

'I'll do that. Good morning, Mr Chambers.'

'Joseph. Call me Joseph.'

'Goodbye, Joseph.'

'What are you grinning at?' Kevin asked as they stepped out onto O'Connell Street.

'Do you remember the last time I was asked out for a meal?'

He shook his head.

'Well, neither do I. But in the last two days I've got two invitations; dinner with Mark tonight, and lunch with my bank manager in the near future. Must be my new perfume,' she said, sniffing at her wrists.

'The smell of money,' Kevin remarked, as they turned down Henry Street. 'Now, what do we get first? And before we start, how do we get it back to the house?'

'We'll have it delivered, of course!' she said. 'But I may be a while buying the beds. Why don't you go over to Peats and pick out the TVs and and video?'

Kevin smiled in relief. 'Right. We'll meet at Arnotts for lunch at two, okay?.'

* * *

Christine had bought the beds in a matter of minutes. She knew exactly what she wanted when she strolled into the bedding department. When she'd first walked into the master bedroom in Island View, she'd promised herself the biggest bed she could find, something she could stretch out on, something luxurious and dramatic. She'd spent her whole life in small cramped beds that were either too narrow or too short – or both – and even when she was sleeping with Robert, he usually hogged most of the bed, leaving her hanging onto a thin strip along the edge.

A young man in a crisp white shirt and thin black tie wound his way through the beds towards her. She thought he looked about Kevin's age.

'Can I help you?' he asked politely.

'I'm looking for a bed ... well, two, actually. I want a single bed, and then the largest double bed you have.'

The young man nodded. 'Well, this is our standard single bed. An Odearest ...'

'I'll take it,' Christine said, barely glancing at the bed.

'Don't you want to know the price?' he asked in surprise.

'Not really. I'll take it.'

'Yes, ma'am.' Somewhat bemused, the sales assistant led her across the floor to the array of double beds.

'This is the king-size ...' he began.

'And is this the largest you have?'

'Well, we do have this other model here in stock at the moment. It's two feet wider than the king size.'

It was so big she wouldn't have been able to get it into her old bedroom ... but it was just right for the new house. She had a sudden image of herself lying naked on the bed ...

'I'll take it,' she said, deliberately not looking at the price tag.

'Yes, ma'am!'

'And you will deliver?'

'Of course.' The sales assistant was beginning to realise that this was a genuine sale. The sort that happened once a year, if you were lucky.

The bill came to just under two thousand pounds.

'I'll need your address and phone number,' the assistant said. 'We'll give you a ring before the van goes out.'

'I've just moved in to a new house and the phone isn't in. You'd better let me ring you in the next day or two.' She wrote out her new address – suddenly wondering just how to spell Killiney: with one L or two?

She must have some address cards printed up, and some headed paper too, on really nice-quality paper ... maybe with gold edging ...

'Thank you very much Mrs ...' the assistant glanced at the name and address, '... Mrs Quinn.'

Christine saw him frown; she knew he found the name

vaguely familiar, and he was trying to remember where he'd heard it. Picking up her bags, she turned away before he could ask any questions.

Maybe she'd think seriously about changing her name.

Chapter 47

'Well frankly, Mark, I'm astonished.' Mark Cunningham sat on the end of his mother's bed and watched her devour her usual huge breakfast. She ate as if she hadn't eaten for a month, as usual. Despite her enormous appetite, she remained a tiny bird-like woman, and she used her deceptively frail and fragile appearance to her advantage.

'You should have asked me first,' she said querulously.

'I did, Mother,' he said defensively. He was thirty-eight, and yet she still managed to make him feel like an eight-year-old.

'You told me you were inviting our new neighbour over for dinner ...' she began.

'And you agreed. In fact, you said it was a very good idea,' he added.

'But you didn't tell me she was this lottery winner I've read about in the newspaper.' Her mouth twisted as she said the words 'lottery' and 'newspaper' as if she'd tasted something bitter. 'A now you tell me she's a separated woman with a seventeen-year-old son.'

'Does that make a difference?' he asked.

'Mark, you're being deliberately obtuse. Of course it makes a difference.' Celeste Cunningham pushed herself higher in the bed. Against her pale face and snow-white hair, her blue eyes burned fiercely. 'I'm mean, we really don't want you associating with people of that sort.'

'Mother!' Mark Cunningham took a deep breath and counted slowly to ten. 'You haven't met the woman. I have. She is a perfectly nice, perfectly ordinary young woman, who has had a stroke of good fortune, and has used some of that good fortune to buy the house next door. That's all.'

'You spent a lot of time around there yesterday.'

'I was pulling weeds out of the pond. And you were the person who promised the Kellys that I'd look after the garden. As if I'd nothing else to do.'

Celeste Cunningham ignored him. 'And then you brought that snack around to her.'

'She hadn't eaten all day. It was the least I could do. And I would have done it for anyone.'

'I wonder. Is she blond?' she asked suddenly. She nodded decisively. 'I bet she's blond.'

'What's that got to do with it?' he asked blankly.

'All of your girlfriends have been blond.'

'Susan was a brunette.'

'That was dyed.'

Mark sighed in exasperation. 'Mother; I've just met the woman. I've absolutely no interest in her,' he said quickly.

'I'm sure,' she said in disbelief. 'You said the same about Annette, and you nearly married her!'

'I did not.'

'I read it in the newspaper.'

'So you knew it was true!'

'If it wasn't true, you would have sued them. But you didn't sue, so it must have been true,' she said triumphantly. 'Your own mother, and I had to read about it in the newspaper,' she added.

'Mother, that was gossip column tittle-tattle. If they see you with the same person more than once, then you're engaged. And you don't sue the papers over rubbish like that.'

'Your brother never got his name in the paper.'

'James is an accountant, not exactly a high-profile job.'

'He's not photographed in night clubs.'

'One night club.'

'And he's not seen at the races with some dolly-bird on his arm, and what about the photograph of you at the première of *Les Miserables* a few months ago with two women! You'd never see James doing that.'

Mark grinned. 'James is fifteen years older than me, bald as a coot and, in my professional opinion, about seven stone overweight. And if Moira saw him even look at another woman, she'd run a knife through him.'

'If you're not careful, you'll have people saying you're merry.' She nodded firmly. 'That's what they'll say.'

'Merry?' he said blankly.

'Merry. Happy. Gay.'

'Mother! You're impossible.'

'I'm only looking out for you, Mark,' she said. 'Someone has to.'

'Yes, God knows. How I managed to live this long, make my way through college, survive three years in a New York casualty department, and now hold down this job without your assistance is quite beyond me.'

'Don't be sarcastic. It doesn't suit you.' She lifted the tray and handed it to him. 'Here, you can take this now. I've lost my appetite; I couldn't eat another morsel.'

Mark looked at the tray. There wasn't another morsel left to eat.

'I don't think I'm well enough to prepare a meal,' she said. 'I'm seventy-seven. You know that. I'm not as strong as I used to be.'

'As your doctor, I can confirm that you are the healthiest woman I know. You've the constitution of a horse.'

'That's all very well for you to say. But I haven't got long left. My mother died when she was forty.'

'She died in childbirth. I think the chances of you going that way are slim enough!' he grinned.

Celeste Cunningham snuggled deeper under the covers, until only the top of her snow-white hair showed. 'I don't think I'll get up today,' she said weakly. 'I feel far too tired. You'll have to cancel this Christina woman.'

'Christine, Mother, Christine.'

'Whatever.'

Mark turned away, pausing by the door. 'I'm sure I couldn't do that, Mother. I mean, I have extended the invitation; it would be ill-mannered and not very neighbourly to cancel now. I think I'd better book some place for dinner. I wonder if the Grey Door or the Old Dublin would be able to fit us in.' He pulled the door closed before she could respond, and then hurried downstairs, a broad smile on his face.

If his mother behaved true to form, she'd phone him in his surgery around noon, and tell him that she had managed to drag herself out of bed for his sake. She'd tell him that she might be able to throw together a few things for supper, just so long as he wasn't expecting something grand.

He'd thank her for making the effort on his behalf, and bring her home a big bunch of flowers ... and find she had prepared a banquet.

As usual.

Chapter 48

Robert Quinn pressed the thin sliver of metal into the lock, turned it, turned it again, then jerked it up. The door clicked open. Without turning round, he stepped into the hall and closed the door behind him. Easier than opening it with a key and as quick.

The hall was awash with letters. His thin lips twisted in an ugly smile: these losers stood no chance, begging for a hand-out. If you wanted anything in this world, you didn't ask, you took. Mind you, Christine was so soft, she'd probably end up giving a load of money away. Well, she could give it out of her share.

Taking care not to step on any of the letters in case he left the imprint of his shoe, Robert quickly checked through the down-stairs rooms, then upstairs, to make sure the house was empty. The last thing he needed now was to discover that there was someone in the house. He wasn't going to go back to prison, not when he was so close to the jackpot. When he was satisfied that the house was empty, he began a methodical search.

He started with Christine's bedroom. She hadn't changed a thing since he'd last slept in the house – except, strangely enough, the bed, he noticed, smirking at the single bed. She must have dumped the bed they'd bought together when they moved in. She probably still kept everything where she used to keep it: in the bottom drawer of the bedside locker.

Kneeling on the floor, he pulled the drawer open. Right again. His gloved fingers sorted systematically through the material in the drawer, but it was the usual assortment of electricity and gas bills, old bingo books, miscellaneous receipts, ads torn from magazines, knitting patterns.

At the bottom of the drawer he discovered a black-and-white picture of Christine and himself standing outside the registry office in Molesworth Street. He almost didn't recognise the two people in the photograph. He looked so young and gawky, she pretty and unsure in her light suit. Another time, another place. Different people. He remembered the date well: 21 June 1980. The worst mistake he had ever made. He was about to put the picture back into the drawer when he realised that Webb would probably pay good money for it for his book.

Shoving it into an inside pocket, he checked through the other drawers in the bedside locker, then moved on to the dressing table, careful not to disturb anything, though the room was in such a mess that it was doubtful if anything he did now would be noticed. That was unlike Christine; she was usually so tidy, she used to drive him mad. She'd probably made the mess when she packed her bags ... and that was another sign that she wouldn't be back. Finally, he ran his hands under the mattress and under her pillow.

Nothing.

Frustrated, Robert crouched in front of the dressing table and stared at his reflection. He was tempted to drive his fist through the glass, but he knew if he released the rage that bubbled constantly inside him now, he would probably trash the house. And besides, he didn't want his dear wife to even suspect that he was looking for her. He wanted his appearance to be a big surprise.

He took a deep breath, calming himself. Okay. So there was nothing here; maybe downstairs, then.

There were more begging letters in the kitchen. Christine had obviously read through these. Some had been crumpled and thrown on the floor, a few others were spread out on the table. Ignoring them, Robert first spread a sheet of newspaper on the floor, then emptied the contents of the flap-top bin out onto it, and poked through the sticky mess, looking for anything with an address on it.

Nothing.

Folding the newspaper, catching up the rubbish, he dumped everything back into the bin and then moved on to the notice-board, his gloved fingers lifting the numerous scraps of paper, notices, reminders, bills and special offers.

Nothing.

He went through the sitting room quickly. They rarely used the room even when he was living there. It was set aside for visitors, and there had been precious few of those over the years.

Less then fifteen minutes from the moment he entered the house, Robert returned to the kitchen, convinced that there were no hints, no clues to her present whereabouts. Maybe she had simply walked out of the house, determined to stay in the first guest house or hotel that came to mind. Maybe they'd gone down the country, or gone away ... but no, they hadn't gone away because he'd come across her passport in one of the drawers upstairs.

He'd have to talk to Helen Keogh then. Christine had, obviously.

There were two cups on the draining board. Robert slumped at the kitchen table and looked at them. He remembered Webb had told him that Keogh had come around the morning Christine left – yesterday morning, in fact. Robert nodded. They'd sat at this table and made their plans. What had they talked about? He could ask Helen Keogh – politely or not – but if he did that, Christine would know he was around, and then she'd disappear for good. And yet if he didn't soon find out where she was, she would start to blend into her new life, maybe even change her name, and then he'd never get to her.

'Fuck it!' In a fit of frustration, he swept his hand across the table, scattering the letters onto the floor.

Colour flickered among them.

Reaching down, Robert plucked an estate agent's advertisement sheet from the assortment of fallen letters. Turning it over, he looked at a colour picture of a house, large, red-bricked, ancient and pretentious. His lips drew back in a feral grin; now he knew what the two women had been talking about. Turning over the sheet again, he read the name aloud, the sound echoing flatly in the empty kitchen.

'Island View, Killiney Hill.'

Chapter 49

'That's terrible. Terrible.' Harry Webb nodded sympathetically and checked his tape recorder to make sure there was enough tape left. This was great stuff; he could already see the headline:

SORROW OF JILTED LOTTERY
WINNER'S FIANCEE

Pretty Sandra Miller, fiancée of Kevin Quinn, son of the lottery multi-millionaire, Christine Quinn, wept today as she described how her boyfriend had jilted her even as plans for their wedding were well underway. 'He lost all interest in me when he won the money,' she said.

Mrs Betty Miller put down her teacup and stared at the reporter. 'I have taken legal advice,' she said importantly. 'And I have been told that I have an excellent case for breach of contract.'

Sandra Miller turned to look at her mother, eyes and mouth wide in astonishment. This was obviously news to her.

'After all, he proposed to my Sandra. We'd even started looking at hotels for the reception.'

'Ma ...' Sandra began.

Betty Miller kicked her daughter's ankles.

'Of course, I'm sure the lad had nothing to do with it. It's that mother of his. She always considered herself too grand for the likes of us. Probably thinks that now she has money she'd be able to make a better match for her son.'

'Ma ...'

'She's never liked me of course, but that's because she knew

I could see right through the likes of her.' Betty Miller took a deep breath and sighed almost sadly. 'But he proposed and my Sandra accepted, and in law, that's as good as a written contract ...'

Harry Webb leaned over, pretending to look at his tape, but in reality to hide the smile on his face. Was this woman for real? And who was it had said that a verbal contract wasn't worth the paper it was written on?

'If he doesn't want to marry my Sandra that's fine. We won't force him to do anything he doesn't want to, of course. But ...' she lowered her voice and leaned across the table, 'he slept with her.'

'Ah, Ma, for Christ's sake,' Sandra snapped, and stormed out of the room.

'You can see how upset she is,' Betty Miller said sympathetically. She leaned across the table again. 'And ... she was a virgin until they slept together.'

LOTTERY WINNER TOOK MY VIRGINITY

Webb took another biscuit; this was getting better and better.

Chapter 50

They had lunch in the restaurant in Arnotts. Christine stood in the queue to pay for their lunch while Kevin looked for seats. While she was waiting, she worked out what she had spent. In the past three hours she had bought two beds — one for herself, the biggest she could find, a smaller one for Kevin — a gorgeous Persian rug for the bedroom floor, three standard lamps, two bedside lamps with leaded-glass shades, two sets of cream silk sheets, a handwoven beaded quilt, a complete set of copper saucepans, a complete set of Le Creuset pots, an Italian espresso coffee maker ...

She stopped. How much had she spent? She tried to total the items in her head. And she hadn't even counted the scarves, the handknit cotton sweaters ... She stood rigid in stunned shock when she realised she must have spent about ten thousand pounds.

Without noticing. And in less than less than three hours.

And they still hadn't bought the TV and the video.

The highest wage Robert ever earned had been ten thousand a year.

But it was still only nine days' interest on her winnings, wasn't it? And the two million was still intact, wasn't it? She broke out in a cold sweat as she tried frantically to calculate it all.

Finally she realised that the money she was spending now *did* come from the two hundred and twenty-five thousand, seven hundred and ninety-five pounds she had also won. Even when she bought the house, she still wouldn't have broken into the two million. Suddenly the amount of money, the sheer enormity of it began to sink in. She could spend like that and still be safe.

But what had she just done? She didn't actually *want* half of that stuff; she'd probably never even use it. Why, for God's sake, had she bought three lamps? And where was she going to put them? And she didn't even know how to use the espresso maker. In fact, she hated strong Italian coffee.

But, to be able spend like that without thinking, without counting the cost, was exhilarating ... and absolutely terrifying. If she kept this up, she'd run through the two million in no time at all. What she had just done was stupid – a binge – and now that she'd got it out of her system, she wouldn't do it again.

Christine slid into a seat opposite Kevin and began unloading the tray. 'Chilli for you, is that all right?'

'Yea, fine. I was thinking,' he said immediately, as he tucked into the food, 'I was thinking, we should get a car.'

Christine nodded. 'I agree.'

He looked up, eyes wide with surprise. 'You do?'

'I do,' she smiled. She had picked the lasagne for herself and was beginning to regret it. She didn't want to spoil her appetite for dinner with the Cunninghams. 'What should we get?'

'Something fast, a GTI ...'

Christine shook her head. 'I was thinking more along the lines of a Merc or a BMW.'

'Bit stodgy. Not quite your image. Your new image,' he added. 'When can we get it? he asked.

'Well, you know we *could* go out right this minute and buy one ... however, there is one slight problem.'

Kevin paused with a forkful of chilli half-way to his mouth.

'I can't drive.'

'Yes, you can. What about that car Dad – Robert – had? You drove that.'

Christine stared at her plate. She hadn't thought about Robert's car for a long time. When he'd changed jobs, they'd been forced to let it go, but it had been fun while they had it. She smiled, remembering his attempts to teach her to drive. Every lesson had ended in an argument. Eventually Tommy Keogh, Helen's husband, had shown her the basics in two lessons. She remembered Sunday afternoon trips to Dollymount, Glendalough, Greystones, the three of them singing in the car at the tops of their voices.

That was another time, another world entirely.

'It's been more than ten years since I last sat behind the wheel of a car. And I haven't got a licence. We'll get lessons first – both of us – and then we'll choose a car.'

'Great. When will we start?'

'Well, let's leave it a week or two first. Let's take things slowly.' Christine pushed her lasagne around the plate. 'What are you going to do this afternoon?'

He shook his head. 'I'd nothing planned. Why?'

'I was thinking you should buy yourself some new clothes for tonight's dinner. Maybe a nice sports coat and a pair of cords. Get yourself a pair of shoes too.'

'Aw, Mum, you're not serious!'

'I am. I don't want you making a show of me by turning up in jeans and a tee-shirt.'

Kevin sighed. 'Look, Mum, about this dinner tonight. I really don't want to go.'

'You have to.'

'No, I don't.'

'Kevin,' Christine warned.

'Look,' he said reasonably. 'I'd be bored. And if I'm bored you're going to get pissed off with me, and that means we'll have an argument later. If I don't go,' he added, 'it'll means you get to chat to your Doctor Cunningham all by yourself.'

'Doctor Cunningham's mother will be there too.'

'The old biddy will probably nod off during the soup.' When he made her smile, he pressed home his advantage. 'Come on, you know what I'm saying makes sense. You'll have a much better time without me. You know you'd be on edge all through the meal, making sure I used the right knife and didn't drink soup with a fork, and hoping I wouldn't say something you don't want them to know.'

Christine chewed on the inside of her lip. What Kevin said made perfect sense; she would be more at ease without him there. 'But what'll you do while I'm gone?' she asked eventually.

Bending his head to hide his triumphant smile, Kevin reached down into the bag at his feet and produced a box. 'I used some of the money you gave me to buy a portable CD player.' He opened the box, showing her a flat black machine with a raised circular section. 'It's like a walkman, but it plays CDs. Works off the mains or batteries. And the sound, Mum, you have to hear the sound to believe it: the sound is just incredible, so clear you'd think you were there with the band. I was going to go into Virgin and get myself some CDs.' He pushed the CD player back into its box. 'So you see, it won't bother me staying at home.'

Christine looked uncertain, though they both knew she had already reached a decision. 'We'll talk about it later. Now, I want you to do something for me. I want you to take the parcels back to the new house and wait for me.'

'Sure. Where will you be?'

'I've a few bits and pieces to do around town. Then I want to go out to the old house just to see if there's any post and sort out things like the change of address.'

'You'd better not give the new address in the local post office. It'd be all over the estate in hours.'

'You're right.' She hadn't thought of that. 'What should I do?'

'Maybe have Helen collect all the mail and forward it to you?' he suggested.

Christine nodded. 'Yes. I'm sure Helen wouldn't mind. I'll do that.'

'What time will you be home?'

'Around tea time. Maybe you could stop at the shops and get some milk, tea and sugar. We'll shop properly when we get a fridge.'

'We can always use the fridge in the house,' he suggested.

Christine paused. 'No, Kevin. I've spent a lifetime using other people's cast-offs. We'll go into Power City or the ESB and have a look at fridges and freezers in the morning.'

Kevin gathered up the parcels. 'How am I going to get all these home?' he grumbled.

'Treat yourself to a taxi.'

'Another taxi! I've been in more taxis in the last few days ... At this rate we're going to run through the two mil in no time.'

'We won't,' she promised, sincerely. 'This money is going to see us through for the rest of our lives. I swear it.'

* * *

'I've been invited to dinner,' Christine confided to Maurice O'Connor.

The hairdresser nodded but said nothing. He had long ago realised that most of his clients weren't really interested in what he had to say; they were only interested in listening to themselves talk.

'I want a particular look ...' she said slowly.

'What sort of look: casual, sophisticated, sporty, professional?'

'I'm not sure,' she confessed. She raised her head and looked into the mirror. With the towel around her neck, her damp hair hanging lank around her face and without make-up, it was very easy to see the old Christine Quinn. Last week's Christine Quinn.

'Is this someone you wish to impress?' Maurice asked.

'Yes. Absolutely.'

'A man?'

Christine felt colour rise on her cheeks. She nodded. 'A man.'

'Will you be dining alone?'

'No. With his mother,' she smiled.

'Must be serious, then,' Maurice grinned.

'He's my new neighbour.'

'What sort of person is he?'

'I don't know,' Christine confessed. 'I know very little about him. He's a doctor.'

Maurice placed his hands on either side of her head, straightening her hair, and watched her reflection in the mirror. 'Okay, so he's a professional man. Young?'

'Late thirties.'

'Still only a child, then! How about a very elegant, swept-back look?' He caught her damp hair and piled it up on top of her head. 'It will show off your long neck and fine cheekbones. And when you're finished you simply pull out the pins and shake it loose.'

Christine tried to imagine herself with the new hairstyle, but couldn't. 'Do it,' she said. 'I'm entirely in your hands.'

'What are you going to wear?' Maurice asked, his hands busy in her hair.

'I've just bought something new.' She had spotted the peacock-blue silk sheath dress in Brown Thomas's window on her way up to the hairdresser's. It was cut in a vaguely oriental design, with a very proper high collar and long sleeves, and it ended just above the knees. It was also slit along the left side almost to the hip. She had gone into the shop with the vague idea of trying it on and maybe looking for something else. She knew some of the new clothes she'd bought would do for the evening, but, for reasons which she couldn't entirely explain to herself, she wanted to impress Mark Cunningham. Once she tried the dress on and saw herself in the full-length mirror, she couldn't resist it. The delicate cloth moulded itself to her body, emphasising her slender figure, accentuating her breasts, and the daring slit showed off her legs. The young female assistant told her that it was by Jean-Louis Scherrer, whom Christine supposed was a fashion designer, but the name meant nothing to her. It was reduced to three hundred pounds and she bought it on impulse. She seemed to be buying a lot of things on impulse now, but, having spent a lifetime of scrimping and saving and counting every penny, it gave her a great deal of pleasure just to be able to say, 'I'll take it,' without having to check the price first.

However, now she was beginning to regret buying the dress. Maybe it was too much, too flashy. She didn't want to turn up overdressed.

'Don't frown,' Maurice said gently. 'You'll give yourself lines.'

'I was thinking,' she said, slowly. 'Can I ask your advice?'

'Of course. I get more confessions in this chair than a priest does in a confessional. And they're treated with the same confidence.'

'I told you I was invited to dinner by my new neighbour.'

'And his mother.'

'And his mother. I want to make a good impression. I've just bought a new dress, which is absolutely stunning, but a little ...' she paused, hunting for the proper word.

'*Risqué* ... revealing?' Maurice supplied.

'Daring,' she said eventually. 'It's very dramatic, and fairly demure except for a long slit up the side. I'm just wondering whether I should I wear it or not. I don't want to appear overdressed. What do you think?'

'Is this your first visit to your neighbours?'

'It is.'

'And it is a wealthy neighbourhood?'

'Very.'

'Have you met the mother yet?'

'No.'

'I'm not sure about your neighbour. Maybe he'll be casual, but you can be sure the mother won't be. And if she's dressed to the nines and you're casual, you'll be intimidated. If you want him to notice you, if you want to make an impression, then wear it. Knock him dead!'

Christine nodded decisively. 'I will.'

Chapter 51

'Christine? Christine!' Helen Keogh stepped back from the door. 'My God, I almost didn't recognise you.'

Helen had been surprised by her friend's appearance yesterday, but now she was astonished. The transformation was sensational. Christine's hair had been swept back and up, giving her a sophisticated and regal look, and adding two inches to her height. With the dark glasses over her eyes and her flattering make-up, she was virtually unrecognisable as the woman who had lived down the street.

'You look beautiful,' Helen said simply. And it was true. When she saw Christine yesterday morning, she was pretty; now she was stunning. 'If that's what money can do for you, then I want some too,' she smiled, leading the way into the kitchen.

'I won't tell you how much it cost. It would frighten you,' Christine said with a tight grin. She was disturbed because she felt unaccountably ill at ease in her friend's presence. For the first time in her life, she noticed the bleakness of Helen's kitchen, the spatters of grease on the wall behind the cooker, the broken tile above the sink, the cracked lino, the ugly speckling of rust on the fridge door. But she was sure that if she looked at her old house with new eyes, she would see exactly the same faults – and more.

'How's the new house?'

'Oh, it's lovely, Helen. You'll have to come and see it. I bought some things for it today. I just can't wait to see it furnished.' She stopped suddenly, realising that it must sound like boasting.

But Helen was nodding, happy with her friend's good fortune. 'Go on. What did you get?'

'Actually, I went a bit crazy, Helen. I don't know what came over me. Let me see, I got several lamps – about five altogether, I think – and the slinkiest sheets you ever saw, and a really expensive Persian rug for beside the bed, and scarves, and a coffee maker ... Oh, I can't remember it all. I really can't.'

'And that was just this morning?' Helen asked.

'Three hours. God knows what's going to happen when I get a full day in town. Then I went and got my hair done. I know I only had it done the day before yesterday, but I'm having dinner tonight with my next-door neighbour,' she added.

Helen looked up in surprise.

'Doctor Mark Cunningham. Tall, dark, very handsome, a surgeon.'

'Married?'

'Single.'

Helen started laughing. 'Now that was very quick. You only moved in yesterday.'

'You can take that smirk off your face, Helen Keogh. He's perfectly charming ...'

'I can tell that from your description.'

'... and his mother will be there too.'

Helen poured tea into two cups and put one down in front of Christine. She sat down at the other side of the table, resting her elbows on the scored surface. 'I've nothing to offer you. There's not a biscuit in the house,' she said. 'I haven't gone shopping yet. I'm waiting for Tommy to come in with his wages. Money's tight this week because we bought some of Miranda's schoolbooks. Forty-eight pounds, and that's only for three subjects. The fella in the shop said the entire list would come close to ninety.'

'Let me help,' Christine said immediately, reaching for her bag.

'No,' Helen said sharply, then lowered her voice. 'No, Christine. It's very kind of you, but I wasn't telling you just so that you'd offer me money.'

'I know that. It never even crossed my mind,' she lied. 'But whenever I was short, you helped me when you had it. And now I have it; let me give it to you ... let me pay you back a little for all that you've given me down through the years.'

Helen shook her head.

'It's not charity,' Christine said quickly. 'I wouldn't offer you charity. Look on it as repayment of a loan. And no-one will know, not even Tommy. It'll be just between you and me.'

Helen shook her head again, but less forcefully.

Christine opened her bag, reached into the envelope and pulled out ten fifties, folded them over twice, and pushed them across the table into her friend's hand, without letting her see how much there was. 'Please take it,' she whispered. 'It would make me very happy.'

Helen started to shake her head, but Christine squeezed her fingers tightly. 'Please.'

Helen's fingers tightened over the money, and then she drew it down and shoved it into her apron pocket without looking at it.

The two women sat in silence for a while. Five hundred pounds meant absolutely nothing to Christine, and yet she knew how much it would mean to Helen; she knew how much it would have meant to herself last week.

Christine finally raised her head. 'I've come back to ask you a favour.'

'Of course,' Helen said immediately. 'You know you only have to ask.'

'I was going to go down to the post office and give them the new address to have my post re-directed, but Kevin reminded me that if we did, the news would be around the whole estate in hours.'

'What don't you let me collect it and send it on to you?'

Helen suggested immediately.

'That's just what I was going to ask.'

'What are you going to do about the begging letters? I saw the postman this morning. He came in a van just to do your delivery.'

'I haven't even thought about it,' Christine admitted. 'There are so many deserving cases, I'm not sure who to give it to, and I suppose some of the letters must be hoaxes. I'll give some money to the Vincent de Paul and the Samaritans, and I thought about giving some to Childline.' She suddenly looked at Helen. 'Maybe we could go through them together. You could help me choose the more deserving cases. You're better at reading people than I am.'

Helen nodded. 'I'll do that. If fact, what I'll do,' she added, 'is sort through them here and send you on those I think are genuine.'

'That's a super idea.' Christine stood up. 'I'm sorry for rushing, but I've got to get back. I was just going to go around to the house to see if there was anything I wanted.'

'I'll come with you,' Helen said.

* * *

Christine turned the key in the lock and was about to open the door, pushing against the piled-up post, when a car pulled into the kerb and a voice called, 'Christine! Oh, Christine!'

Christine Quinn's face was an expressionless mask as she turned. Her sister Sheila jumped out of the Volvo Estate, all nervous energy and smiles. Obsessed with her weight, constantly dieting, her younger sister had always been thin, but she was now skinny to the point of ugliness. Today her hair was red. Nick's grinning face appeared on the opposite side of the car, sweat gleaming on his bald head.

Sheila swept up the path and wrapped her arms around

Christine, enveloping her in a cloud of floral perfume. 'Oh, I'm so delighted for you. Isn't it wonderful news? Marvellous. And you look so lovely. Did you get your hair done locally? I must recommend my own hairdresser. I mean, he's just excellent.' She lowered her voice to a confidential whisper. 'He'd do it much better than that. It doesn't really suit you that way.'

'I'm busy, Sheila,' Christine said icily, embarrassed and annoyed by her sister's display of affection.

'Oh, I'm sure you are. So much to do. Look, Nick has booked dinner for the four of us – the pair of us, you and Kevin – at this rather lovely little restaurant he knows. We can have a good old chin wag over a meal.'

'I can't,' Christine said shortly.

'Why not?' Sheila pouted. 'Nick has booked a table for eight o'clock.'

'Well, you should have asked me first.'

'But we knew you'd be here. You're always here. You never go anywhere.'

It gave Christine a great deal of satisfaction to say, 'I have a dinner engagement tonight. And now,' she added, 'you really must excuse me.' Stepping into the hall, she slammed the door with unnecessary force. It was something she'd wanted to do for years.

Sheila and Nick stood on the footpath and stared open-mouthed at the house. Finally, Sheila took a deep breath and cried, 'Well ...!'

They were turning back to the car when a small man with bad teeth stepped into their path. 'I'm Harry Webb, investigative reporter. I wonder if I could have a few words with you?'

Chapter 52

Christine deliberately dressed with her back to the mirrored doors of the wardrobes. She was determined not to look at herself until she was completely ready. Silk underwear. No bra – she didn't really need one and she didn't want the straps to show. No stockings. She opened her jewellery box and looked inside. She lifted out her mother's string of pearls and looked at them for a few moments before returning them to the box. No rings and no watch. She would go into town in the morning and buy a new watch to replace the tiny square-faced one she'd bought herself as a twenty-first birthday present. She would also look at a gold necklace and some earrings. Finally the dress. She stepped into it and buttoned up the many tiny pearl buttons that fastened along the left side. She straightened the collar and tugged the sleeves straight. She slipped into a pair of midnight-blue shoes she had bought to match the dress ... and then turned around.

A dozen images of an elegant, sophisticated woman stared back at her.

Christine walked up to the mirror and looked critically at her reflection. Less than a week ago she had been doing exactly the same thing – staring at her reflection in a mirror. But the woman who had looked back then was not the woman who was looking at her now.

As she stepped away from the mirror, she realised, once again, that money did make a difference. And what a difference!

The hall door was open as she came down the stairs, walking carefully on the high heels, one hand trailing on the banister. She had filed and painted her nails, the pale red lacquer matching her lipstick, but she wished now she'd had them done properly in town.

Her high heels tapped as she walked out onto the step. The atmosphere was still and silent, the heavy, almost cloying scents of earth and greenery sharpened by the salt air of the sea. She breathed deeply, filling her lungs with the air. Fresh air. Clean air. The smells of the day had stayed with her until now. The metal and sulphur of the city air, the sour odour of stale cooking from Helen's house, and the musty, dry smell of her old house still lingered in her nostrils.

'It's six minutes to eight, Mum,' Kevin called, hurrying down the stairs. He stepped out onto the porch, shading his eyes with his hand.

'There's plenty of time. It will take me exactly three minutes to reach the Cunninghams',' Christine said.

'How do you know?'

'I timed it earlier,' she smiled.

Kevin shook his head. 'It's only dinner, for fuck's sake ...'

'Language!'

'Sorry, Mum. You look amazing,' he added, quickly changing the subject.

'You don't think it's too much?'

'I think it's definitely too much,' he grinned.

'I just want to make a good impression.'

'You'll certainly make an impression.'

Christine turned to look at her son. 'Are you sure you don't want to come?'

He shook his head, pushing strands of blond hair out of his eyes. 'Look, you know I don't. I'm going to stay here and listen to my new CD player. You go and enjoy yourself.'

She nodded uncertainly. 'I'll only be next door if you need me.'

'I'm seventeen,' he reminded her. 'I can look after myself.'

'I'm sure you can,' she said quickly.

'Don't drink too much and be home before midnight,' he said

with a grin, the same advice she always gave him when he was going out for the night.

'I have my key,' she said, giving him the same answer he invariably gave her. She had only taken half a dozen steps down the drive when Kevin called after her. Christine turned round. He was holding the enormous bunch of flowers and the bottle of wine, which she had brought home from town with her.

'You know, Mum,' Kevin said, leaning forward and giving her a quick kiss on the cheek, 'if I didn't know you better, I'd be inclined to think you were as nervous as a girl going on her first date.'

'Don't be ridiculous!' She turned away before he could see the colour on her cheeks.

The gates automatically swung open as she approached and she knew Kevin was watching her in the camera. Juggling the flowers and wine, she waved to him through the camera, then turned right and headed for the Cunninghams'.

Kevin was right. She *was* as nervous as a girl on her first date. But this wasn't a date, she reminded herself. This was a social evening, simply one neighbour inviting a new neighbour to dinner. It had happened on her own estate all the time ... in a smaller way of course. Newcomers would be invited in for a cup of tea or they'd be bought a drink in the pub.

She hoped bringing the flowers and wine was the right thing to do. The flowers cost her twenty pounds in the florist's off Dawson Street and the wine was just under thirty pounds in the wine merchant's just up the road from the National Library. The softly-spoken young man in the shop assured her that it was a very fine wine, showing her the label, pointing out the vintage. It meant nothing to her; Christine usually bought a bottle of wine in the local supermarket every December to go with the turkey on Christmas Day. The last bottle she bought had cost three pounds ninety-nine. Kevin drank most of it, she remembered.

Christine slowed as she approached the Cunningham house. The gates were open, but she wondered if she should press the call button to let them know she was coming.

No. He was expecting her; that's why the gates were open. Taking a deep breath, she turned and walked up the drive, butterflies fluttering in her stomach, suddenly wondering if this was a good idea after all.

Chapter 53

Harry Webb's finger pressed the button again and again, and another half-dozen shots clicked off in rapid succession.

Christine Quinn coming through the gates of Island View ...

A close-up of her face, beautifully made-up, relaxed, smiling, a new elegant hair-style ...

Christine Quinn's head and shoulders against the tree-lined street ...

Christine Quinn balancing a huge bouquet of flowers and a long rectangular box – a wine box – in either arm ...

Christine Quinn striding forward, revealing a daring length of leg through the slit in her vaguely oriental-looking dress ...

Christine Quinn turning into a neighbour's house ...

'That's it,' Webb said. 'Got them all.' He turned to look at Robert Quinn who was sitting behind the wheel. Quinn had insisted on driving and Webb felt he was in no position to argue. He had tried to find out how Quinn had discovered his ex-wife's address, but the big man simply stared at him and said nothing.

'It's hard to believe it's the same woman,' Webb remarked.

Robert Quinn was thinking the same thing. It was hard to believe that this was the woman he'd married years ago. Here was proof, if proof he needed, that with money you could achieve anything. He wondered how much she'd spent in the past week: a fortune if looks were anything to go by. She was obviously spending it as if it was going out of fashion. If he didn't stake his claim soon, there'd be nothing left. He drummed his fingers on the steering wheel of Webb's battered Toyota, thinking furiously. He had been planning on waiting a while, but he would have to move soon.

'What do we do now?' Webb asked.

'We wait.'

'For what?'

'Until she comes out.'

'But that could be ages,' Webb protested. There was a movie on the box he wanted to see.

'We wait until she comes out,' Quinn snapped.

Chapter 54

Kevin watched his mother disappear through the gates, then flicked the switch, locking them again. She had the remote control on her key-ring, she would be able to open them when she came home. He stood at the open door and pulled his earphones onto his head, racking the sound of the portable CD player up to max. Megadeth's *Go to Hell* drowned out the irritating chittering and twittering of the birds and the rattling hiss of the leaves in the trees.

He was bored.

Eight o'clock on a Friday evening. He couldn't remember the last time he spent a Friday evening at home. Right now he should be heading out, meeting a few friends, having a few drinks, maybe taking in a gig, stopping in on a party on the way home.

But that wasn't possible anymore. And all because they had won the money.

That fucking money!

He turned back into the hall and slammed the door behind him. With his hands tucked into the back pockets of his jeans, he wandered from room to room. Maybe it might have been easier if they'd won a smaller amount: a couple of thousand would have made all the difference to their lives, paid off a few bills, bought them a couple of luxuries ... but it wouldn't have completely destroyed their lives in the way that their win had. Two million was just too much. Oh sure, it allowed them to have anything they wanted, to do anything they wanted to do, go anywhere they wanted to go ... except do the things *he* wanted to do, go where *he* wanted to go. The money had made him a prisoner.

Kevin strolled into the kitchen and took the six pack of coke out of the fridge. Pulling one of the cans free, he snapped the tab and drank deeply as he walked up the stairs.

The house was so fucking big! He was never going to be comfortable here, he knew that. And he had a feeling he was never going to be able to get his mother to sell. She was going to blow their fortune on this place, and that really pissed him off. What he needed right now was to get set up in a place of his own. He was wondering how he was going to swing that as he nudged the door of his room closed with his foot. He had access to the bank account; he had a cheque book, and the credit cards would be arriving any day now. Theoretically, he could spend as much as he wanted; his mother had put no limits on him. But he knew there was no way she would let him go and live on his own.

Kevin slumped down on the padded sleeping bag, his back to the wall. He rolled the frosted can against his forehead. Jesus, but he was wound up as tight as a drum, completely wired.

He drank some more coke and reached for a cassette case. The five white tablets he'd bought from Skinny yesterday were concealed inside the empty case. Kevin shook them onto the floor in front of him, arranging them in a straight line. Picking up the first of the small white tablets, he popped it under his tongue, then took a mouthful of coke, allowing the liquid to dissolve the E. Someone had told him once that if you held E under your tongue then it was absorbed quicker into the bloodstream. He didn't know if it was true, but he was willing to try it.

He swallowed the second tablet and then, on impulse, took a third. It'd take about half an hour for the E to hit, and then he'd buzz for a couple of hours. The E would relax him, allow him to think calmly and clearly, make him feel real good, and help him get a good night's sleep. Maybe he'd even come up with some way of making his mother see sense.

He swallowed a fourth tablet.

Chapter 55

'Christine!' Mark Cunningham smiled warmly, but she could see his eyes widening slightly as he took in her outfit. 'You're very welcome.' He stood back to allow her to step into the circular hall. Somewhere in the low sprawling bungalow a series of clocks were pinging and chiming the hour. 'You look stunning,' he said simply.

'Thank you.' Christine smiled. Mark was casually, but stylishly dressed in a pair of light tan cord trousers, a check shirt and a pair of brown loafers. He had obviously recently showered because she could smell soap and aftershave from him. 'I'm not too early, am I?' she asked anxiously.

'Bang on time,' he said. 'Did your son not come?'

'No.' She was about to lie, to make up some excuse, but instead, she said, 'He thought he would be bored and decided to stay at home. I hope that's not a problem.'

'No, of course not. And he's probably right: he might well have been bored. I can remember many dinners my parents dragged me along to ... and it was always on a night when there was something good on the box. Besides,' he added, 'if he was bored, you wouldn't be at your ease.'

Suddenly realising she was still holding onto the flowers and wine, she handed them to Mark. 'The flowers are for your mother. I hope she likes flowers.'

'I adore flowers.' A woman's voice came from behind Christine.

Christine turned as a tiny woman swept out of one of the rooms. Christine wasn't tall, but this woman barely came to her chin. Her skin was smoothly-polished ivory, patterned with tiny hair-thin wrinkles, and she could have been anything from fifty to eighty, although the loose skin on her throat gave a closer indication of her real age. Her white hair was pulled back severely off her face and held in a tight bun at the base of her skull. She stopped in the centre of the hall, directly under a circular skylight which threw a disc of warm evening sunlight onto the highly-polished wooden floor. 'Celeste Cunningham,' she said dramatically, extending a slightly claw-like hand.

Christine stepped forward and held the woman's hand lightly, the skin dry and smooth, almost like paper. She was afraid to press too hard in case she hurt her. 'Christine Quinn,' she smiled. Mrs Cunningham was dressed entirely in black, in a dress that had all the appearance of a nun's habit. The severity was relieved by a string of magnificent pearls and a large cameo broach that sat high on her left shoulder. Christine was relieved she hadn't worn her mother's pearls; they would have looked positively shabby beside Celeste Cunningham's.

Mark handed his mother the flowers. She dipped her head, nostrils flaring. 'These are magnificent. You have excellent taste, my dear. But you shouldn't have.'

She pushed the flowers back into her son's arms. 'Leave these in the kitchen for me, Mark. I'll put them in water presently.' Sliding her arm through Christine's, she led her into a large sitting room, leaving Mark standing in the hall.

'Oh, this is beautiful,' Christine breathed as she stepped into the room. One wall had been replaced by floor-to-ceiling windows and sliding glass doors. The view out over the landscaped gardens was breath-taking.

'It is very pleasant now, although in December it can be a little stark for my taste.' Celeste released Christine's arm and sank into a rigid high-backed armchair. 'Please sit down.' She watched, her face impassive, as Christine sat on the sofa opposite, her dress parting to reveal her thigh. 'How are you settling in? Mark tells me you've bought the Kelly house. Such a nice couple, and a lovely house, though a little old-fashioned for my taste. He was in the computer business, a consultant I believe.'

Christine nodded, unsure of what to say. She had always been sensitive to people's moods and she was becoming increasingly uncomfortable in the old woman's presence. She could sense that, although outwardly polite and charming, Mark's mother didn't welcome her. She had a feeling that this was going to be a long evening.

'Have you lived here long, Mrs Cunningham?' she asked.

'Oh, do call me Celeste. Yes, we've lived here for nearly forty years. My late husband and I moved here before Mark was born. Of course the house was entirely different then. We've changed it bit by bit over the years. The glass wall for example, was Mark's father's idea: he was a surgeon too. You might have heard of him, Dr James Cunningham. He was quite famous in his day. He attended all the best people.'

Christine shook her head.

'But no, I suppose he'd be a little before your time, my dear.'

Christine swivelled around in her seat to look through the windows again. 'Your gardens are magnificent,' she said to break the uneasy silence that followed.

'Yes. Mark looks after the garden. If he hadn't been a doctor, he would have become a gardener.'

'I should have been a gardener,' Mark said, coming into the room and sitting down on the sofa beside Christine. 'The pay is okay, the hours are shorter, there's less hassle and damn all paperwork.'

Celeste Cunningham folded her hands into her lap. 'Ignore him. He was destined to be a doctor from the day he was born.'

Mark glanced at Christine and winked. 'My brother James was the one who was destined to be a doctor, but when he decided that accountancy was his vocation, my destiny was rewritten.'

Celeste sighed. 'Mark, you're impossible. Now, don't embarrass our guest with family gossip. Go and get us some drinks.'

Mark stood up. 'Christine. What will you have? A gin and tonic? Whiskey? Wine?'

'Just some fruit juice, please,' said Christine.

'Oh, you'll have something stronger than that!' Celeste insisted. 'It's not as if you're driving.'

'Actually, I don't take alcohol, except a little wine with food,' replied Christine.

'Well, then, some wine! We have an excellent cellar.'

'Really, I'd prefer not,' said Christine firmly.

'And the usual for you, Mother?' Mark butted in, putting an end to the exchange.

Celeste nodded. There was quite a long pause. 'Do you have children, Christine?'

'A son. Kevin. He's seventeen.'

.

Mark handed around the drinks and then sat down beside Christine again with a glass of red wine in his hand.

'What does your son want to be?' Celeste inquired.

Christine sipped her fresh orange juice carefully. She was conscious of Mark's presence beside her, aware that his eyes had moved down her body, lingered on her legs as he handed her the drink. 'Kevin hasn't made any decisions about his future yet,' she said slowly. 'He's just finished school,' she added.

Celeste sipped her drink. 'Mark knew what he was going to be when he was fourteen.'

'I was *told* what I was going to be ...'

'And college? What about college?' Mrs Cunningham interrupted.

'We haven't even thought about it.'

'Well, you should. I would recommend Trinity. Both my boys went to Trinity. And their father, and his father. Young people will get nowhere without an education these days. Without an education, they stand no chance of a job, and with no jobs, they'll end up sponging off the state and living in some wretched housing estate.'

Christine raised her head and looked into Mrs Cunningham's eyes. 'I've lived all my life on a variety of housing estates,' she said quietly.

'Of course you have, my dear, but now you've moved beyond that.'

'Only through chance. You do know that I won the lottery last Saturday night. Over two and a quarter million pounds. If I hadn't, I'd still be living on that housing estate.' She sipped her drink.

Celeste smiled thinly, coldly. 'You will excuse me, Christine,' she said, suddenly standing up, 'I'll just go and check that everything is in order for dinner. Mark rather sprang this on me!'

'I do hope you haven't gone to any trouble.'

'None at all,' the old woman said sweetly.

Mark remained standing until his mother had left the room, then his shoulders slumped as he relaxed. 'Would you like to walk in the garden?' he asked.

'I'd love to.'

'Take your drink,' he said, pushing back the long glass door. The fragrance of lavender wafted into the room. 'You will have to excuse my mother,' Mark said as they stepped off the patio and onto the lawn. 'She can be somewhat unfriendly and ... old-fashioned at times.'

'She's entitled to be.'

'She doesn't mean to be rude, but at her age, her ideas are fairly entrenched.'

Christine raised her glass and described a semi-circle, encompassing the rigid lines of bushes and shrubs intersected with perfectly circular beds of flowers. The garden was a blaze of colour.

'Did you do all this yourself?' she asked, changing the subject.

'No indeed.' He looked around. 'My father started it, and I try to keep it up. It's far too strict and formal for my taste, but that's how mother likes it ... and so that's how it stays. I prefer informality, naturalness in a garden. Maybe that's why I like yours so much.'

'You know you're welcome any time,' she said quickly.

'Thank you for coming tonight,' he said.

'Thank you for asking me.'

They walked in silence for a while, sipping their drinks, the evening sun warm on their faces. Mark stopped occasionally to pull a dead head off a flower, or pluck off withered leaves. They were both aware that it was a comfortable silence; neither felt under any pressure to fill the stillness with idle chatter.

Christine realised that it was a long time since she had felt so at ease in a man's presence.

He wasn't a threat.

The realisation astonished her. She didn't view Mark as a threat. All her life – from her earliest encounters with her father, then her boyfriend, then the boyfriends before Robert – men had threatened her in one way or another. Nowadays, they simply made her nervous; she was constantly wondering what they wanted from her. In the last couple of years, there had been no man in her life: nor had she missed one in her closed and miserable little world. But now that world had opened up. She watched Mark bending over a shrub, and wondered if there was any chance ...

No such luck, she thought ruefully.

Mark glanced up at his companion. She was not beautiful, in the classical sense, he thought. But she was quite lovely. She carried herself well, and there was an aura of stillness about her which he found intriguing. He guessed that she must be terribly nervous: a young woman plucked from the world she had grown up in and thrust into this strange new life of wealth, where everything had a price, and she could afford it all. But if she was nervous, she disguised it well; she seemed so calm, so still. She didn't rattle on endlessly, nor did she move restlessly. Mark had encountered women like her before, especially when he was working in the casualty wards in New York. They were usually women who had been abused by life, and yet had survived, and by surviving had become stronger. He wondered if his assessment of Christine was correct. He wondered if life had treated her badly. He hoped he was wrong.

The dinner gong rang out and broke his reverie.

'Don't let mother get at you during dinner,' Mark said as they crossed the lawn. He saw Christine's surprised look. 'Oh, she may be my own mother, but I'm not blind to her faults. Her favourite hobby nowadays is baiting people. She thinks because she's so old and frail-looking, she can get away with murder. And she's usually right. People don't answer back.'

'Maybe they should,' Christine said softly.

Chapter 56

Kevin took a deep breath, then blew hard, feeling the tension flow out of him, leaving his entire body tingling. Working his head from side to side, he opened his mouth wide, hearing jaw muscles crack and pop, and yawned hard.

This was just what he needed. A little E to ease away the tensions, allow him to think, make a few plans, sort things out. When you'd got all those other pressures piling up on you, how could you possibly think straight?

The music stopped, but he continued hearing it inside his head, his foot twitching in time to the last beats of the music. His fingers felt numb as he struggled to eject the CD and insert another into the player. The disc tumbled from his hand and rolled away across the floor. Kevin sat and watched it. He couldn't be bothered to stand up and get it and, besides, the play of light across the CD painted it in shimmers of rainbow colours.

He was reaching for the coke can when he knocked it over, the dark liquid foaming across the floor. 'Fuck it,' he giggled. 'Oh shit,' he said suddenly as the coke touched the last of the white tablets he'd laid out, staining it brown. He picked it up and popped it into his dry mouth, swallowed hard, then washed it down with more coke.

He'd taken all five now. Maybe he shouldn't have taken the last one, but he couldn't waste it. It would have been a sin to allow it to dissolve in the coke. They were too expensive for that.

The thought struck him as very funny, and he held himself, arms wrapped tightly around his body, as he giggled uncontrollably. He was aware that under his right hand his heart was pounding hard.

Chapter 57

'Mark didn't give me a lot of time for preparation, so I'm afraid you'll just have to take us as you find us,' Celeste Cunningham said. 'This is just a little everyday supper I threw together earlier ...'

Christine bit the inside of her cheek and deliberately kept her face expressionless as she looked at the table. She was quite sure even the Queen of England didn't eat with her best silver every night.

The Cunninghams' furniture tended to the modern style, smoked glass and metal bars. Christine found it cold and impersonal but she had to admit that, against the dark glass of the circular dining-room table, the display of sparkling cutlery and gleaming crockery was impressive. The flowers she brought had been arranged in an enormous Waterford crystal vase on the table.

'You sit here,' Mrs Cunningham said, indicating a chair to her left, 'where I can talk to you without shouting across the table. Mark, you're in your usual place.' She seemed momentarily puzzled by the fourth setting that had been laid.

'Christine's son, Kevin, had already made arrangements for tonight and couldn't come,' Mark explained.

Brenda, the part-time cook, who was almost as old as Mrs

Cunningham, moved silently around the table, ladling consommé in bowls.

Mark Cunningham sat directly across from Christine. He smiled encouragingly; he was rapidly coming to the conclusion that bringing Christine here tonight, before she even had a chance to settle into the new house, probably wasn't fair. He should have taken her out someplace ... but would that have seemed as if he was asking her out on a date? For all he knew she might have a boyfriend.

Almost as if she read his mind, Celeste Cunningham looked at Christine and said, 'And is there a Mr Quinn anywhere around?'

'There is,' Christine said immediately.

Mark was surprised by his own reaction; he wondered why he felt so disappointed.

'We've been separated for years now,' Christine added. She was looking at the array of knives, forks and spoons laid out on either side of her plate, wondering which one to use first. She remembered reading that you started at the outside and worked in ... or did your start on the inside and work out? She glanced surreptitiously at Mark, watching him reach for a spoon, and she copied him.

'And does your boy ever get to see his father?' Celeste asked.

Christine knew what was happening. The old bitch was pumping her for information which she could then spread around the district. All the gossip about the newcomer; it happened on every estate, rich or poor.

She had two choices. She could tell the truth now or she could lie and tell the old bag a story; but there was every chance that the true story would get out sooner or later, and then she would be branded a liar.

'Robert – my ex – isn't Kevin's father,' she said, not looking at the old woman, her eyes on Mark as she drank a spoonful of the clear consommé.

'Oh.' Celeste Cunningham put a wealth of meaning into the word.

'I was very young when it happened. Young and stupid. The boy told me he loved me, until I became pregnant. Then he changed his mind, or his parents changed it for him. He went on to college. I believe he even became a doctor,' she added, glancing sidelong at the woman.

'What's his name?' Mrs Cunningham asked immediately. 'Mark is sure to know him.'

'I think that's precisely why I won't tell you his name.' Christine smiled to take the sting from her words.

'It must have been very hard bringing up a boy all by yourself,' Celeste persisted, after an awkward pause.

Christine was about to say: I sponged off the state, but said, instead: 'I worked when I could ... and when I couldn't the state supported me.'

'And is Kevin your only child?'

'Yes.'

'Have you no family?'

'I have a sister, but I rarely see her. She has a young family of her own to bring up.'

Celeste Cunningham tut-tutted. 'It must have been very hard,' she repeated, but there was no sympathy in her voice.

'It was hard, but I had good neighbours,' Christine said quietly.

'Well, you'll have good neighbours here too,' Mark said immediately. 'If you want anything, all you have to do is ask. We'll do everything we can to make you welcome, won't we, Mother?'

'How is your consommé, my dear?' Celeste asked, not answering the question.

'Lovely,' Christine said, even though she found it almost tasteless. But she wasn't sure if that was because the clear soup *was* tasteless or because she was aware that Mark was watching her constantly. Curiously, she didn't resent his gaze. She didn't find it intrusive. He wasn't looking at her in the way that some men did, trying to undress her with their eyes. He watched her face, her eyes, her lips, her throat, almost as if he was trying to memorise her features.

Brenda moved around the table, serving lamb, mint sauce, bowls of roast potatoes, string beans, cauliflower and carrots. Christine declined the potatoes, but took a little of everything else.

The conversation centred around the lottery, Celeste sniping away at every opportunity, until Mark changed the topic suddenly.

'Tell me, what do you think of your new house?' he asked.

Christine smiled warmly. 'Oh, it's magnificent ...'

'Well, I've always thought that the master bedroom was particularly gaudy,' Celeste sniffed.

'I especially like the master bedroom,' Christine continued. 'In fact, just today, I bought the largest bed I could find for it.'

'King-size,' Celeste Cunningham stated flatly.

'Bigger than that!' Christine concentrated on cutting the tender lamb. 'King-size is only five feet wide, but I managed to get one seven-and-half feet wide!'

'Where?' Mark asked.

'Arnotts.'

'Oh, I wouldn't shop *there*,' Celeste said, archly.

'Mother shops by catalogue now,' Mark said, irritated by his mother's constant negative tone.

'But only from the best catalogues.' She turned to Christine. 'Are you enjoying your meal, my dear?'

'I am, thank you,' she said quickly. She was hardly tasting it.

'Yes, Brenda is an excellent cook. You will really have to get a daily woman in to help you in that big house. You can get them quite reasonably these days, because many of their husbands are unemployed. Twenty-five or thirty pounds a week is a sufficient wage nowadays.'

'Oh, I'm sure I could afford more. Especially if the husband is unemployed.'

Celeste glanced sharply at her, unsure if the younger woman was mocking her. 'You will need a gardener too. I can recommend Seamus ...'

'Mother, Seamus is ancient. Any one of these days he's going to keel over in the garden. I watched him out there yesterday and I thought he was going to have a pulmonary embolism on the spot.'

'Seamus does all the gardens around here. I believe it would be a mistake to bring in someone new.' Celeste was watching Christine as she was speaking. 'I mean, he's completely trustworthy.'

'He's also pricey, inefficient, slow and neither terribly good nor terribly reliable. He spends more time having cups of tea in the kitchen than he does in the garden. And who cut down my black irises?' Mark demanded.

'That was an accident.'

'Rare black irises,' he said to Christine. 'It took me four years to bring them on, and then, when they finally blossomed, they were stunning. Even you have to admit that, Mother.'

'If you say so.'

'And what did our gardener do? First he cut them down, then he dumped them on the compost heap.' Mark turned back to his mother. 'That's because he was trying to hide them!' He looked at Christine again. 'You don't need a gardener. All you need to do is keep the grass down on the lawn and keep the beds weeded. Your garden is low maintenance; it's designed to look wild and untrammelled.'

Christine wasn't sure what 'untrammelled' meant, but she

had a rough idea.

'If your son takes care of the grass, I'll show you what to do with the rest of the garden. That's if you'd like to learn about gardening.'

Their eyes met, and this time neither looked away.

'I would.'

Celeste Cunningham looked from her son to the young woman, aware that she was missing something, but not sure what. 'Brenda, bring the dessert,' she said loudly. 'Then we'll have coffee in the sitting room.'

Chapter 58

'I really don't think your mother likes me very much,' Christine said softly.

'I'm not sure if my mother likes anyone very much anymore,' Mark replied. They turned at the bottom of the driveway to wave at Celeste Cunningham who had been outlined against the lighted hallway as they'd walked away from the door, but she had turned away.

'You really don't have to walk me home,' Christine said. 'I only live next door, remember.'

'I just thought I'd use the opportunity to apologise for my mother's behaviour,' he said in embarrassment.

'Don't apologise,' Christine said quickly. 'You're not responsible for it.'

'The evening was not a great success,' Mark admitted. He fell into step beside her, his hands tucked deep into his pockets.

It had been a disaster, and had become more and more uncomfortable as the night progressed. Celeste had continued sniping at Christine throughout the meal and on into the evening. The younger woman had impressed Mark by retaining a dignified silence; she simply hadn't risen to most of his mother's gibes. However, this had only infuriated Mrs Cunningham until, by the end of the evening, she had become positively rude. Mark attempted to come to Christine's assistance again and again, but when his mother started putting him down with her caustic remarks, commenting on his social life and bringing up his previous girlfriends, he realised what she was trying to do and decided it was time to call it a night.

'I told you, she didn't like me. I'm not from her class,' she added, sliding her arm through his; it seemed entirely natural.

Mark pretended not to notice her arm, although he was intensely conscious of the heat of her flesh against his. He shook his head. 'It's not that. I thought it would be different with you, because you're a neighbour. But I've seen her do something similar with other women I've brought home ... and they were from her class,' he said. 'In fact that's probably one of the reasons I've no-one at the moment,' he added, suddenly wanting her to know that there was no woman in his life, 'why I remain a so-called eligible bachelor. I bring women home for dinner, my mother insults them, makes them uncomfortable, and drives them away.' He laughed softly. 'God, what must that sound like! A real mammy's boy.'

'It sounds as if your mother isn't really a nice person.'

'I know that.'

'And it sounds as if you've been bringing home the wrong sort of women.' They slowed as they came to Christine's gate. 'Because if they were interested, they wouldn't have allowed themselves to be driven away so easily.'

'Maybe you're right,' he said gently.

Christine lifted her key-ring and pressed the remote control. The gates swung open, hinges squeaking slightly.

'But let me make it up to you,' Mark continued. 'Let's have

dinner again, without my mother this time. What do you say?'

'Yes.'

'Yes? Just like that? Most women I know would have to consult their diary and get back to me.'

'I'm not most women, Mark.'

'I'm coming to realise that,' he said very quietly. 'When?'

'Whenever,' she shrugged.

'Tomorrow night, same time? I'll pick you up,' he suggested. 'But maybe you've something planned?'

Christine leaned forward and brushed her lips against his cheek. 'I've nothing planned for tomorrow night.'

Chapter 59

Robert Quinn drove his elbow into Webb's ribs, waking him with a start. 'Here they come,' he muttered.

Webb scrambled into a sitting position, neck and back muscles protesting. 'What time is it?' he mumbled, digging the heels of his palms into his eyes. 'I feel like shit.'

'Quarter to midnight. Now, shut up.'

They watched the couple walk slowly down the road. Christine was linking the man, her arm pressed lightly against his body. There were deep in conversation.

'Jesus, she's a fast worker,' Webb muttered. 'She can't have known him before yesterday.'

Quinn leaned forward on the steering wheel, staring hard at the couple, trying to make out the man's features in the dim light. Now, just who was this fucker? Some waster out to try and grab a chunk of Christine's fortune, no doubt. Robert's teeth bared in a humourless grin. Well, he was going to be sadly disappointed.

'I can get hold of the electoral register tomorrow and find out who the neighbours are,' Webb muttered.

Neither said anything as Christine leaned forward to kiss the man on the cheek, then she turned and vanished into the shadows. The man remained standing by the gate for a few seconds longer before he too turned away and retraced his steps.

'Now what?' Webb demanded.

'We wait.'

'For what! The night is over.'

'We wait.'

'For how long?'

'We'll give it an hour and see what happens.'

Webb slumped resignedly. What a waste of a fucking night!

*　*　*

But it didn't take an hour. Christine was gone less then five minutes before the gates swung open again and she re-appeared, running fast. Her new hair-style was awry and she was in her bare feet.

The two men looked at each other, saying nothing.

When Christine returned at a run, the dark-haired stranger was running alongside her. He was carrying a black medical bag in his left hand. They raced up Christine's drive.

'Stay here,' Quinn snapped. He hopped out of the car and darted across the road, keeping to the shadows. In his customary black polo-neck jumper and black trousers, he was almost completely invisible and even Webb found it difficult to follow his progress.

Quinn stepped through the open gates and into the bushes. Then, moving as cautiously and as silently as possible, he made his way towards the house. The bottom of the house was in darkness, but the top floor was lit up. Parting leaves, he stared across the drive. The front door was open and he could see into the hall, the light dancing off the marbled floors and polished banisters. He idly wondered how much this place had cost – a fortune probably.

He caught a flicker of movement in one of the bedroom windows and stepped further back into the bushes to get a better angle. He could see the top half of Christine's body. Both her hands were pressed against the sides of her face and she seemed distraught.

Something was very wrong here.

When he heard the siren, his heart began to thunder. Then he identified the sounds as ambulance rather than police. They must have phoned the ambulance from the neighbour's house. It could only be Kevin, he reasoned. He hadn't seen him all evening. Something must have happened to the boy.

He shrank back as Christine came running down the stairs and out into the night. The ambulance was very close now, and she'd obviously gone out onto the road to bring it in.

The house and garden lit up with strobing red and blue lights as the ambulance appeared. The doors were opening even before it came to a stop and the two attendants hopped out as Christine came running back into the garden. She led the two men carrying the stretcher into the house.

When they re-appeared, a blanket-wrapped bundle on the stretcher, Quinn's teeth flashed in a wolfish smile. He was right, it was the boy. Obviously while Mammy was away, Kevin had been a naughty boy. Robert watched as Christine's new boyfriend draped a coat over her shoulders, his hands resting there, close to her neck. As he helped her into the back of the ambulance, Robert heard him ask where they were going.

'Mater Hospital,' said the driver, and Robert's smile broadened. As the ambulance sped away, the boyfriend pulled the hall door closed and ran down the drive.

Robert Quinn had always been an opportunist ... and this was an opportunity not to be missed.

'What's happened? What's going on?' Webb demanded frantically as Quinn slid in behind the wheel.

'The boy's sick. Overdose, I'll bet.'

'Aw, magic! Well, come on, let's go.'

'Wait.'

'What are waiting for?'

Headlights flashed on the road. A sleek black BMW turned out of the neighbour's drive and sped off after the ambulance. Robert turned the key in the ignition and gunned the engine to life.

'That's what we were waiting for. I wanted to make sure that we were behind him, rather than him behind us.'

'But we'll lose him. We can't keep up with that car.'

'We don't need to. I know where they're going.'

Saturday, 17 July

Chapter 60

Mark drove Christine home just after seven in the morning. Neither of them spoke on the long drive back to Island View. Christine was numb; she felt cold and empty inside. She hadn't got a headache, but she could feel a solid pressure at the base of her skull; there was a sour, sick feeling in the pit of her stomach and her throat felt raw, her eyes gritty. She hadn't cried; that would come later, much later.

She flinched when the house appeared. Suddenly, she wasn't sure she could bear to go back into it again. It was no longer the happy place full of promise and magic that it had been yesterday.

There were some images from her life which would remain with her to her grave: her last memory of her mother; her baby daughter's broken body, the tiny white coffin; Robert standing over her, hands closed into fists; and now, Kevin sprawled in a pool of vomit, his breath rasping in his lungs like an asthmatic. She wasn't even sure why she had looked in on him ... instinct, she supposed, and the faintest hint of vomit on the air. Even as she was bending over him, she knew what had happened. Drugs.

Methylenedioxymethylamphetamine, the doctor had called them, pronouncing the long word carefully. Now the commonest drug on the market. The street name was easier to remember. Ecstasy.

They drove through the open gates and Mark stopped the heavy car in front of the house. Christine sat looking at it, seeing it now in an entirely new light.

Maybe this wasn't going to be her lucky house after all. Maybe she should think about moving. She didn't have to buy it; she could walk away tomorrow if she wanted to. Certainly she couldn't have asked for a worse omen.

'Christine ...'

But if she hadn't been living in this house, and Kevin hadn't overdosed, then she wouldn't have been able to call on Mark, and Mark wouldn't have been able to save him ... but maybe if she hadn't been living in this house, Kevin wouldn't have taken the drugs.

Too many maybes.

'Christine ...'

The last week had been like a dream and she'd really believed that her luck had changed. Last night reminded her that all dreams ended.

What use would her money be if anything happened to Kevin? He was all she had; the best thing she had ever done. Her life hadn't amounted to much until she had won the money, but she was determined that Kevin's would be better, much better.

'Christine.'

Christine turned, suddenly aware that Mark was talking to her. She looked at him blankly, then unsnapped the seatbelt and climbed out onto the gravel. Mark came round the car and wrapped her in his arms, holding her tightly. 'You're exhausted,' he said gently. 'You need some rest.'

'Last night ...'

'We'll talk about last night when you're rested.'

'I can never thank you ...' she mumbled.

Mark reached into her pocket and pulled out her keys, shuffling through them until he found the one which opened the hall door.

She wasn't sure how she would have survived last night without Mark's help. He had saved Kevin's life, she was convinced of that. When she'd run, almost hysterical and incoherent back to his house, he was so calm, and his calmness transferred itself to her. He phoned the ambulance before they left his house, saving precious minutes. Then, while waiting, he tended to Kevin, easing his breathing, making sure his air passages were free.

And later, in the hospital, he had been very much in charge; he knew all the doctors personally and this had helped tremendously. He sat with her in the casualty department, holding her hand, explaining everything that was happening, until eventually, when they had pumped Kevin's stomach, and run blood tests and determined that he was out of danger, he insisted that he take her home.

'It's every mother's nightmare,' Christine said, and she slumped on the stairs.

Mark sat beside her, his arm around her shoulder. 'Everything is fine now. He's out of danger. And this scare should put him off them for life.'

'Could there be complications?'

'It's too early to tell. But he's young and healthy. I think he's going to be all right.'

'I've read of people dying from these Ecstasy tablets.'

'That has happened. He'll be kept in for a day or two for observation. I'd say he'll be home on Monday.'

Christine suddenly stood up.

Mark came to his feet. 'Easy, now,' he said.

'I'll go and clean up Kevin's room,' she said, then gripped the banisters as she swayed.

'I'll take care of that,' he said firmly.

'No, that's not fair on you.'

Mark suddenly stooped and swept her up in his arms, cradling her like a baby. 'Bed,' he said. 'Doctor's orders.'

Too tired, too numb to protest, Christine wrapped her arms around his neck and pressed her head against his chest. His heart beat solidly, reassuringly, in her ear.

She was asleep before he had gently laid her down on the sleeping bag.

Chapter 61

LOTTERY WINNER'S ANGUISH

Ireland's latest lottery millionaire, Christine Quinn (38) was today passing an anguished vigil at the bedside of her son, Kevin. Kevin Quinn (18) was admitted late last night to the Mater Hospital with a suspected drugs overdose. A source close to the family, said, 'Kevin was depressed because his mother had moved out of the estate where he'd grown up.'

LOTTERY WINNER'S DRUGS
OVERDOSE

Kevin Quinn (18) who had shared in his mother's recent two-and-a-quarter million pound lottery win, was today fighting for his life in a Dublin hospital. The hospital has refused to confirm that he overdosed on heroin, though they have confirmed that he is being treated for an overdose.

Kevin's pretty fiancée, Sandra Miller (18), was bitterly disappointed because she had been refused access to Kevin. 'This is all his mother's fault,' she is reported as saying. 'She's trying to keep us apart. That's why she moved away as soon as she won the money. I'm sure it's the pressure she's put on him that has caused him to do this. He's never used drugs before.'

EXCLUSIVE: I LOST MY SISTER WHEN SHE WON THE LOTTERY

In an exclusive interview, Sheila Newman, sister of multi-millionaire lottery winner, Christine Quinn, reveals how winning the lottery completely changed her sister's personality.

'We were always a very close family,' she said, 'but when Christine won the lottery, she became a different person overnight: cold, distant and withdrawn. She is now refusing to pay for urgent hospital treatment for our father ...'

Chapter 62

The smell of coffee brought her to consciousness.

Christine sat up slowly, fragmented images of her nightmare slipping away, thankfully vanishing ... until she realised that it hadn't been a nightmare. It was real. She *had* come home last night to find Kevin had passed out in a pool of vomit, overdosed on drugs.

'Can I come in?' Mark peered round the corner of the door.

'Mark? Mark ...' Christine mumbled, pushing herself up in the sleeping bag. 'What time is it?'

'Three,' Mark said, crouching down beside her, placing a cloth-covered tray on the sleeping bag between them.

'Three!' She struggled to sit up. 'Kevin! I've got to get ...'

Mark put his hand on her shoulder. 'I've just spoken to the hospital. Kevin is awake and alert. Looking and feeling a bit sorry for himself. He's fine, Christine. He'll have a stomach ache to end all stomach aches and a throat like sandpaper, but that's a small price to pay for what might have happened. The duty doctor will have a look at him this afternoon, and then, if he's okay, he'll give him a lecture on drug abuse and send him home.'

'I thought you said it would be Monday.'

'Shortage of beds,' he shrugged.

Christine sat with her back to the wall, and ran her fingers through her ruined hair-style, pushing her hair back off her face. Now that Kevin was out of danger, her worry crystallised into rage. 'Stupid little bastard. Just wait till I get him home.'

'Well, let's get him home first,' Mark said, and whipped the cloth off the tray, revealing cups, an enormous jug of coffee, fresh croissants, Danish pastries, butter and an assortment of jams. 'Breakfast, brunch, lunch and afternoon tea is served. This will bring up your blood-sugar level.' He poured a large cup of coffee, the rich aroma filling the room. Christine accepted it eagerly, wrapping her hands around it, drawing its warmth into her. Mark poured himself a cup, then pulled a newspaper out of his back pocket. 'I think you'd better have a look at this.'

Christine read the minor headline on page two: LOTTERY WINNER'S DRUGS OVERDOSE.

'How did they find out?' she asked eventually.

Mark sat cross-legged beside her, squinting in the afternoon sunlight. 'I initially thought that you might have been spotted and recognised at the hospital,' he suggested. 'But this is the first edition, which went to press in the early hours of the morning. I'm not sure how they would have got the news so quickly.'

'Webb,' Christine said finally, nodding slowly. 'Harry Webb. Reporter. When he discovered I won the lottery he set about spreading the story. He's been hounding me, offering me money to co-operate in some story with him. He probably found out where I live. He's probably even now watching the house,' she said in alarm.

'Describe him.'

'Short, bald, ugly, dirty, bad teeth.'

'Stay here,' Mark said, coming fluidly to his feet. 'I'll take a look outside.'

'He drives an old red Toyota. Be careful, Mark. Please.'

'I'll be careful.'

Christine scrambled to her feet and stood by the bedroom window watching Mark trot down the drive and disappear into the bushes. He reappeared several anxious minutes later with a broad smile on his face. She hurried out onto the landing to meet him at the top of the stairs. 'Well?'

Mark stopped on the stair directly below her, so that his face was on a level with hers. 'You were right. An old rust-bucket parked on the corner. He fitted your description to a T.'

'What did you do?'

'I called the police.'

'You *what*?'

'I called the police. Suspicious-looking character, lurking in a car, watching the houses.' He shrugged, a boyish grin on his face, his eyes wide and innocent. 'It's all true, isn't it? The local lads are very good. They'll come and take him away, check out whatever story he gives them, and by the time he's out, we'll have Kevin home here.'

Christine started to laugh.

'It's good to hear you laughing,' he said.

Christine stepped close to the edge of the stairs and stretched out her hands, resting both forearms on Mark's shoulders. He put his hands on her hips, steadying them both.

'Thank you,' she said softly, kissing him lightly on the lips.

'For what?'

'For everything.' She kissed him again.

Mark pressed himself closer to her, his hands moving up along her sides and around her back.

'I know we've only just met,' Christine breathed, 'but I feel ...'

'I know,' he said softly, turning his head slightly, kissing her warm lips.

On the road outside a police siren wailed, startling them. Then they started laughing again. Christine was shaking so hard she almost fell over.

'Careful.' Mark held her tightly, their faces inches apart. Then, simultaneously, they kissed each other, gently, delicately, tentatively.

Christine broke away first, stepping backwards, catching hold of Mark's hand, drawing him with her, pulling him back to the bedroom.

'Christine ...' Mark began, as she stood in front of him and began to unbutton his shirt. 'You don't have to do this.'

'I want to,' she said simply. 'Don't you?'

'Yes.' He kissed her again, tasting her lips, tracing the line of her jaw with his tongue, while his fingers worked at the innumerable buttons along the side of her dress. 'Oh, yes.'

Christine peeled back his shirt, then ran her hands across his chest, fingernails rasping through the thick mat of coarse hair. His stomach muscles tightened as she pressed her hand to them and began working on his belt.

All the buttons undone, Mark slid his hand along her side, gently touching the edge of her breast, then moving around to trace the line of her spine downwards, until he touched silk.

Placing both hands flat against his chest, Christine stepped backwards away from Mark. Puzzled, he watched her, until he realised that she was pulling her dress over her head. She felt her nipples harden as his eyes roved over her body and when he reached out and pressed his hand against her breast – delicately, tenderly – his touch was electric, sending shivers deep into the core of her being.

When they were both naked, he drew her down onto the

sleeping bag, lying beneath her, holding her as she climbed onto him, her pale flesh contrasting sharply with his deeply-tanned skin.

Christine leaned forward, her breasts brushing against his chest, the touch sensuous and erotic. 'I haven't done this for a long time, Mark ... I'm a little nervous ...'

'Don't be,' he said, pressing his mouth to hers, swallowing whatever else she was going to say.

They made love gently, easily, taking their time, exploring each other's bodies, their desire matching their hunger. They managed to keep their passion under control, toying with each other, arousing each other, teasing, until he entered her, and then their lovemaking became wild, abandoned, the pleasure so intense it became almost painful, Mark's fingers squeezing her thighs as he clutched at her in his passion, her nails leaving red half-moons on his shoulders as she shuddered above him, back arched, head thrown back.

Finally, lying side by side, still wrapped in each other's bodies, they fell into a doze, the sweat of their lovemaking cooling on their skin.

Christine woke first. Sunlight and shadow had moved around the room and she knew it was late afternoon. She was intensely aware that all her muscles were aching, especially along her thighs and into her groin, but it was a pleasurable, satisfying ache, and her breasts felt heavy, bruised, the flesh scored where Mark had clutched at her.

Moving quietly, so as not to wake him, she slid out of his arms, and then knelt by the side of the sleeping bag, simply looking at him, noting the marks of her own passion on his skin.

She wasn't sure if she loved him – she was still too cautious for that – but she was drawn to him, and he to her, and that was enough for the moment.

Mark found her standing naked by the window, bathed in

sunlight, staring out over the long sloping lawn. He came up behind her, pressing his naked body against hers, wrapping his arms around her body. She pressed her hands on his, squeezing lightly.

Tilting his head, he kissed her shoulder, then the line of her throat. He stopped when he felt her tremble and turned her around to face him. She was weeping, huge silent tears that curled down her cheeks and splashed onto her breasts.

'Why so sad?' he whispered, brushing away the tears.

Christine shook her head. 'Not sad. Happy. Really happy. For the first time in my life.' Standing on her toes, she kissed him lightly on the lips.

'Marry me,' he said, very slowly.

She looked at him, eyes wide in shock. She started to smile, thinking it was a joke.

'I mean it.'

'You can't. We've just met.'

'You told me if you saw something you wanted, then you went for it. I'm like that too. I want you, Christine Quinn.'

'We barely know each other.'

'Then we'll have a lifetime to get to know each other. What do you say?'

Christine pressed herself against his chest, holding tightly, afraid she was going to fall.

'Ask me tomorrow,' she said shakily.

Chapter 63

Kevin's bed was empty when Christine and Mark walked into the ward. Christine was relieved. At least he was well enough to be up and about. She looked around but couldn't see him and his locker was empty, so she stopped a nurse. 'Excuse me, but do you know where Kevin Quinn is?'

The young nurse smiled. 'I'll find out for you now.'

'He's probably in the TV room, or gone down to the shop,' Mark said.

Christine nudged him in the side. 'You have your doctor's look on now!' she teased.

Mark unfolded his hands from behind his back and made a conscious effort to relax his straight shoulders. 'I am a doctor,' he reminded her.

'With an excellent bedside manner,' she smiled.

He was about to reply, when the nurse returned, looking from Christine to Mark. 'Kevin Quinn has gone home,' she said. 'He left about an hour ago with his father.'

'His father!' Christine felt as if someone had kicked her in the stomach.

The nurse passed across an envelope. 'This was left at the nurses' station for you, Mrs Quinn.'

'Get me the matron on duty,' Mark snapped as Christine tore the envelope open.

'No ... no ...' Christine said, resting her hand on his arm. 'It's all right. Everything is all right.' She smiled shakily at the nurse. 'Just a breakdown in communications.' She handed Mark the single sheet of paper. The words had been printed in block capitals:

BE WAITING AT THE PHONE NEAREST THE WIN-
DOW IN THE ENTRANCE LOBBY AT 5:00.

Mark looked at his watch. It was three minutes to five. Catching Christine's hand, he dragged her past the startled nurse.

*   *   *

The phone was ringing as they raced into the foyer. A very pregnant young woman, cradling a young child on her hip, looked up in surprise. She'd only ever seen the phone used for making out-going calls. She was just getting slowly to her feet when a man rushed in front of her and snatched it up. Then, instead of answering it himself, he passed it to the blond, wild-eyed woman by his side.

The line was crystal clear and he might have been standing at her shoulder. 'Long time no see, Christine.'

The voice sent icy chills down Christine's spine. Maybe she had once loved Robert Quinn, but that had been a long time ago, and too many years of beatings and abuse had destroyed any love there might have been between them.

'What do you want?' she hissed. 'Where's Kevin? What have you done with him?' She tilted the phone so that Mark could listen.

'Safe. For the moment.'

'Where is he?' she demanded.

'I've told you. Safe. And well. Delighted to see his step-father of course.'

'What do you want?'

'To share in your good fortune.' He had lost some of his flat Dublin accent, she realised. Now his voice was sibilant, hissing, like a snake's.

'What do you want?' she asked for a third time.

'A million,' he said calmly. 'Less than half what you won. In return for your son. Quite a bargain.'

'This is blackmail!' she whispered.

'That's what it's called,' he agreed pleasantly. 'And before you have any foolish ideas about police, you should remember that I would really become upset if you did that. I'd hate for this boy to become a liability to me.'

'Please don't harm him. Let me talk to him.'

'No. This is the deal. Monday morning at noon, you bring a million in unmarked notes to the warehouse on the quay I used to use. You remember the one?'

'Where you stored your books? I remember it,' she said numbly.

'No tricks, Christine. If you try anything stupid, I'll start sending your precious boy back to you a piece at a time. Do you hear me?'

'I hear you. Please don't hurt him.'

'Well, that's entirely up to you, isn't it?' he said, and hung up.

Monday, 19 July

Chapter 64

Sunday remained little more than a dream. What she did remember, however, was that the entire day dragged, each minute ticking away with interminable slowness.

She didn't know what she did for the day. She remembered eating, because Mark had forced her, but she didn't taste the food, and she threw it up later.

And every time she looked at Mark, she felt guilty. If she hadn't been making love to Mark, she would have been at the hospital, and if she'd been at the hospital, then Kevin wouldn't have been kidnapped. She knew if anything happened to the boy, she would never be able to forgive herself. And if anything happened to Kevin, it would also destroy any chance she had for a relationship with Mark.

Robert had destroyed her life up to this, and now he was doing the same to her second chance. And it was all because of the lottery win. She was beginning to wish she'd never won the money. It had certainly changed her life, but not in the way she'd planned.

* * *

At two minutes to ten, on Monday morning, Mark pulled the BMW into the kerb at Christine's bank. 'Are you sure you want to go through with this?' he asked for the hundredth time.

'Absolutely. The money means nothing to me. I'd gladly give it all just to have Kevin back.'

Mark nodded. 'Then do what you have to do,' he said, and flipped down his Doctor on Call sign under the sunflap. He pulled a lever which popped the boot open and Christine took out a small suitcase and carried it up the steps to the bank just as the doors were opening.

Joseph Chambers was entering his office when he saw Mrs Quinn step into the bank. Smiling delightedly, idly wondering if he was free for lunch today, he came out from behind the counter. The smile faded when he saw the suitcase in Christine's hand. 'Mrs Quinn, how lovely to see you. Are you off somewhere?'

'Something like that, Mr Chambers.'

'Joseph,' he reminded her. 'Call me Joseph. What can I do for you?'

'I'd like to make a withdrawal.'

'Of course. I'll look after it myself. How much?'

Christine lowered her voice. 'A million.'

Chambers started to laugh – until he realised that she wasn't amused. This wasn't a joke. His own smile faded. 'I'm afraid that's out of the question,' he said firmly.

'You told me I could take out any amount at any time,' she snapped.

'Well yes, I did, but ... I mean ... a million ... What do you want a million for anyway?'

'It's none of your damn business! Now, are you going to give me my money or not?'

'I cannot.'

'Why not?' Christine demanded frantically, her voice rising.

'I simply don't have that amount of money here in cash.'

'How long would it take you to get it?'

'Three days, maybe four.'

'I must have it this morning.'

'Why? Mrs Quinn, is everything all right?'

'Everything – is – fine.' Christine pronounced each word slowly and distinctly through gritted teeth. 'Everything is fine.' She took a deep breath. 'Okay. How much money could you let me have right now in cash?'

'I don't know. I'd have to see what we have in stock. You'd

better come into my office.'

'And hurry, Mr Chambers.'

'You're going to buy something,' Chambers said quickly.

Christine nodded.

'Something expensive.'

'Very precious,' she agreed.

'Well, why don't you offer a guaranteed bank cheque? It's as good as money in the bank.'

'This deal is strictly for cash.'

Chambers's fingers were moving over his computer keyboard. 'I could probably let you have fifty thousand.'

'I'll take it,' she said immediately.

'I'll go and make the arrangements,' he said, completely puzzled at this stage. First she wanted a million, now she'd settle for fifty thousand. The huge win must have gone to her head.

'Make it in small notes,' she said as he left the room. 'Nothing bigger than a tenner.'

'That will be a huge amount of money,' he protested, 'Quite bulky.'

'That's why I brought the suitcase.'

* * *

Joseph Chambers escorted Christine Quinn to the door. He offered to carry the suitcase for her, but she adamantly refused. He saw her dump the bag into the boot of a BMW and then climb into the passenger seat alongside a distinguished-looking young man. Shaking his head, completely mystified, Chambers returned to his office. Somehow, he didn't think he'd be having lunch with the lady.

He didn't realise until the afternoon that all his European phone directories were missing, even the out-of-date ones, which were absolutely of no use to anyone. He never did find out what happened to them.

Chapter 65

'Stop here,' Christine said quietly. Mark turned the heavy car in off the road until its bumper was almost resting against the metal barrier at the edge of the water.

Christine pointed through the windscreen. 'It's that one there.'

'Are you sure?'

She nodded, reading the faded sign. 'Uniport Importers. When Robert was bringing in books, these people handled the shipping. He often stored consignments of books in their warehouse.' She looked over the building again. 'They must have gone bust a couple of years ago.'

'More than a couple,' Robert said.

Christine looked at the clock on the dashboard. 11:30.

'I'd better go. You stay here.' She leaned across the seat and kissed him quickly on the lips. 'Don't follow me. If Robert sees you, he might get scared and do something foolish. I'm just going to give him the money and get Kevin. I promise.'

'I'll stay here,' Mark said unhappily. 'But I wish there was more I could do.'

'I couldn't have come this far without you,' she said.

Mark pulled the lever which popped open the boot, then he reached over and caught Christine's arm as she was opening the door, pulling her back into the car, and kissed her deeply. 'Please be careful. You're very precious to me. I don't want anything to happen to you. Just give him the money, take Kevin and walk away.'

Christine looked at him for a moment, then she nodded. 'I'll be careful,' she promised, but somehow she didn't think it was going to be a simple matter of handing over the money and walking away. There was too much unfinished business between Robert and herself.

Christine hauled the heavy suitcase out of the back of the car. Holding it in both hands, the handle cutting into her fingers, she lugged it towards the warehouse.

Seven years ago, carrying a single small suitcase she stood outside her own house, holding Kevin by the hand, as Robert slammed the door in her face.

And later, when she managed to get an eviction order and a barring order, she had stood on her doorstep with the same suitcase in her hand and heard Robert hurl obscenities at her from the gate.

The warehouse backed directly onto the quays, a relic of the days when ships actually docked right up against the quay walls. It had once been one complete building, but over the years it had been divided and subdivided into scores of smaller buildings and units and while she remembered it as a thriving business from the few occasions she had been there with Robert, now it was nothing more than a vandalised ruin.

Christine ducked through a hole in the torn wire-mesh fencing, wondering how she was going to make her way into the building. The area between the fence and the building was piled high with rubbish. She picked her way carefully through the mess, trying desperately to ignore the squeaks she heard from the shadows. She didn't want to even try to guess what they were.

Christine stopped when she realised she was following a rough trail through the rubbish, as bottles, cans, cardboard boxes compacted underfoot. Someone used this building on a regular basis: down-and-outs, junkies? Christine shivered. She hoped none of them were at home right now.

A stunted bush grew out of a hole in the wall almost directly in front of her. Most of its leaves were withered and those that clung stubbornly to its branches had a diseased and blotched appearance. Christine was brushing past the bush, when she spotted the door, half-hidden behind it. Heaving the suitcase before her, she pushed her way through the opening.

She was standing in what had once been a small reception hall, although it had now been vandalised almost beyond recognition. It stank of rot and urine, proof that the building was still used, at least for one purpose. A fire had once blazed in the corner; long black marks streaked up the wall to the ceiling, where plastic piping now hung in melted stalactites. The barrel of an empty syringe rolled away from her feet.

Moving through the office, Christine stepped out into a long narrow corridor, with a half-dozen doors opening off on either side. She made her way cautiously down the corridor, peering into each room, wondering how she was ever going to find Robert in this maze.

She put down the suitcase and sat on it, breathing hard. Where was he? He could be anywhere ... that's if he was even here in the first place. He had a vicious and perverse sense of humour. In the silence she heard church bells tolling noon. Frightened now that Robert would do something to Kevin, she picked up the heavy suitcase and hurried down the corridor.

She had to think fast. Where would Robert meet her? It had to be some place they both knew. When he had used this place he had a small storage area quite close to the river ... She turned to the left and hurried down another dilapidated corridor, not checking the rooms now, frantic to reach Robert before he harmed Kevin.

She stumbled and almost fell; a scream stopped in her throat as a pigeon fluttered out from one of the rooms. It flapped down the corridor before her, wings clapping loudly, and then disappeared into silence. On impulse, Christine followed it, knowing it had to have flown towards an exit. At the bottom of the corridor, she turned right and found that she was looking into a room which had a large chunk missing out of one wall. And through the hole in the wall, she could see out into the body of the warehouse.

There were two figures on the opposite side of the warehouse, outlined against the noonday sky and the filthy water, standing at the edge of the river.

Straightening her shoulders, gripping the suitcase tightly, Christine strode across the filthy floor to meet her past.

She was twenty-seven when she left Robert, twenty-seven before she finally plucked up the courage to walk away from him. She'd chosen that as one of her significant lottery numbers because she felt it marked the start of a new phase of her life. A life without Robert, a life of freedom.

But it had been neither, of course. He was always there, at the back of every thought, and there was always the possibility that he would return. When she won the lottery it was one of the first things she thought about.

As she approached him, she felt the years slip away and suddenly she was twenty-seven again.

... bruises on her body, where they weren't visible, scars on her soul ...

She couldn't remember exactly when the beating started. It became worse after Baby Margaret's death though. Robert held her responsible, not only for that tragedy but for everything else that had happened in his life. He didn't love her anymore, he freely admitted that, and so he used her, but he wouldn't free her, wouldn't allow her to walk away, because that would have shown him up as a loser who couldn't hold onto his job, couldn't protect his child, couldn't control his wife.

Her high heels tapped on the concrete, splashing through the puddles. Her eyes were fixed on his face, remembering ...

... she knew when he was going to beat her by the expression in his eyes. So cold, so dispassionate. He didn't seem to take any pleasure out of striking at her; he approached it almost as if it

were some kind of duty. On the one occasion when she struck back, hitting out at him with a soup ladle, he broke three of her ribs.

His eyes were implacable now.

Christine stopped ten feet away from her ex-husband. He had changed. His physique was magnificent and his tightly cut, cropped hair gave a cruel, arrogant cast to his features. She wasn't sure that she would have recognised him if she'd passed him in the street. Then she looked into his eyes again, and realised that she would always know him.

Ignoring him, she spoke directly to Kevin. He was sitting on a bollard with his back to the water.

'Are you okay?' Her voice echoed slightly in the vastness of the warehouse.

He nodded. He was looking pale and drawn, there were deep dark circles under his eyes and she thought he might have been crying, but he looked unharmed.

'You look good, Christine,' Robert said, stepping forward, stretching out a hand for the suitcase.

Christine took a step back.

Robert smiled tightly. 'Money obviously suits you.' He folded his arms across his broad chest. 'I thought of you often while I was in prison. Sometimes I felt that if we had never met, I would have been a great success.'

'You were a loser, Robert. You were always a loser.'

The smiled faded.

'*... don't you dare speak to me like that, you bitch.' The blow had broken three of her teeth, impacting two of them into her gums. The surgery was agony; she told the dentist she'd fallen downstairs.*

'You always were an arrogant cow,' he sneered. 'I think the mistake I made was not keeping you in line.'

'What do you call keeping me in line?' She asked coldly.

'Beating me until I could barely walk? Taking my shoes so that I couldn't leave the house, doling out every single penny so that I never had anything for myself, and then raping me whenever you felt like it? Is that what you call keeping me in line?'

'I suppose that's what you've told the boy here. Told him what a monster I was.'

'I didn't need to tell him. He knew,' Christine said bitterly. 'He wasn't blind.'

... Kevin launching himself on Robert's back, clawing at his step-father's face, pummelling him, trying to pull him off his mother ...

Robert turned to look at Kevin. 'She was never satisfied,' he said mildly. 'She would never let things alone. She was always making demands, she always wanted, wanted, wanted ... And I could never give her enough. And no matter what I gave her, she always wanted more. Sure, I smacked her a couple of times, but only when she really needed it.'

'You sicken me,' Christine said tightly. 'Come on. Let's get this over with. I've brought you your money. One million pounds.'

'In a rush to get back to your new lifestyle, Christine? New house, new boyfriend too, I see. I was watching you with him on Friday night. Very cosy that was. And while you were partying the night away, your poor son was overdosing ...' He tousled Kevin's hair. The boy twisted away quickly, and Christine saw that his hands were taped together. 'What will the papers make of it? I'm sure that slimy little rat Webb is already selling the rights. He's going to make your life one fucking misery.'

'I don't care about that. I want my son back.'

'Your son. At least be thankful that you can have your son back. What about my daughter? I'll never have her back.'

Christine stared him in the face. 'Sometimes – like now – I'm glad she died, because God knows what you would have done to her if you'd remained in the house.'

Robert paled, his big hand closing in fists.

... *The fists pummelling, punching at her stomach, her breasts* ...

Quinn saw the fear in her eyes and smiled triumphantly. Despite her bluster, she was still the same woman, still frightened of him, still aware of his power. Reaching over he caught hold of Kevin and flung him across the floor. The young man rolled to a stop at his mother's feet.

'You bastard,' she snarled, crouching down beside Kevin. He had skinned his forehead and cheeks.

Quinn strode forward and snatched the suitcase off the ground where Christine had dropped it as she reached for her son. He thumbed the locks, but nothing happened.

'Key,' he snapped.

'I haven't got it,' she lied.

'Lying bitch.' Digging into his pocket he produced a long-bladed hunting knife. He looked at her for a moment ... then jammed the blade of the knife beneath one of the locks and started to prise it upwards.

'You wouldn't try and cheat me, would you, Christine?' he whispered.

Christine hauled Kevin roughly to his feet.

'Mum?'

'Just walk,' she hissed. 'Walk away.'

'Mum?' There was stark terror in his eyes as he looked from Robert to his mother. 'What's going on?'

Holding Kevin tightly by the arm, Christine pulled him away from the water's edge.

'I'll tell you what's going on, boy,' Robert called after them.

One of the locks clicked open.

'Your mother and me came to a little agreement on how much you're worth. Most people go through this life not knowing their worth, but if anyone ever asks you ... you can say that you're worth a cool million!'

The second lock snapped open.

Christine glanced over her shoulder. Robert was crouching down with the open suitcase on the ground, bundles of money in either hand. Then he froze.

'Kevin,' Christine whispered urgently, 'when I say go, I want you to run. Go through that opening, then down the corridor to your right. Mark is outside in a car.' She looked over her shoulder again. 'We'll split up. He can't chase both of us.'

Kevin started to shake his head. 'He's not going to come after us. He has the money ...'

Robert screamed. It was a sound of pure animal rage.

'But not enough.' Christine pushed Kevin away from her. 'Go on. Run.' She turned back to face her ex-husband. He was holding a thick yellow phone directory in one hand.

'I should have known,' he shouted. He flung the book at her. 'I should have known.' Snapping the locks shut, gripping the suitcase in his left hand, the knife in his right, he advanced towards her. 'You always thought you were the clever one.'

Christine took a step backwards. She realised Kevin was still standing by her side, frozen with shock. She pushed him away. 'Go, Kevin,' she pleaded.

Robert lifted the knife. 'Maybe I should cut that fucking arrogant smile off your face. See how much your new boyfriend likes you then, eh?'

'Run!' Christine screamed. Kevin darted to the right, while Christine deliberately ran off to the left, leading Robert away from her son. The big man hesitated a moment, then turned to follow Christine.

She kicked off her high heels and ran barefoot across the broken floor, fragments of glass and stone cutting into her feet. Robert pounded after her, screaming obscenities, almost incoherent with rage. She risked a quick glance over shoulder. His face was a mask of anger, white spittle flecking his lips. He would kill her if he got her. He had threatened it often enough as he'd beaten and kicked her. Something had always held him back, but there were no restraints now.

He was close now, so close. He had stopped roaring, but she could hear his heavy rasping breath, and her shoulder muscles tensed, expecting to feel the hot touch of the knife.

She turned quickly to the left, stumbling, bare feet sliding on the oily floor, but managing to keep upright. Robert turned sharply, leather-soled boots skating out from under him, sending him crashing to the floor.

Christine dashed through an opening. And stopped, swaying back and forth, tottering on the edge of the wall. Ten feet below her a filthy Liffey lapped against the slimy stones.

She turned. Robert was climbing to his feet. There was blood on his chin, where he had bitten into his tongue when he'd fallen. Lips peeled back from his bloody teeth in a parody of a smile, he advanced on Christine, knife clutched in a white-knuckled grip.

'Nowhere to go, Chrissy. No-one to turn to this time.'

Christine turned and hauled herself up the rotting fire-escape that ran along the outside of the building. Flakes of rust stung her feet, bit into her hands, stained her flesh a blood-red as she climbed. She felt the whole construction sway and shift beneath her weight, threatening to pull out from the wall, sending her plummeting into the dark river below.

Robert pounded after her, the metal fire escape vibrating with his every step.

He was close now. So close.

He slashed at Christine. The knife nicked the back of her calf, the touch red-hot, searing, numbing.

Christine's naked foot suddenly punched through a rotten step, shards of metal scoring her leg. Dragging her leg free, she pulled herself up to the next step. She couldn't go much further. A portion of the rusty rail snapped away in her hand, leaving her with a two-foot length of metal. Another step crumbled beneath her weight, sending her crashing to the ground, the force of the blow numbing her chest and arms.

Robert loomed over her, knife raised. 'Oh, I'm going to get you this time, you bitch!'

With the last of her strength, Christine struck out with the metal bar in her hand, catching him across the shins. The force of the blow snapped the metal in half – and sent Robert tumbling backwards. He managed a single terrified scream before his head banged off a metal stair. He fell the rest of the way in silence.

Christine watched his body tumble and twist through the steps. A whole section of the fire escape suddenly gave way beneath his weight, plummeting him into the filthy river below. He was still clutching the suitcase as he hit the water.

Christine watched the rippling circle of slime and bubbles until they had vanished, then she raised her eyes, looking away from the river and her past. From this height, she thought she could see Killiney in the distance.

Chapter 66

Christine Quinn crouched by the pool and fished long strands of weed from the murky water, enjoying the feel of the cool water on her flesh. Robert's reflection swam up over her left shoulder, bringing her to her feet with a scream. Mark Cunningham caught her before she tumbled into the pool.

'Mark! You frightened me.'

He held her close, stroking her hair. 'I'm sorry. I was talking to you as I came down the lawn, but you were obviously miles away.'

'How's Kevin?'

'I gave him something that will help him sleep. He'll be out until morning.'

'He's going to be all right?' she asked anxiously.

'He's going to be fine. How are you?'

'Sore ... and getting sorer.' Both legs, from ankles to knee were swathed in bandages, and Mark had wrapped her bruised and scraped hands in gauze.

They strolled arm in arm through the garden, enjoying the late afternoon sunshine. 'What will happen, Mark?' she asked eventually, 'about Robert ...'

'I would imagine there will be a police investigation, and you'll probably have to appear at an inquest,' he said slowly. 'But it's a fairly straightforward case. Robert kidnapped your son, attempted to blackmail you, and then attempted to kill you. He fell when you hit him in self-defence. It was an accident. The verdict will be accidental death or death through mis-adventure.'

Christine suddenly shivered, the realisation sinking in that Robert had tried to kill her. Mark put his arm around her shoulders and squeezed hard. 'It's all right. It's all over now.'

Christine nodded. It *was* all over.

And now it could begin properly. Her new life.

She was finally free of her past.

They wandered through the trees until they came to the gate that led down to the sea. With everything that had happened over the past few days, she hadn't even had a chance to go down onto the beach and walk along the shore. Gripping the iron bars tightly, she stared at the brilliantly blue water.

'Do you know what I've just realised, Mark? I have the money a week today,' she said slowly. 'A week.'

'And it's changed your life completely.'

She nodded. But there was one other change she could still make. Glancing sidelong at Mark, she said, 'You asked me a question on Saturday ...'

'And you said to ask you again,' he smiled.

'Ask me again.'